SNOWDROPS FOR ADA

by

Virginia Aitken

First published in Great Britain by
Pen Press Publishers Ltd
39-41, North Road
Islington
London N7 9DP

ISBN 1-904754-70-8

Printed and bound in the UK

A catalogue record of this book is available from
the British Library

Cover design by Jacqueline Abromeit
www.geminivision.co.uk

For Audrey

About the Author

Virginia Aitken was born in Preston, but now lives with her husband Henry in Magherafelt, a rural town set in the heart of Northern Ireland.

Having spent much of her career as a teacher of English and Drama in grammar schools, she is now a tutor at Queen's University, Belfast. She has written widely within the educational sphere, and has had her three plays performed on the amateur stage.

Snowdrops for Ada is the sequel to her first novel *Oh My Child*, which was published in 2002.

She and her husband share the same hobbies of gardening, painting, and boating. They spend much of their holiday time travelling along the French waterways on their river cruiser, and are frequent visitors to the south of England, where all their grown up family live.

Acknowledgements

I would like to thank all those who have helped in the making of this book:

my husband Henry Aitken, for his unfailing support and encouragement;

my mother Audrey Goodwin, for sharing with me her memories of her mother, Ada;

my sister Shirley Arends for recollections of her conversations with our grandmother, Ada;

Bert Henderson, for gathering family information;

my daughters Lynne Green and Clare Scott for their ideas and suggestions;

my two sons Ian Aitken and John Aitken, for their ongoing interest;

my daughter-in-law, Antonia, who was impatient to read this sequel to *Oh My Child*;

my niece, Carol MacLean, a published writer, for her enthusiastic chats about writing;

the Harris Museum, Preston, for biographical information;

and all those in Cambridgeshire who kindly sent additional historical information.

Preface

Snowdrops for Ada, a fictionalised biography set in Ely, Cambridge, London and Preston, at the turn of the twentieth century, is the sequel to *Oh My Child*. The story covers a nine-year period in Ada's turbulent childhood, exploring her growing understanding of life, through peaks of happiness and troughs of sadness. Her hopes and disappointments intertwine with the serious issues of protection of children and the rights of women, no less important today than they were a hundred years ago.

The facts and events of the novel have been gleaned from information found in wills, parish records, archive material, letters, diaries, and stories in living memory. The thoughts, feelings and motivation of the real people in this story are based on the author's assumptions, deductions and conclusions drawn from that information.

The fictitious people in the novel provide a colourful backdrop, but any similarity to persons living or dead is purely coincidental.

CHAPTER 1
ADA

Part 1

In the early morning on the first day of spring, in the year of 1893, Ada was a shivering bundle of excitement. This was the day she had been looking forward to. She was tired of wearing her black taffeta mourning dress with its little detachable and detestable, prickly lace collar. She longed to wear her pink brocade dress again with its long white sash and its twenty-two shiny, satin buttons down the front of the trim bodice. She was only five years old, after all.

It was ever so cold in her bedroom, and the bedclothes were ever so cosy, but neither of these would deter her from getting out of bed and tiptoeing to the curtained sash window. She pulled back the mint-green, velvet drapes to look down on to the walled garden below, her very own secret garden, with its fragile and fading memories. But where she expected to see a host of yellow and purple crocuses under the beech tree, she saw instead an impenetrable blanket of snow, a bleak and hostile white landscape.

She cried out, a long and sorrowful wail. The snow-laden beech tree with outstretched arms reached out to this little girl in her disappointment, but, just as its tender shade had been powerless to nurse her poor mother back to health, so now was it unable to dry away Ada's tears.

Ada suddenly found herself being gathered up into the enveloping arms of Maud Harrison, the housekeeper, being wrapped up in a woollen blanket and taken to the warm kitchen, where the range was already throwing out a comforting heat. The kitchen maid, Ellen, a buxom lass in her late teens, was about her morning chores. The kettle was singing on the hob, and scones were rising in the top oven, emitting a mouth-watering aroma.

"Now sit on my knee, my pretty one," Maud Harrison was cooing gently, "and we'll see if we can rock these tears away. Ellen will bring you some warm milk and a freshly baked scone heaped with strawberry jam." She soothingly stroked the child's head of golden curls as she gently rocked backwards and forwards, backwards and forwards, on the old rocking chair beside the range, until Ada's sobs began to subside.

"Here's your warm milk, miss," coaxed Ellen, wanting to offer some comfort. "I put an extra spoonful of sugar in it for you as a treat." A toothy smile of encouragement and sympathy split her heated face from side to side.

"Mind you drink it all up now," instructed Maud, as she sat Ada in a more upright position for the purpose.

A little later, when they returned to the bedroom, Maud was in the process of getting Ada's clothes from the wardrobe, when the child suddenly asked, "Why are there no spring flowers today?"

"Because of all the snow," Maud replied. "It's still winter."

"No, it's not," said Ada, her brown eyes flashing. "You said it would be spring today."

"So I did, young lady."

There was no getting away from the fact, and Maud looked thoughtful. For the past fortnight, each night as she had tucked her young charge in bed, Ada had asked, "Is it spring tomorrow?"

Each night Maud had said, "Not yet, my pretty one. It's still February."

Each night the child had sighed resignedly, patiently saying her prayers, ending with, "Please, God, make the spring come quickly!"

Bedtime last night was different.

Maud had answered, "Yes, this is the last day of winter and tomorrow will be March 1st, the first day of spring."

Ada had flung her arms round Maud's neck and snuggled

down to sleep with a contented smile on her face.

"Is that what made you cry?"

Ada's lower lip began to tremble.

So that was the trouble: her promise to the child had been broken.

"The good Lord has decided to make us wait for a few more days yet." It seemed expedient to blame a higher authority, if she was to regain Ada's trust – though what was so important about the first day of spring Maud was at a loss to understand.

*

"I would like to have a little sleep now," Matilda had announced one afternoon the previous July, as she sat in her wicker chair in the garden.

"Shall I fetch you your shawl, my dear?" Richard had asked.

"Oh, no. It is so lovely and balmy. Just perfect." Matilda had determined that her husband should not yet know the ugly truth that she was dying of consumption, like her mother and sister before her. Time enough for that.

Time enough for "Phthisis" to be written on her death certificate, time enough for retrospective medical terms to hide the fearful reality that she was suffering from that killer disease, tuberculosis. It grieved her more than words could ever express that there was so little time to spend with Ada, her little daughter. She would keep going as long as possible.

"I live for my little girl," Matilda had said quietly, her determination tinged with fearful hopelessness, to Ada, who laughed and played at her feet. How she wished it would be so!

Richard had left them both to enjoy the peace and humming quiet of that summer afternoon. On his way through the vestibule to the front drawing room, he had heard Matilda's fit of stifled coughing. Of course, he had seen the signs of hollowness in her cheeks, her clothes beginning to hang on her body, and knew in his heart that there was little time left to them. His young wife would not outlive him after all: that was not in God's great plan.

What was he to do? A man in his late seventies, with a five-year old daughter to look after, and very few years left to him! The future looked bleak indeed.

Then, all too soon, on that raw February morning just a few weeks ago, Ada and her father had gone out into the walled garden together in silent grief and picked just five snowdrops, to put in her dead mother's hands. There had been only five: "A snowdrop for every year of your life," her father had told her, adding, "Snowdrops are nature's teardrops, and when they dry, spring flowers will bloom and we will be happy again."

*

Since the funeral, Waddington Terrace, Ada's home, had been shrouded in sadness and gloom. The blinds remained drawn at the front of the house, though the Ely citizens passing along St Mary's Street looked down at the pavement as they passed the house of mourning. Should the blinds have been raised, the passers-by, out of sympathetic courtesy, would not have intruded upon Richard's private grief at such a time as this – the death of his second wife. First, the lovely, red-haired Frances, mother to Richard's two sons, now in their forties with children of their own; and second, the gentle Matilda, almost half his age, taken away from him in her prime.

Visitors, friends and relatives, some of whom came by train from as far away as Cambridge, spoke in hushed whispers in the drawing room; Richard brooded for hours alone with his memories and his books; and Ada had to wear that hateful, black, taffeta dress. She longed for things to be happy again.

Part 2

"What's the hullabaloo!" exclaimed Ellen in the kitchen.

Every now and again Ellen, born and bred just a few miles outside Ely in Wilburton village, indulged in these mysterious pseudo-Irishisms for effect. She claimed it was in her blood. Her grandmother was a County Wicklow girl who in 1848, through "services rendered", had managed to secure a passage for herself and her younger brother on a packet-boat from Dublin to the mainland, thereby escaping inevitable death from starvation during Ireland's Great Famine.

"I can 'ardly 'ear myself think with all the racket!" Reverting to her more normal vocabulary, Ellen now clapped her floury hands over her ears, as she stood over a large ball of dough, which she was in the process of kneading into small rolls to be baked in readiness for lunch that day.

There was such a cacaphonic commotion outside: the midday cathedral bells boomed through the streets of this ancient city of Queen Etheldreda; the chimes of St Mary's church, towering above the coach house at the far end of the walled garden at the back of Waddington Terrace, rang out in synchrony; just round the corner in Barton Road, Colonel Wale's militia band was practising a rousing military number; all of which was accompanied by a loud knocking at the front door.

Miss Maud Harrison was not one to be easily intimidated, and strident knocking was something she abhorred, even in normal circumstances, let alone at the
door of a house in mourning. She would greet whoever was making such a din with a frosty look of disapproval. She signalled to Ada to stay upstairs, for such visitors were not for the likes of Ada, the daughter of a gentleman.

On opening the door, however, she greeted the visitor politely enough. "Good morning, Mr Porter, sir," she said deferentially, all the bluster and annoyance now gone, for she rather admired Mr Henry John, her master's younger brother.

"Where's that brother of mine?" demanded Henry John in a loud, but not unkind voice. There was a slight note of uncertainty, or perhaps embarrassment underneath the confident exterior. He rarely called to see his brother: they did not see eye-to-eye on certain matters. As he stood there on the doorstep, he reflected that, although he had tried to smooth over the acrimony following the reading of their father's will by sending a special telegram to Richard and Matilda at the time of their marriage, he had only stepped across the threshold of Waddington Terrace, over that shiny brass sill, three times since their father had died, and that was for two funerals and one christening.

But today was different: he was on a mission. His wife, Mary Ann, had sent him.

Ada peeped round the newel post at the top of the stairs, to catch a glimpse of this bold individual. She dimly thought she recognised the voice, but had no clear recollection of seeing this man before. Nevertheless, he was a welcome distraction, something to relieve the sad boredom which was beginning to permeate through the household. In real chronological terms only four short weeks had elapsed since her mother's death, but such is the resilience of childhood, and such was her own special stoicism and impatience, that she had had enough of mourning. She was ready to move on and enjoy what life had to offer.

"Are you going to keep me on the doorstep all morning, Maud? The snow may be thawing, but I tell you, it's bitterly cold out here."

Maud took Henry John's coat and hat, and ushered him into the drawing room.

"I'll inform the master that you're here," she said, closing the door behind her.

Ada was confused. She knew her Uncle Charles, for he lived on Forehill, a road in the centre of town, not far away, and he came to see her father every Wednesday without fail. That was her father's brother. She liked him very much. Her father had never talked about another brother, not that she could remember.

She sat on the top stair, intrigued, but not daring to disobey Maud's instructions to stay upstairs: to begin with, that is. Finally, curiosity got the better of her and she determined that she had to quiz Maud about it. She crept downstairs and, as she passed the drawing room door, she heard a snippet of the conversation within.

"I shall never set foot in Vine House again," her father was saying. "You know my reasons, and I will *not* be dissuaded. That is final."

The visitor was persisting. "Think of Ada, Richard. Let her come to Vine House on her own, without you, if you feel so strongly about it. She needs to get away, to see her cousins. She would enjoy playing with Olive. After all, there's only a couple of years between them. She needs to be with young people, not cooped up here with adults all day."

Richard may have appeared dismissive of Henry John, but the latter's words were true. Richard had not been thinking about his daughter: he had been thinking about his own loss. This kindly old man looked down with a perplexed and troubled expression.

"And you need some time to yourself, to help you get your mental strength back." Henry John was a compassionate man, when all was said and done, and a good father to his ten surviving children, whose ages spanned nineteen years. And he remembered what a good older brother Richard had been to him in the past: there were nineteen years between them too.

"You forget, Henry John. I'm an old man."

"Pooh! You're as fit as a fiddle, and if it wasn't for this sad business, you'd be out skating down at Middle Fen, taking Ada with you too, now that she's five."

It was true. Richard nodded. He had indeed intended taking Ada skating this winter, and had already gone as far as approaching Mr Legge, the boot-maker, about a pair of skating boots to be made specially for her. He cast his mind back down the years to when he was five, and his father had taken him to Legge's to get fitted for a pair of leather boots. What a bond had been made between father and child then! He could feel that warmth even now, more than seventy years later.

"You have a responsibility to your child," Henry John was continuing. He could see that he had gained ground and clinched the argument with a neat summary. "Take her out and about, entertain her, instruct her, before you really *are* too old."

Ada hardly heard the last two sentences, for she fairly skipped down the vestibule, the thoughts in her head revolving like prizes in a fairground tombola: a visit to Vine House, cousins, skating with her father!

"Maud! Maud!" She was a breathless parcel of excitement as she rushed into the kitchen. "I'm going to Vine House to play with my cousins and I'm going skating!"

The child was not given to telling lies, and could only have got information such as this by one means.

"Were you listening at the door?" Maud looked stern.

Ada hung her head for a moment, and then said, "Yes."

The next moment she was dancing round Maud's skirts and chanting, "I'm going to Vine House! I'm going to play with my cousins! I'm going to go skating!"

Maud had not the heart to chastise the child. It warmed her to see Ada smile and sing.

The next moment Ada was tugging her hand, pulling her towards the back door. "Come on!" she said.

"Not outside, surely!" Maud knew it was cold out there.

Ada persisted. "Let's go and see if they've come."

Maud was at a loss to understand what was going through the child's mind, but she would indulge her, for she was pleased Ada was so cheerful.

"Put this round you, my pretty, or you'll catch your death." Maud could have bitten her tongue, but the child seemed not to notice as the door latch was lifted and they stepped carefully through the melting snow.

Ada stopped and pointed. "There they are!"

Under the beech tree, in a shaft of sunlight, where the rich earth was beginning to show through the patchy snow, just peeping through was a delicate cluster of yellow and purple crocuses.

"See! See! Spring flowers! Now we'll all be happy again."

Part 3

"Stop fidgeting, child," Maud gently admonished Ada, who was standing on a chair before the dressmaker. "Do you wish the pins to stick in to you?" Ada shook her head. "Well stand still, and let Miss Sneed finish the hem-line in peace."

Miss Sneed had been commissioned by Richard to fit his daughter out with some new clothes. This was the third and final fitting. Frances, Richard's first wife, had had all her clothes made by Miss Sneed and her employees in the years gone by, and only last summer Miss Sneed had been called to adjust one of Matilda's dresses which was beginning to hang on her. Miss Sneed had been a fine couturier in her time and, even now in her declining years, she still worked with painstaking precision performed by deft and nimble fingers. To young Ada, however, this fitting, like the two preceding ones, was a painfully slow procedure, requiring the patience of a saint.

Maud had respectfully suggested to Richard that, as Ada had been invited to stay with her cousins in Vine House for a few weeks, it would inappropriate for her to be wearing mourning weeds.

"You see, sir, it would cast an unfortunate blackness over everyone, and would defeat the whole purpose of Ada's visit."

Richard had readily agreed, for the words of his youngest brother were still ringing in his ears. Ada needed young company, and he needed some time to be rejuvenated, so that he could be a good father to his little girl.

In the end it had been decided that she should spend a month in Vine House, his old family home. By rights it should now be *her* family home, not simply a place to visit. Try as he might, Richard could not forget that, as the eldest son of the Haddenham Porters, this house should have been his.

"One day, son, all this will be yours." He could hear his father's voice loud and clear, saying over and over again: "Vine House will be yours, when I die."

Since the seventeenth century, Vine House had always been passed on to the eldest Porter son. Why his father should have bequeathed it to the youngest son, Henry John, Richard still found hard to comprehend or to bear, even after these twelve years since his father's death.

Ada watched, fascinated, as Miss Sneed put yet another handful of pins into her mouth, chawing on them in such a way that each one was manoeuvred and singly delivered head first through her pursed lips. What with the silver winking of these pins and the gold glinting of her pince-nez rims, Miss Sneed was as strange a person as Ada had ever seen.

Strange she may have looked, but whatever else Miss Sneed could lay claim to, there was one thing for certain: no-one ever had cause to complain about the standard of work carried out by her team of seamstresses, who laboured tirelessly at the back of her costumier establishment on Forehill; and no-one ever had to wait long for their costumes, ball-gowns, shifts, blouses and other garments to be completed, boxed and delivered to the door.

So it was that the following day no less than five brand new dress boxes were delivered to Waddington Terrace. As Ada peeled back the delicate white tissue paper, which had been gently folded round each colourful item of clothing, her eyes grew wider and wider. The fittings were over; the clothes were really hers to wear. The full realisation that she would never have to put that black taffeta dress on ever again made her smile, and then giggle delightedly.

Lying in bed that night, she could hardly wait till the next day, when it was all arranged that Mr Stokes, the coachman, would take her in the Victoria to Vine House.

"You'll be just like a lady," Maud had enthused, hoping that the child would not pine or fret without her. She knew that she would certainly miss Ada. A whole month without seeing that pretty, little face, and brushing those golden curls seemed a very long time.

For Ada herself, a child of five who had lived in a house filled with sickness, death and mourning for so long, meeting her cousins and playing at Vine House were wonderful attractions. Wearing her new clothes was the icing on the cake. She snuggled deep under the blankets and the mint-green satin eiderdown. Before Maud had turned down the lamp and closed the door, Ada had slipped into a contented and dreamy sleep.

Part 4

Uncle Charles was pointing through the right window of the Victoria, saying, "And if you look across the fen, right in the distance, you'll see…" But Ada was not listening. The swaying motion of the carriage, as it rumbled on towards Haddenham across the fenland causeway, had finally lulled her to sleep.

It had been decided that Charles would accompany his young niece on her journey, as Richard was still adamant that he would not set foot inside Vine House for as long as he lived. Although Charles could understand his older brother's sense of grievance, he was not of the opinion that it should be indulged to such an extent that it divided the family. However, that was not his reason for looking after Ada on her journey: he was glad of a ready-made opportunity, an excuse even, to visit Henry John and Mary Ann, and it would give him time to spend with his nieces and nephews at Vine House. He liked children and young people in general. He always had been a gregarious fellow, had married young and his wife Mary had borne him eight children, all of them surviving. That was a long time ago, for even his youngest was nearly thirty-three and his eldest was over fifty.

Charles was in his own way an educationalist. Now a retired veterinary surgeon, he had always loved Cambridgeshire, and the fenland region in and around Ely in particular.

"What Charles Porter doesn't know is not worth knowing," Mr Ingle, a one-time resident of one of the other big late-Georgian design houses of Waddington Terrace, would tell his family. "A regular fount of knowledge."

Nowadays Charles would have liked nothing better than to instruct his grandchildren about the locality in which he lived, but they all lived far away, two of them in Australia and the other three in California. His only grand-daughter, Agnes, who lived in Sydney, was the same age as Ada. He liked to think sometimes that Ada was Agnes. It was Charles who had helped to persuade Henry John to swallow his pride and call on Richard, with the invitation for Ada to visit Vine House. On his Wednesday mornings in Waddington Terrace, it had saddened him to see little Ada in her house of mourning, with scant opportunity to mix with children. He had felt an urge to do something to help.

Even at the start of this journey, even before Ada had finished waving her little lace handkerchief through the back window of the Victoria to the diminishing figures of Maud and Ellen, Charles was pointing out various buildings and giving a potted history.

"Now, child, look out to your left and you'll see Oliver Cromwell's House." He then told her a little about Roundheads and Royalists and the Civil War, most of which was way beyond Ada's comprehension, but she was a polite little girl and listened as attentively as she could, with a look of interest on her face.

You may assume he did not tell her about the house opposite, which was known locally as "Cromwell's knocking-shop". This was where all kinds of shenanigans had gone on between the soldiers in Cromwell's Model Army and the Ely ladies of ill repute.

"Round this corner, now keep looking to your left, there's a building you know well. Isn't that so?"

Ada peered through the Victoria's side window at the Eagle and Lamb. This was a public house. You may wonder why a young child like Ada should know a place such as this, but the truth of the matter is that it was the inn attached to the Eagle Brewery, which was owned by her father.

The Eagle Brewery was still a going concern, and still belonged to Richard, though there had been regular offers to amalgamate with other brewers in the town. Mr Hall and Mr Harlock had put forward favourable terms which Richard was beginning to think might be a sound investment for Ada's future. He would give it some serious thought in the New Year. Time enough for decisions like that.

"Look over there!" Charles was pointing in another direction. "That's the militia's parade ground," he said, before shaking his head and tutting his disapproval, "though I hear some new houses are to be built on it. Scandalous! I hope Colonel Wale is not too late to put a stop to it."

And so it went on, till eventually Ada could keep her eyes open no longer.

She woke to find that the carriage had already turned off Haddenham's main road, swept up a gravelly driveway and had stopped outside the front door of a fine country house with a thatched roof. The late afternoon sun cast long shadows across the lawn, and, when Ada opened her eyes and saw a haze of purple and yellow crocuses in bloom, she knew that she would be happy here.

A very fine lady was waiting on the doorstep. This was Aunt Mary Ann, who had decided that she herself would open the door to her niece, rather than leave it, as was customary, to the housekeeper. What Ada noticed was the abundance of her aunt's greying curly hair, which had been scooped up onto the top of her head, allowing coils to fall from the crown all around, even onto her forehead. She smiled a warm welcome and, with outstretched arms, embraced Ada and kissed her lightly on the cheek, before whisking her into the house and into the drawing room to meet her uncle and her cousins.

Ada looked anxiously back towards the Victoria and Uncle Charles, worried that her trunk with her new clothes would somehow be forgotten, but she need not have worried, for Mr Stokes was already seeing to all the necessary lifting down of the luggage: Ada's trunk and boxes were first; then two wicker baskets filled with jars of Maud's speciality jams, tangy chutneys and a rich fruit cake; and finally a case of port sent by Richard to Henry John.

"Welcome, child, welcome!" Uncle Henry John's voice seemed to resonate in the hallway. "Now, make yourself at home!"

With that he marched out into the driveway to greet his

brother. His voice could be heard right to the front door and beyond. "Charles, my dear fellow. Come in out of the cold and have a glass of port. Now tell me, how was your journey?"

"Ada," Aunt Mary Ann was making the necessary introductions. "These are your cousins."

Ada clung to her aunt's long skirts in an attempt to hide from the row of three faces which looked at her.

"Hilda, Florence and Olive. This is your cousin Ada."

Ada knew that there were ten Vine House cousins, for her Uncle Charles had told her all the names.

"Let me see," he had said, rubbing his silver, bearded chin as he tried to recall all the names. "There's Everard. Of course, he lives in a house of his own next door. Your grandfather built it years ago. It was where he retired to when your uncle Henry John got married."

Already this was getting complicated for Ada, but Charles persevered with as good a family history as he could, with the best intentions. He did not want Ada to feel over-awed and at a loss among strangers. He had thought that, if he told her all about her cousins, then they would not seem like strangers to her.

"Then there's Clara. Now she lives two doors away with my sister Ann. Takes good care of her, you understand. Let me see who's next. Is it Gertrude or Emeline? Anyway, Mabel is the one after that. She must be about seventeen years old."

Seventeen had sounded very old indeed to Ada.

"Then there's Henry. A fine fellow! He will go far, mark my words. Jessie is next."

He had then told her about Hilda and Florence, thirteen and twelve respectively, assuring her that they would look after her very well.

"Olive is the youngest. The two of you will be good friends."

"How old is Olive?" Ada had asked, hoping that she was not also seventeen.

"She's just seven. Yes. You and she will get on like a house on fire."

Ada now looked at the happy faces of her three cousins. Thirteen year-old Hilda was smiling at her to make her feel welcome and loved. Florence was grinning cheerily for she was a naturally jolly twelve year-old, and Olive was smiling because she would not be the baby of the household for four whole weeks.

Ada was never to forget this moment. She smiled back, shyly, and the beginnings of friendships were forged.

Part 5

Right from the start, Hilda saw to it that Ada settled in well. She and her sister Florence felt very sorry for this pretty fair-haired cousin, whom they had never met before. They thought it must be just dreadful if their own mother should die, and were determined to do everything they could to help Ada to be cheerful.

On that first day their mother said, "Now, Hilda, I want you and Florence to show Ada all round the house, so that she doesn't get lost. Olive, you go along with them too. And then it will be time for supper."

Supper for the children was eaten in the warm morning-room adjoining the kitchen. The old table was always covered with a blue, pink and white seersucker tablecloth and the meal usually featured eggs in some form or another - poached, boiled, fried or as an omelette. There was plenty of freshly baked bread and butter, with homemade jam to follow, all washed down with warm milk. This meal was generally a cosy affair, but lately Hilda had not really enjoyed it as much as she used to. She was irked and becoming impatient. There was a rule in Vine House that the younger children ate supper in the morning room at six o'clock, whereas the older ones were allowed to eat dinner with the adults in the dining room at half-past seven. One had to be fourteen to be classified an older child and Hilda would have to wait eight more weeks till her fourteenth birthday. Ada would be a welcome diversion at supper-time for four of those weeks.

"Leave out the study on your tour," Aunt Mary Ann was saying. "Your father and Uncle Charles will be discussing business." She knew that her husband valued Charles's opinion on many matters, for Charles's reputation as a fund of information was recognised by all with whom he came in contact.

Henry John ran the prosperous Porter wheat-crop farmlands over on the Hillrow side of Haddenham, and was also the director of the Porter brick-works and clay-pits down at Haddenham End. At present, he was in the process of setting up a butcher's shop in the old Porter brewery premises adjoining Vine House, and it was this latest venture which he wanted to discuss with Charles. Charles was knowledgeable about such a vast array of subjects that he was invaluable when decisions had to be reached.

Hilda took Ada by the hand, Florence led the way down the terrazzo hallway, and Olive trotted behind. They began their tour round the house with the library, the room next to the drawing room. The panelled oak door opened into a sombre room with dark brown velvet curtains, reading lamps on mahogany tables, and an Indian carpet on the floor.

"This is the library," said Florence, with pride. Most people did not have a library.

Ada looked at the book cases, but there were not half so many books as there were in the library at Waddington Terrace, where the ceiling-to-floor shelves on three sides of the room were filled with hundreds of books of all shapes and sizes.

"Can you read yet?" asked Hilda.

"Oh yes!" Ada replied confidently. She could hardly remember a time when she could not read. Like her father, she loved books. Her favourites were *Alice in Wonderland* and *Through the Looking Glass*. She never tired of the lateness of the White Rabbit, the rhymes of the odd duo Tweedledum and Tweedledee, and even the wickedness of the Queen of Hearts who would shriek: "Off with her head! Off with her head!" Richard used to sit Ada on his knee on a Sunday afternoon and read to her, and she loved to hear about the adventures of characters such as Robinson Crusoe and Man Friday. On the last three or four occasions, however, he had taken to reading some of Mr Tennyson's poetry to her, which she found to be rather dull in comparison. The sad life and death of The Lady of Shalott had made her cry when her father had read it to her.

The lady in her white gown, who sang "Tirra, lirra!" as she lay dying in the little boat which floated down the river towards Camelot, reminded Ada of her own mother lying coldly and stiffly in her white gown on her death bed.

"What's your favourite story?" asked Olive, who was doing her level best to be a little lady.

"*Alice in Wonderland*, of course." Ada had meant to be polite in her reply, but the words came out all wrong, and Olive turned away, feeling that she had been reprimanded in some way for asking such a silly question.

Next Florence led the way through another panelled door under the main stairs, down some fifteen brick steps, polished and worn through centuries of use.

"Be careful you don't fall!" warned Hilda. "Hold my hand really tightly. The steps are ever so slippery. And, Olive, you keep a tight hold of the hand-rail, like Mama always tells you." Hilda was a considerate girl, always looking out for others, but on these dimly-lit steps she did not notice that Olive was pouting.

They descended to the three cellar apartments: one was the cold room containing marble slabs, on which were placed cooked meats, Cottenham cheese and butter under wire mesh frames, and hanging in the corner was a side of cured and smoked bacon; another was the dry room containing neatly stacked apples and potatoes from last year's crop, and plaited onions hanging in the corner; and finally a locked room which was the house-servant's quarters.

Clambering up the stairs, they jostled into the morning-room, already with its table in the process of being laid for supper.

"Far too early!" Janet, the house-servant, crossly said to the flushed faces. "Wait for the gong, as usual. Be off with you!"

"We're only exploring and showing our cousin round the house," Hilda answered.

"Well, go and explore somewhere else and don't be under my feet."

They tiptoed across the wide kitchen, so that Janet would not hear them, to peep into the rooms adjoining, which were to be converted into the butcher's shop. As they came back across the kitchen, Ada thought that it looked very similar to the kitchen in Waddington Terrace, but it was not quite so warm and friendly. Leading up from the kitchen, in the far corner, was a narrow, spiral staircase, which the four children now climbed.

"These are the back stairs," said Florence. "They used to be for the servants in the old days, when they used to live in."

Ada was not very sure what Florence meant. She was about to ask "Live in what?" but they had now reached the top of the stairs, and were at one end of a long corridor with dark oak flooring. How it creaked when they walked on it! More panelled doors! Florence was giving a running commentary as she opened each door on the landing,

"This is Gertrude and Emeline's room, but they're away in France at the moment, learning how to be real French ladies. This used to be Everard's room, but he doesn't live here any more. He's going to be married next month and we're all going to be bridesmaids. And this used to be Clara's room before she moved in with old Aunt Ann."

"This is Jessie's and Mabel's room." Hilda now took over, for Florence had been talking so fast that she had become quite breathless. "You won't see them, because they're away at boarding school. They only come home in the holidays. I'm going to go next September too."

As Hilda divulged this piece of information, it would have been difficult to determine whether she spoke with enthusiasm and anticipated pleasure at the prospect being too old to attend the local girls' school in Haddenham and moving on to a boarding school for older girls, or whether she felt apprehensive about a new life away from her Mama and Papa. Family values were very important in Hilda's estimation of things.

One thing was for sure: Florence was dreading the time when her sister would go away to boarding school, so for a few moments her natural ebullience gave way to thoughtful reflection as the tour continued.

Next, on the left of this corridor, there was the bathroom,

with a black and white chequered linoleum floor covering. Under the frosted window was a huge, white, enamel bath, with eagle claw feet which grasped golden orbs. Cork mats, mirrors and towel stands stood against the walls, and Margerison 'White Windsor' toilet soap tablets were resting in brass soap-containers shaped like clam shells. Ada liked the fresh, clean smell in this room.

Closing the bathroom door, they were now at a kind of crossroads. Ahead there was the main flight of stairs leading back down to the terrazzo hallway. There was a corridor to the left, leading to the bedroom Ada was to share with Olive, and Henry's bedroom was next to that. Ada learnt later that he was also away at a boarding school.

"This is Mama's and Papa's bedroom," said Hilda, "but we're never allowed in there."

"Unless there's an emergency," added Florence.

Off the final corridor to the right was a dressing room, complete with a walk-in hot-press where the family's clothes were warmed and aired. To the left was a study, used as a schoolroom in years gone by, but now used as a quiet family work-room.

It was a whirlwind tour and, although its purpose was to help Ada not get lost, she now was well and truly disorientated and had no notion how she would ever find her way on her own. However, any fears she may have had were soon to evaporate when the final door was opened. They had reached the last room on their tour: the nursery.

Ada stood open-eyed and open-mouthed at what was before her: she had never seen so many toys!

It was nothing short of a wonderland of teddy bears, Russian dolls, rag dolls, hoops, wooden tops and striped skittles, with a magnificent rocking horse regally overseeing his realm of playthings. How Ada longed to touch his noble head and look deep into his lustrous brown eyes.

Also, set neatly in an open wooden chest beneath the window was a collection of musical instruments, including a cornet, a flute, cymbals, a triangle, a tambourine, a soldier's tin drum and a miniature piano.

"You can play these whenever you like," Hilda smiled with encouragement.

Ada hung her head and said nothing.

Olive, sensing that somehow she might be able to regain some ground, immediately chimed in, "What instrument do you play?"

"I can't play any at all," replied Ada simply.

Hilda came to the rescue, "Never mind! We'll teach you how to play while you're here." She gave her sister one of her looks as if to say, "Be nice!"

Hilda was in fact true to her word and, even though her pupil was to prove musically inept, she persevered and succeeded in getting Ada to strike the triangle at the correct time in a little musical ensemble, which these four youngest members of the household performed on the following Sunday in the drawing room.

To the right hand side of the fireplace, three dolls, dressed as fine gentlewomen in silk dresses with frills, sat on small chairs at a round table, which was laid with a real Wedgewood china tea-set, finely crafted in miniature. Ada wished she could become small like Alice and pour tea for these ladies. But it would be a much more orderly tea-party than the Mad Hatter's, and there would be no rudeness!

"Come and have a look at this!" Hilda had run over to the other side of the room to where a tall dresser stood against the high wall with a set of wooden steps placed in front of it. "Mind you don't fall! The steps are a bit rickety."

When Ada had climbed up the three steps, there before her was a toy farm, destined one day to become a collector's item. Someone had arranged all the two hundred and forty lead pieces, collected over a period of some twenty years, into a replica of a working farm complete with farm-house and farmer, barn and farm-labourer, glossily painted fences and trees, farming implements and a plough, water-trough and buckets, cart-horses and carts, cows and even a milkmaid on a three-legged milking stool, sheep and pigs, and finally hens no bigger than her fingernail in the farmyard.

Ada was not sure whether this was a toy or an ornament and she determined that she had better not touch any of it during her stay.

Finally, the pièce de resistance for Ada was a fully furnished doll's house with little hinged doors, see-through windows with lace curtains, real pieces of furniture and even little dolls inside.

Olive desperately wanted to be nice, to get into her sister's good books again, and said, "Let's play with the doll's house together."

Ada's eyes glowed with pleasure. So it was, that on that first afternoon, with only two years between them, Ada and Olive could be observed playing contentedly together, absorbed in the world of the doll's house, until the gong rang for supper.

Florence and Hilda sat at a writing table. Florence, who was quite an artist, was designing the bridesmaid's dress which she would like to wear at her brother's wedding, if she were to have her way. Hilda was composing a letter to her sister Jessie, smiling and satisfied, pleased that she had helped to make her sad little cousin's first day at Vine House a happy one.

Part 6

Ada was not sure if she was dreaming or whether she was awake. Everything was hot and confused.

Someone was saying, "She's delirious. Get some cold flannels!"

The damp bed-clothes were thrown back, her nightdress press-studs were opened and then she felt the delicious shock of icy cold cloths pressed on her forehead, chest and wrists.

Then the White Rabbit was looking irritably at her. "I'm late! I'm late! And it is all your fault!"

"No, it's not!" she managed to say, though her throat hurt horribly.

"We must send for Richard!" Mary Ann was earnestly imploring her husband's assent to what she knew was imperative.

"He refuses to set foot in Vine House." Henry John remembered his brother's words during their last meeting. It was difficult to explain to his wife just how adamant and stubborn his brother had become over this matter.

"Papa!" Ada croaked.

She saw his face smiling at her, but he was in the middle of a framed picture. He wasn't real. It was only a painting. She remembered looking at that very painting before she was carried up to bed. But she did not know when that was.

By the time Sunday had come, Ada was one of the family, taking afternoon lessons with Olive in the school-room. Miss Taylor, spinster of Haddenham parish, was Olive's tutor who called each weekday afternoon, once Olive had returned from morning school in Haddenham village, to encourage lady-like pursuits such as sewing, painting and playing the pianoforte.

Sunday afternoon had found Ada sitting on the sofa beside Hilda in the drawing room.

"Are you excited?" Hilda had asked.

Ada had just nodded. She had in fact been very apprehensive, for this was the day she was to take part in the regular Sunday afternoon entertainment. Everyone performed a little party piece. It was a pleasant way of passing the time between lunch and afternoon tea, but to Ada it was torture. Wearing her Sunday best, her pretty new mauve, organza frock fashioned by Miss Sneed, had helped not a jot. All she could think about was whether she would strike the triangle at the right moment in the quartet with Hilda, Florence and Olive.

She had felt very hot and her head ached. Every time she looked at the French window, she winced as the light seemed to sear her eyeballs.

"It will be our turn next," Hilda was saying in a whisper, as Henry John had set forth upon a rousing rendition of his father's favourite, Burns's poem *My Love is Like a Red, Red Rose.*

Ada had looked one by one at the old portraits of generations of Porters glowering down at her from the walls. They were all there in their gilt frames watching her, waiting for her to make a mistake. She had felt herself beginning to shiver. She had wanted to cry, to run from the room, to go home, anything rather than strike that triangle!

Just when she thought she could bear it no longer, her gaze had fallen upon the face of her father, smiling down at her. For there too was his portrait, showing his kind eyes, his tickly beard which she loved to stroke and curl her fingers through, his starched wing-collar with the spiky points, and his looped fob-watch chain shining on his moderate corporation. She had felt cheered, encouraged, and knew that she would strike that triangle at the right time, especially for him.

"But his child needs him," Mary Ann was saying. She was not a lady to give in so easily. "He may never see her again. I, for one, could not live with myself if that were to happen. I'll go myself. He'll listen to me."

Without further ado, she bustled out of the room, and Ada could hear her order the carriage.

"Off with her head! Off with her head!" the Queen was shrieking.

"No! No!" Ada was afraid, and wanted to run, but which way? Which way? Across the snowdrop field to the lady in a white gown, or across the purple and yellow crocus lawn to the portrait in the gilt picture frame? All her bones ached. Her knees and elbows and wrists and fingers were stiff and sore.

"There, there!" a soothing voice was drying her tears and smoothing her brow. "Sit up now, child, and take some of this warm milk."

How spiky her throat felt, but the milk was sweet and warm and slipped down without too much discomfort.

"I think she should sleep now, sir." It was Janet's voice, no longer cross and bossy, but concerned and compassionate. "I'll keep watch over her if you wish, sir, until Dr Granger calls."

Henry John was glad to leave the sick-room and go down to his study. He hardly dared think about his young niece, for three of his own children had died in infancy upstairs in that very room.

When Ada woke again, there were hushed voices.

"How is the patient, doctor?" Henry John bit his lip as he waited for the inevitable reply.

"Too early to tell yet, I'm afraid." Dr Granger spoke quietly, with a tone of authority, disguising the fact that the prognosis was not good. It was an automatic response, borne of many such inquiries during his forty years of attending the sick. Some patients suffering from a high fever and an inflamed throat survived, and some did not.

Ada did not like this stranger who smelt of camphor and menthyl. She wanted to get out of bed and tell him she was "very well, thank you". She struggled desperately to free herself from the bed-clothes, but there were hands keeping her down. She fell back, physically too exhausted to fight. Inside her head the Mad Hatter was singing "tirra lirra" over and over again.

When the old grandfather clock in the dining-room below began to chime midnight, Ada listened, her eyes closed. She heard herself counting out loud, in a voice that was so croaky she hardly recognised it as her own: "...five, six, seven..."

"...eight, nine, ten, eleven, twelve," continued another voice beside her. She dared not think the voice was real.

Ada was scared to open her eyes. In her fever-dreams she had seen so many different faces careering before her bewildered eyes that she could not tell what was real and what was imaginary any more. But the hand which held her hand felt real, and the lips which kissed her forehead felt real.

"Is that really you, Papa?"

She opened her eyes and there was her father.

Richard nodded and smiled. "How's my little girl?"

"Getting better."

"That's good. Now get some sleep and I'll read you a story in the morning."

CHAPTER 2
RICHARD

Part 1

"The best picnic," Richard corrected Ada.

"That's what I said: the bestest picnic in the whole world!"

Richard was relaxing in one of the new-fangled deck-chairs which Mr Stokes had recommended he buy, once the picnic at Wicken Fen had been suggested. What a palaver there had been trying to work out how to manoeuvre all the hinged struts and bars to form a support for the red and yellow striped material serving as the seat! How Ada had laughed and clapped her hands with glee, as she watched the antics of Mr Stokes grappling with wood and canvas! Richard had been quite bemused and amused by such a contraption, but he had to admit that it was remarkably comfortable.

The idyllic meadow overlooking Wicken Fen on this summer day was swathed in rainbow flowers. A golden profusion of celandines, buttercups, primroses and kingcups, merged with the ethereal delicate blues of speedwell and the fiery glow of red campion.

To the few passers-by in this remote beauty spot a few miles south of Ely, the picnic party must have seemed a motley assortment of people. First, there was an old gentleman in plus-fours and a lightweight colonial jacket, dozing in a modern, garish deck-chair. Seated on the shaded step of a Victoria carriage, an ageing red-faced coachman was fanning himself: he was an incongruous sight in his heavy dark green livery and a knotted white handkerchief serving as a hat. The middle-aged woman, kneeling as she cleared away the remains of the picnic into a wicker basket, was probably a servant of some sort, judging by her home-spun bonnet. The little girl in a frilly white dress, with a multi-coloured smocked bodice, must be the old man's grand-daughter. She was a picture of contentment, surrounded by a carpet of wild flowers.

"What's this one called, Papa?" Ada tapped Richard on the arm, as she presented a flower for his inspection.

"Now let me see," he said, opening his eyes and yawning. It had been many years since he had been called upon to name wild flowers, but his memory was serving him well, for this must be the ninth or tenth wild flower Ada had brought for him to identify. "This, my dear," he said examining the fresh pinkness of the small petals, "is called willowherb."

"It's bending down!" Ada observed as the willowherb flower began to droop in her hot and clammy hand.

"It's very flimsy, but pretty. Put it in your box very carefully with the others."

He watched her as she trotted back to the coach.

"Look, Mr Stokes," he heard her say. "Isn't this a nice one? I think it's my favourite."

Richard soaked up the warmth of the day, smelt the perfumes of meadowsweet and flowering grasses, and even thought he caught a whiff of the fragrant southern marsh orchid down in the fenland below. He could hear the grasshopper warblers calling to one another in the distance. Life was good.

He had Mary Ann and Henry John to thank for today.

"You need to get away every now and again," Mary Ann had bluntly, though kindly, stated the obvious, on that last day in Vine House. She was a strong-willed lady who rarely accepted "no" for an answer. She had won her brother-in-law over once before and would do so again, for his own good, and for Ada's.

"Go on a few picnics! Show Ada the sights!" Henry John had said. "Stokes can organise the itinerary, and Maud will be in her element filling a hamper with all kinds of interesting delicacies. Have her go with you, to serve up the food and so forth."

Charles had played his part too. "Nothing like a change of air to make the horses gallop faster," he added, chuckling. He had been thinking back to one Maid Marilyn, a sickly filly which he had attended on the outskirts of Ely some forty years before, in his capacity as veterinary surgeon. This three-year old had sniffed, snorted and savoured the different air at Newmarket, then had astounded trainers and punters alike when she ran the race of her life. Charles's reputation as a "horse-doctor" was made.

And obscurely, Matilda had played a part as well. One Sunday afternoon in late May, Richard had taken down a large book for Ada to look at. Ada was sitting at her mother's old escritoire in the drawing-room with *The Complete Works of William Shakespeare* before her. The navy blue, leather-backed volume was heavily embossed, with the familiar bust of the bard taking centre position on the front cover.

"It's the biggest book in the world, bigger than all the books at Vine House," she commented with the confidence of one who knew. During her four-week stay in Vine House, she had been allowed to take down each book in the library, one at a time, to peruse. She had felt the weight of many big books, and she knew that none could compare with this huge tome. "May I open it, Papa?"

"Of course, but very carefully. Books are always to be treated with love and affection."

Ada had opened it somewhere near the middle. She let out a gasp of surprise. Between the two pages was a folded piece of white tissue paper.

"Look, Papa!" she called, her eyes wide with excitement at finding such buried treasure.

Together, the two of them had gently unfolded the paper, and inside was a pressed flower of faded yellow, with the name "Toadflax" carefully inscribed in black ink on a little card. It was Matilda's distinctive, sprawling hand-writing. Richard had been shaken to the core: another reminder of the unfairness of that grim reaper, Death.

"Is this a real flower?" Ada wanted to know.

"Yes indeed," whispered Richard, gathering his composure. "Would you like to pick your very own flowers, and press them, like your dear Mama did?" he had asked. It had seemed the right thing to say. Matilda would have been pleased.

"You mean, pick the flowers in the garden?" Ada had looked worried, a little frown appearing on her brow. It took a few seconds for Richard to appreciate what was wrong. He looked into her wide brown eyes; then understood. She was thinking back to the time, nearly four months ago, when the two of them had gathered snowdrops.

"Not garden flowers, but wild flowers," he quickly assured her, a gentle smile on his kindly face. His words had an immediate effect, for her frown lines disappeared. "Flowers which grow in the countryside," he continued. "And to the countryside we shall go."

"When, Papa, when?" Ada's face had lit up.

"Midsummer."

"Papa! Papa!" Ada now came running up to Richard. "Mr Stokes says I have to collect another two flowers and then I'll have twelve altogether."

Richard smiled, his memories fading. "Twelve! That's good."

"And he says they will be my twelve discipoles."

"Do you mean 'disciples'?"

"I don't know." Ada bit her lip and was silent for a moment. "Papa," she continued, "what are discipoles?"

Richard sighed. Here was something else he had neglected. When they got home that evening, he would take her on his knee and tell her all about the 'discipoles'.

Part 2

Richard led Ada blindfold into the morning room. Maud looked on with her hands clasped together in joyful expectation. Ellen stood transfixed at the doorway into the kitchen, mouth open, watching the young mistress of the house.

"You can have a peep now, my birthday girl."

On the morning-room table, now protected by its day-time burgundy chenille cover, the breakfast things having been cleared away, was a large strangely angular package, tied up with a bright pink bow. Ada simply stood before this parcel wrapped in shiny brown paper, not quite knowing whether to open it or not. Richard nodded to her in encouragement, and then looked at Maud.

"Go ahead, my pretty," coaxed Maud, "you can't keep your father waiting. Open it and see what's inside!"

"Shall I help you?" suggested Richard.

"I can manage, thank you, Papa."

And manage she did, though it was a lengthy process, for the paper was tough.

Amidst the rustling and crumpling of the paper, Richard thought back to other birthdays, so many years ago. The excited, shining birthday faces of his two sons, Alfred and Frank, careered before his inward eye.

Alfred and Frank, both in their forties, were like strangers to him now. Why had they voiced so many objections to his marriage with Matilda? It was inconceivable that they could have harboured such a dislike of her. She had even been a relation: the daughter of his own cousin, Marshall. Trying to be reasonable, he thought that perhaps they had objected to her youth, her lack of wealth perhaps? Did they think she had been a gold-digger? Now that Matilda was dead and buried, God rest her soul, why did they show so little interest in his darling daughter, Ada, their own half-sister? It was all very perplexing and hurtful. It distressed him more than words could express. He longed to talk with them again; they had common interests: the three of them were all master brewers, after all. They had so much still to share.

His reverie was broken.

"My very own writing desk!" Ada exclaimed, and then she flung her arms round Richard and hugged him so tight about the knees that he almost fell over.

"Steady, steady, child!" Maud came to the rescue.

The miniature escritoire was of the type which had no legs, for it was designed to sit on a lady's lap, or on an occasional table in the drawing-room. It was fashioned from expertly crafted, inlaid mahogany, with a sloping hinged lid covered in fine crimson leather. The brass inkwell fitted delicately in the right-hand corner of the top beside a runnel for a pen to rest in.

"Have you had a look inside?" Richard asked. "Lift the lid and see!"

What Ada saw inside filled her heart with happiness. Ever since her stay in Vine House in the spring, she and her cousin Hilda had exchanged letters. Hilda's were full of news of the cousins, her day as a bridesmaid at her brother's wedding, and how she was looking forward to going away to school. Ada's little notes were concise accounts of her walks round Ely with her father, visits to the May Fair in Market Place and the Horse Fair on the Green, the picnic at Wicken Fen, and her pressed flower collection. Everything an apprentice epistolarian could ever want was inside the writing desk: bottles of coloured ink, quill pens, watermarked vellum writing paper and delicate envelopes, and some pink blotting paper.

"And see here. This is a new kind of pen. A fountain pen."

Everyone peered as Richard unscrewed the top revealing a bright shiny nib.

"This is a gold nib! Real gold!" he enthused. "It will last for years."

Ellen, still standing in the kitchen doorway, craned her neck to get a better view of this modern invention. Her loud intake of breath voiced her sense of wonderment.

Then Richard unscrewed the nib section from the barrel of the pen to show a rubber tube inside. "You can fill this up with ink and the pen keeps writing and writing."

Ellen's eyes protruded even further from her head, and her individual toothy grin split her face.

"A fountain pen that goes on writing!" she dared to say aloud. Her amazement had made her bold. "Whatever will they invent next?"

"Now you'll be able to write letters to your heart's content," Maud commented, though she was not quite as awe-struck as Ellen. For a traditionalist at heart, modern inventions were a troublesome addition to an otherwise ordered life.

"May I write one now?" Ada asked.

"No time like the present, eh!" Richard was completely satisfied that this was a grand gift for his daughter.

Maud, as ever an expert time-keeper, felt it encumbent upon herself to remind the master of the morning's proposed agenda.

"What time would you like Ada ready for, sir?" she enquired.

"Ready, Maud?" In all the excitement of the opening of the present, he had obviously forgotten.

"The birthday visits, sir," she gently reminded him.

"To be sure, to be sure! The three birthday visits. Shall we say half-past ten?"

As he left the room, Ada was kneeling on the chair, carefully extracting a piece of white vellum notepaper from the writing-case.

"I shall write to Hilda," she said emphatically.

Richard shot a quick look at Maud, for he now remembered what was to happen after the morning visits.

There was to be a special surprise luncheon party for Ada, and Hilda was to come for lunch that day, with her parents and her two youngest sisters, Florence and Olive.

Maud quickly suggested that Ada write a different letter: a thank-you note to Richard. Ada acquiesced with no inkling of what lay in store for her later that day, after the morning visits.

All was going well until the third visit. They had enjoyed good company and savoured hot muffins in the drawing room of Charles and Mary's house on Forehill. Richard could see that Ada loved being the centre of attention. Posing in Mr Bolton's photographic studio, she sat prettily and demurely in her little sailor suit dress and straw hat, knowing that she was special.

But at the Allens something was not right. Ada looked uncomfortable.

The Allens also lived on Forehill, but unlike Charles, Philip Allen did not own his own accommodation: he and his wife Caroline and daughter Annie lodged in the house of George Minns, a music teacher in the town. Richard had great admiration for Philip Allen, who had been his clerk in the Eagle brewery for fifteen years. He was an upright and honest individual. Richard's faith in this man was such that in his will written in the June of 1884, nine years earlier, he had included the following: "I appoint my two sons Alfred Edward Porter and Henry Francis Porter and my friend Philip Spellman Allen of Ely aforesaid executors of my will", adding "I appoint the said Philip Spellman Allen to be the guardian of my infant daughter Ada Porter". In a later codicil, to please Matilda, he had also appointed their friend, William Sayer, a bank manager in Holt in Norfolk, to be joint guardian.

Ada stood quietly, a serious look on her birthday face, as the Allens made a great fuss of her. There was no doubt that they were kindness itself, sharing in her excitement of what her father had given her for her birthday. Annie, a year older than Ada, danced round her, admiring her dress. Caroline told her she was "such a pretty girl, quite grown up!" Philip shook her by the hand and asked her how she was now that she was "a six-year old lady". Richard put his daughter's reticence down to the fact that she was probably tired after all the attention she had received in the morning, nothing more than that. Yes, he inwardly nodded, these were very kind people who would look after Ada well.

He had no reservations about choosing Philip Allen and William Sayer as guardians of his daughter, even though there were so many family members to hand. In his seventy-seven years, Richard had seen too many family divisions, too many family squabbles, and his own sons had as good as rejected his new wife. He ardently believed that Ada would be better off with someone outside the family. She would be adequately provided for financially, his two sons would administer the moneys due to her and her guardians, and she would grow up with either the Allens or the Sayers, good upright citizens. It seemed to him to be a perfectly satisfactory arrangement for when he was dead and gone.

Richard had not noticed the look of envy on Annie's face as she danced, nor Caroline's sorrow that her own daughter was not dressed as prettily and would never receive such expensive birthday presents, and the implications that Ada was a "lady" to Philip were all lost on Richard. But although she did not fully understand, Ada, the centre of attraction, was only too aware of the underlying thoughts and feelings. It cast a shadow on her day.

It had cast a shadow on Richard too, for he wanted this day to be one of glorious surprises for his little girl. Unaware of what was troubling Ada as they walked back home, he knew, however, that what awaited her there would put the twinkle back into her eyes.

"Prepare yourself, my dear, for a huge surprise," he said as he scuffed his shoes on the cast-iron foot-scraper on the doorstep of Waddington Terrace. His shoes were perfectly clean, but this was an accustomed procedure which he performed come rain, come shine.

To Ada's utter astonishment, the door was opened by Hilda. What a hugging and laughing ensued! When Hilda led Ada into the dining room, seated round the luncheon table were Uncle Henry John, Aunt Mary Ann, Florence and Olive. Richard looked on with a heart fit to burst with happiness. Ada's eyes were dancing with delight.

"Ada," exclaimed Henry John, "you look like a little princess today! Imagine that! Two princesses in the one city on the same day!"

There was a hushed silence, a tense pause, as all eyes looked towards Henry John and then to Ada. Unwittingly, he had almost spoilt the last surprise of the day. The whole of Ely knew what was happening in their city on this July day – all except Ada. Richard had pre-warned Charles, Mr Bolton and the Allens to "keep mum" about the event which was to take place later in the afternoon.

"Who's the other one?" Ada asked.

"Why, your cousin Olive!" Henry John hurriedly tried to extricate himself from the awkward situation. The family round the table simultaneously breathed a sigh of relief.

"What about Hilda and Florence? Are they not princesses too?" Ada did not like leaving people out.

"Indeed yes, but they're bigger princesses." Henry John smiled, though he was beginning to look a bit hot under the collar, as he had to extricate himself yet again.

By sheer coincidence, Ada's birthday had fallen on the same day as a royal wedding. Queen Victoria's grandson George, Duke of York and second in line to the throne, had married Princess Mary of Teck. They were to honeymoon up north, it was thought in Scotland, though no-one knew for sure. What was certain was that the royal train would pass though Ely in the late afternoon, on its way northwards from London.

Along with a few thousand other Ely citizens, the family made their way to throng the station platforms and level crossings to catch a glimpse of the royal couple. The platform where they stood was alive with happy, expectant chatter. Streamers and ribbons decked the iron framework of the Grecian and Italian style roof, while Union flags hung from every pillar and post along the platform. Children's white handkerchiefs fluttered back and forth to welcome the newly-weds.

When the sound of a train's whistle was heard, someone shouted, "Here they come!" in a loud bass voice. The crowd broke into a spontaneous singing of the national anthem, followed by cheers which resonated through the station building.

As the immense gleaming Pullman train surged into the station, it seemed to be slowing.

"There it is!" a woman shrieked. "The royal carriage! The one with the royal crest!"

Inside the shining maroon coach, with the royal coat of arms emblazoned on the side, the royal couple smiled gracefully at the people of Ely. The Duke of York raised his right forearm in acknowledgement of the well-wishing crowd, in what was to become his own characteristic regal wave in future years.

What a wonderful experience!

Richard watched Ada as she flapped her lace handkerchief until the train was completely out of sight. He could not help but muse that one day she would be able to tell her children and her grandchildren that she had stood hand in hand with her father on Ely platform and waved to King George and Queen Mary on their wedding day, and that they had waved back to her because it was her sixth birthday.

Part 3

"Bless me! More bits and pieces!" Maud exclaimed as she placed a small parcel, addressed to Ada, on the silver tray used each morning for the day's mail or for visiting cards presented by those who called.

Richard sat in a brass-studded armchair in the quiet room overlooking the back garden. He liked this room. There was a sense of tranquillity and repose there, especially on an autumn morning like this when the sun filtered through the russet leaves of the beech tree, sending slivers of golden light to where he sat.

This had been Matilda's favourite room, where she had helped him with the business accounts for the brewery and the carrier business. It was a place where she had also liked to read, or to work at her tapestries and her flower-presses. She had always been busy, he reflected – until she became ill. Before his fleeting sad thoughts turned to a heaviness which would mar his day, there was a tapping at the door.

"Excuse me, sir," Maud said as she entered the room. "Here's the post. There's a parcel for Ada, too. Though who would be sending her a parcel at this time of year? Christmas is two months away!"

Richard examined the postmark and discovered that the parcel had been posted in the Lancashire town of Preston.

"It must be from Ada's aunt, Priscilla."

Maud sighed.

"Anything wrong, Maud?" Richard enquired, as ever sensitive to the feelings of others.

"Well, sir, it's just that Ada is gathering up little keepsakes and special gifts, but has nowhere to keep them."

"What do you suggest as a solution?"

"Perhaps a vanity case, sir?"

"Excellent idea! A visit to Harvey's is in order, I believe." Richard was already on his feet. "Look sharp, Maud! Coat and hat, please!"

Harvey's was a new establishment at the corner of High Street, just opened a few months, and it reputedly sold everything from light furnishings to underwear, and specialised in ladies' fashions for "the comfort of the home" and for "those occasions when the lady is out and about". Richard had read their advertisement in the September edition of the "Red Book", Mr Tibbit's publication designed to promote old and new places of interest in Ely. Richard remembered, in particular, that ladies' reticules and vanity cases were on sale at Harvey's.

By the time Ada came home from school in the early afternoon, he had returned and was seated in the drawing-room with the wrapped vanity-case on the occasional table by the window, and the small package from Aunt Priscilla beside it.

Miss Brand, Ada's governess, had left in July to be married, and most fortuitously the Misses Bird, spinster ladies of gentle birth who had fallen on comparatively hard times, had taken the brave step of buying the property at the other end of Waddington Terrace and transforming it into a preparatory school. They had thirty children aged between five and nine enrolled in their first term, one of whom was Ada.

"Come in, my dear," Richard said as Ada peeped her head round the door. "Come and show me what you've been doing today."

Ada opened her leather satchel and extracted a slate with a wooden frame. On the one side was a coloured chalk picture of a horse, or was it a cow? It was difficult to decide.

"That's very good," he said. "You're becoming quite an artist!"

Ada beamed. She loved her father's praise. It made her feel ten feet tall. Then her brow puckered.

"These are my home exercises," she said, turning over her slate to show the other side where twelve sums were written. "Sums with tens and units. You have to carry one. They're very hard."

How life went on repeating itself, Richard thought. He remembered being in Vine House sixty years ago, helping his little sister Suzanna as she struggled with addition. How exasperated she had been!

"I hate them, I hate them!" she had exclaimed, throwing down her slate on which were written all the objects of her hate. "I can't do them!"

"They're only sums," Richard had tried to sooth her. "I'll help you, if you like."

Then there was a time, nearly forty years ago, when he and his young family had lived on Main Street in Haddenham. His son Alfred, aged five, had doggedly refused to be helped. Richard had been looking over Alfred's shoulder, and had seen where the problem lay.

"You have to carry the ten," he had offered.

"I can do it, Papa! I can do it!" Alfred had sounded belligerent. He was not one to take defeat kindly, and was not prepared to take help either.

Frank, as a child, had been more willing to listen and before he had entered King's School in Ely as a teenage scholar, he was well on his way to becoming a sound mathematician.

And now Ada!

"Never mind! I'm sure you'll manage famously," Richard said to her. Then, after a brief pause, he added cheerily, "It's your lucky day, you see. You have two packages to open: one from me and one the postman has brought you. Both packages are over there."

How her cherubic face brightened and her brown eyes shone, as she ran over to the occasional table to examine the parcels which were specifically for her.

After supper, when Richard went up to the nursery, Ada was sitting on the floor surrounded with what Maud had called the "bits and pieces". She was examining each one in turn before putting them into her new dove-grey velvety vanity case with its shiny brass clasp.

What an interesting assortment of mementoes and keepsakes

were here! Richard sat on the Ottoman, looking with interest at his daughter's collection. The latest addition was a slim birthday book with just forty pages, called The Glad Year Round. On the frontispiece was written a comprehensive suggestion for how the book should be used by its owner: "A Record of Birthdays and Anniversaries, and Memorable Events, or Engagement Book". This was the present from Aunt Priscilla which had been unwrapped in the drawing room.

Ada had read aloud what her aunt had written inside the front cover: "To my dear niece, Ada from her loving aunt, Priscilla Sellers. October, 1893." She had never met this aunt, but knew she was her mother's sister and lived in a very cold part of England.

There were three crisp card pages devoted to each month. On the first of these was a seasonal watercolour painting in miniature to represent each new month, with an accompanying motto, verse or quotation; and there was a faint imprint of an appropriate flower on a stalk or a leafy twig on the other two pages.

Richard and Ada had turned the pages over until they reached the present month. October's watercolour was a tranquil, pastel river scene, but with storm clouds gathering overhead. Strangely disturbing. The bitter-sweet verse by M Ford was both poignant and comforting to Richard as he read it to himself:

"The flowers are gone, the swallows fled,
But Autumn skies smile sweet and calm,
And those, whom Nature's hands have led
In all hours feel the healing balm."

As Richard was thinking "Perhaps, perhaps", Ada had turned back to the first page, where a poem by Alice Reed was printed.

"Read what it says here, Papa, please."

As he read the delightful rhyming couplets of the poem, Ada had held his hand tightly, listening to his every word.

43

"The glad year round we watch together,
Summer and Spring and Autumn weather.
And Winter merry, with frost and rime,
Sweet with the songs of Christmas-time.
Roses and holly, and lilac and may,
And golden leaves hung loose on the spray,
All like a garland twined together,
All the year round comes birthday weather.
The berries come when the swallows go,
When the sun shines pale the firesides glow,
When the throstle is silent the robin sings,
When roses are falling the snow-flower springs,
Some pleasant thought for every day,
For every step on the onward way,
Some lovely leaf or blossom is found
The glad year round."

Sitting now in the nursery, Ada suddenly asked, "Papa, will you write our names in it, in joined up writing? You can use my fountain pen," she offered, picking it out of her writing case ready for the purpose. She knew that her father could not refuse her request.

Richard wrote two names in the book for her: "Ada Porter", below an arching branch of wild roses, in the space allotted to July 20th; and beside January 19th he penned his own name across a pair of delicate snowdrops, in abbreviated form "Rich. Porter". Ada looked on with admiration as Richard executed his own variety of copperplate handwriting, complete with curled serifs and other flourishes.

"Well now, is everything to your satisfaction, my lady?" he asked, bowing as if he were some learned scribe in days of yore in the employ of Lady Guinevere.

"But what about Mama?"

Richard had tried valiantly to talk less and less of Matilda, for fear of upsetting his daughter, but of course it was only right that the child should have her mother's date of birth recorded too. Consequently, on the first day of December he wrote what in reality was the remembrance of Matilda's birthday, "M. A. Porter". When the ink had dried, he closed the little book, for he could not bear the next question which might have been a request to write in Matilda's date of death as well. He had already completed this unhappy task in Matilda's own birthday book. It seemed to him that their daughter might like to keep this book as well in her vanity case. He would take it out of Matilda's escritoire in the drawing room the next day and present it to Ada, as another keepsake for her to treasure.

"What's in here?" Richard asked, pointing to a small envelope.

"Photographs and special cards," she said in a grown-up manner, nodding her head confidentially. Richard remembered now giving her some photographs, but when the first one was taken out of the envelope, his heart gave a lurch, for it was Matilda's likeness, taken many years ago by Mr Lee, the renowned portrait photographer in Norwich.

"This is Mama, when she was very young," said Ada. "She was very pretty."

Richard sighed in agreement, "Yes, she was. Very pretty indeed."

"Will I be pretty like Mama when I grow up?"

"You're already pretty," Richard said, gently stroking her hair, willing his tears to go away.

"This is you, Papa." She produced a sepia picture of Richard taken when photography was in its infancy. His hair was only just beginning to go grey, he noted, and he was considerably leaner than he was now. He looked quite the man about town. "But where did your whiskers go?" To Ada, her father without whiskers was all wrong.

Then Ada produced another photograph of him. "Look at this one. You look very funny here as well!"

Richard did indeed look very funny, and extremely uncomfortable. He was perched on top of a penny-farthing wedged against the wall outside Waddington Terrace. He recollected how difficult it had been to remain stationary while

Mr Bolton inserted plate after plate into the complex brown box on a tripod, saying "Just another one, Mr Porter. Keep absolutely still." He remembered the blinding magnesium flash as each photograph was taken.

"And this is me!" she said, producing the picture taken on her last birthday.

"You see, my dear, how pretty you are!"

Her two special cards were deftly extracted from the envelope with precision. She looked just like a little lady. Philip Allen was right, Richard thought.

The first card was her christening card, on which Richard had written the words: *"Ada Porter. Born July 20th 1887 at 11.00am. Baptised at St Mary's Church Ely, August 11 1887. Born under the Planet Mars. Richd Porter".*

The second was the card Matilda had written before she died. It had been placed inside a little leather purse which had belonged to her own mother, Ann, a twenty-first birthday present from Ann's father. The words in Matilda's distinctive, sprawling handwriting read: *"My dear little girl, oh my child, I shall soon have to leave you, and when this is given to you, you will be a big girl. This purse was given to my dear mother and now I give it to you."*

"I think you should put this card back inside the purse, my dear," suggested Richard, his heart swelling. It was where Matilda had placed it and where it belonged: along with the lock of Matilda's hair, wrapped in fine paper; and with an 1840 penny black, one of the first day's issue of the very first postage stamp in the world, bought by Ada's great grandfather. He had thought it might be "worth a pretty penny some day".

As all the items were placed neatly in the vanity case and the lid was about to be closed, Richard noticed that a small newspaper cutting had been left out. He knew instantly what it was, and he wondered if Ada might have left it out on purpose.

"Ah-ha!" he exclaimed, with no inconsiderable degree of pride, "I know what this is."

"Read it, please, Papa," she said, with a naughty, expectant twinkle in her eye.

Richard took a deep breath, and puffed out his chest more than the intake of breath necessitated. He began with the title, *"Dernford. Skating!"*

"Go on, go on!" Ada was excited.

He continued to read, *"With his well-known liberality, Mr Evans, of Sawston, provided some good practice for skaters, at the above place. His friends embraced the opportunity in earnest, and the result has been that many who disported themselves upon the ice proved that they were skaters of no mean pretensions. Among the many who attracted particular notice may be mentioned the name of Mr R. Porter of Whittlesford, who was the observed of all observers, and his apparent ease and elegant style won the admiration of all those who are able to appreciate a fleet foot in pattens. January 2nd, 1875."*

"When are we going to go skating, Papa?" Ada's face was a picture of studied innocence.

That evening, when Richard was sitting in the drawing room, sipping his customary tipple of port in the firelight glow, he could not decide whether Ada had engineered the whole episode of him reading the skating article, or whether it had just accidentally happened. In any case, the sure outcome was a proposed visit to Mr Legge, the shoe-maker, whose father had served Richard when he was a boy being treated to a pair of riding-boots.

Ada's feet were to be measured up for skating boots the following day, in readiness for the winter freeze.

Part 4

The New Year came in with a great frost. Fenland farming folk despaired. Not only had Christmas celebrations been marred by extensive flooding of the low-lying land around Ely, but now the waters had frozen solid.

However, there was one group of Ely citizens who were far from miserable. The skating fraternity were cock-a-hoop with excitement, as they walked to the natural ice-arena, wearing their winter woollens, outdoor sports tweeds, mufflers and hats, and carrying their "pattens", the archaic name still commonly used in the Fens for skating boots.

At first light, Richard had come unexpectedly into Ada's bedroom, with an animated lightness in his step, and had gently blown warm breath onto the frosted window-pane to make a clear spy-hole for her.

"Jack Frost has been," he had said. "Come and see!"

Outside, the walled garden was a winter wonderland: the beech tree twigs were coated in furred hoarfrost which twinkled in the wafer-thin shafts of sunlight; blades of grass had become shards and slivers of ice; puddles, lying on the flagstone path after the previous day's rain, had turned to frozen black mirrors.

"Today is very promising, don't you think, my dear?"

She had looked quizzically at him. "Promising?"

"For skating!"

Ada had scarcely been able to contain her enthusiasm, and poor Maud's cold fingers could hardly fasten Ada's new skating outfit quickly enough to satisfy her. Miss Sneed had not been sparing in her provision of buttons on either the warm frock or the outer worsted coat.

Now Richard and Ada were on their way, Richard in the hope that his "apparent ease and elegant style" would still be able to win "the admiration of all those who are able to appreciate a fleet foot in pattens". As Ada walked beside her father down Forehill, she swung her new bladed boots with apparent ease, as if she was an experienced skater of many years.

"Papa," she said, her words belying her nonchalance, "do you think I shall fall over on the ice?"

"You will," he answered with no hesitation. No-one that he knew of had ever learned to skate without a tumble or two.

"But will I hurt myself?"

"Perhaps a little bit," he answered the child kindly, for he did not want to put her off, but at the same time he did not wish her to be unprepared for the usual bumps and bruises.

"Will you fall too?"

"I should hope not, with my years of experience!" he answered with a confident smile, remembering back to the days when he and his friends were the very embodiment of Mr Wordsworth's words from *The Prelude*:

"I wheeled about,
Proud and exulting, like an untired horse,
That cares not for its home. – All shod with steel,
We hissed along the polished ice…"

Nevertheless, doubts crept into the back of his mind: he wondered if his two years away from the sport might have affected his skill. But Henry John had called him "fit as a fiddle". On the other hand, at his age, a fall would do serious damage. He would be seventy-eight in three weeks' time.

Stepping out onto the street was Philip Allen, on his way to work at the Eagle Brewery on the Cambridge Road.

"Good-morning, Mr Porter," he greeted his employer. Then bending down he asked, "And how is Ada today?"

"Very well, thank-you, Mr Allen," she said, fascinated with the white fog which came out of his mouth as he spoke.

"I see you're going skating!" he said, pleasantly enough.

"Yes, we're going down to the ice-lakes. Are you going too?" she politely enquired.

"Good heavens, not me!" Philip Allen replied, perhaps a little too quickly. He was no sportsman, could barely afford the rent of the house outside which he now stood, and the purchase of skates would be out of the question.

Richard sensed his friend's uneasiness but, by gently informing Ada that Mr Allen was "going to work", he inadvertently added to Philip's chagrin.

"Yes, indeed. Sorry. I must be on my way," he said with breathless urgency, his modest employment as brewery clerk taking on disproportionate importance. Raising his hat, he deferentially added, "Good-day to you both."

The "ice-lakes", as Ada called the frozen flooded fenland, were like Christmas card illustrations. Ladies in swirling velvet coats and mink muffs swished effortlessly past. Gentlemen in frock-coats, top hats and mufflers planed past, their hands clasped behind their backs. Lovers with linked arms, glided past in a slow-motion two-step dance. Mature couples danced to Strauss's Skaters' Waltz, audible only to their inner ear. Parents and children came by hand in hand and laughing. Young men dangerously raced each other, shouting and earning the disapproval of those older folks who preferred more leisurely and quieter pursuits on the ice.

Richard tutted and seemed to be critical of these young, riotous lads. Yet he remembered how he and Charles and their cousin Marshall had skated like greased lightning round many a frozen lake on makeshift, wooden pattens when they were boys. What exhilaration! What raucous shouts! What fun they'd had!

"Just remember to keep out of their way," he advised Ada, "for they would knock you down like a feather!"

He saw that one of the lads was particularly skilled and fast, and wondered if he was in fact Albert Tebbitt, the young skater tipped to win the Duddlestone Cup in the near future. He certainly looked like a champion in the making.

Ada's first foray onto the ice was the exact opposite. Her valiant struggles to remain upright resulted in fall after fall, until Richard suggested that she hold on to his coat tails and he would pull her behind him. They were an odd pair to behold: an old man skating like a professional, and a little girl slithering and wobbling in his wake. But the strategy worked. Before long, Ada grew steadier and was soon making sliding steps behind Richard.

"Now you've got the feel for it," Richard encouraged her. "Hold my hand again, and let's see what happens."

Later that day, in the brand new establishment ironically named Ye Olde Tea Rooms, where Richard was treating Ada to afternoon tea, the two of them talked over their wonderful, shared experiences of the day. Mrs Cross, the owner of the tea-room, brought them a tray with a silver pot of tea, a matching hot water pot, milk jug and sugar bowl filled to the brim with cubes of white sugar. Perched on top was a pair of delicate sugar-tongs. Cups, saucers and plates decorated with a pretty rose design were set on the white tablecloth. Then she placed a three-tiered cake stand in the centre of the table. There were hot buttered pancakes at the top, jam tarts made with the local Chivers's speciality strawberry preserve on the middle plate, and slices of Madeira cake at the bottom.

Mrs Cross was not a nosey person, but she could not help but overhear snippets of the conversation between Mr Porter and his daughter. Ada was asking question after question about the names of skating steps, wanting to hear stories of how famous her father had been in his younger days, and needing answers to two repeated questions.

"Am I good skater, Papa?"

He unerringly replied, "You're one of the best, my angel."

"May we go again, Papa?"

"We shall go again and again, every day, until the ice melts. And that is exactly what they did.

Part 5

The morning bells of Ely Cathedral and St Mary's church had rung in Richard's birthday, and it was nothing short of extreme annoyance to him that he was confined to bed. More than anything, he wished to defy the doctor's orders and get up, but the unpalatable truth was that he did not seem to have the energy. The mind, like Barkis, might be willing, but the body was not.

"Complete bed rest," Dr Tulk had advised. He was one of those medical men who used words sparingly yet authoritatively. Inwardly he believed Richard to have been foolhardy during that spell of cold weather: skating at his age! Day after day! It was almost unthinkable. No wonder the old man was suffering from exhaustion.

Just outside his bedroom, Richard had been able to make out Dr Tulk's staccato instructions to Maud. "No disturbances, blinds drawn, beef tea and plenty of rest."

"Ada has a little birthday gift for him. Surely that wouldn't be a disturbance?" Maud had suggested, as she knew how many hours Ada had spent making a special present for this day. It was a gilt-framed picture with the pressed pink willowherb, collected during the midsummer picnic at Wicken Fen, taking pride of place in the centre.

"Complete rest!" was the curt reply, followed by a final directive. "Send for the sons!"

Richard had inwardly snorted. He could not imagine why either of his sons should suddenly come to Ely, seeing that they had not visited him once since Ada was born. They had not even attended Matilda's funeral. He was now beginning to worry whether or not Alfred and Frank would adequately administer monies intended for Ada when he was dead and gone. Would they take sufficient interest when their half-sister was living with a guardian? He decided there and then that he would make doubly sure: in the morning he would send for Mr Rogers, his solicitor, to add a further codicil to his will. He would double the annuity set aside for Ada, thereby safeguarding her future.

And if Ada had made him a special birthday gift, the child should be allowed to give it to him. Such a fuss being made! He rang the little brass bell beside his bed, left there for the purpose of summoning Maud.

"Maud," he said. Now he was actually speaking, he was aware of his breathlessness. "I should like to see Ada now."

"But the doctor…?" To Maud, a doctor's instructions were to be followed to the letter, especially as he had directly forbidden anyone to enter the sick room.

Richard's voice, although quiet and weak, sounded determined and forceful, "Maud, this is my house, Ada is my daughter, this is my birthday, and no young whippersnapper of a doctor has any say in the matter. Now, please ask Ada to come and see me."

"Yes, sir." Maud was so impressed that she even bobbed a little curtsey. She had not done that for many a year!

Ada was as pretty as a picture, Richard thought, as she entered the room on tip-toe, clutching a small parcel tied up with a white satin bow.

"What a very beautiful princess has come a-visiting!" he said to her, trying to make his voice sound less frail. "Come and sit beside me!"

"Go on, child." Maud gently pushed Ada towards the bed. "Show your father what you've brought him."

Ada presented her birthday present. "Many happy returns of the day, Papa." She sounded just like a little lady, Richard thought.

He looked wistful as he thanked his young daughter. "What a lovely reminder of a perfect day!" he said. Then, aware of the incongruity of his own words, given that he was lying ill in bed, helpless like an invalid, with Ada holding his hand, he suddenly became full of promises. "When the weather gets better, we'll take the train to Cambridge, go boating on the Backs, then we'll go to the Gog Magog Hills and visit the old Roman Road, and then we'll see Alfred and Frank." His voice was getting fainter and fainter, almost becoming more distant.

"Your father needs to rest now." Looking at Richard's pallor, Maud knew that he was very tired.

Eager to suggest some pleasurable pursuit to engage Ada's interest, she said, "Let us go into the garden and pick some flowers for your collection."

"Goodnight, Papa. Sleep well," Ada whispered as she kissed him gently on the brow. Slipping her hand out of his, she followed Maud from the room.

Maud was saying, "There are some pretty little snowdrops we can pick."

Ada turned her head, her troubled and frightened eyes meeting Richard's calm gaze.

"No, Maud, no. I hate snowdrops. They're the worstest flowers in the whole world."

"The worst flowers in the whole world," Richard corrected her. And in silent agreement he added, "The very worst."

CHAPTER 3
PHILIP

Part 1

George Minns knocked on the door of the Allens' parlour, one of the four ground-floor rooms which they rented in his town house on Forehill.

"Sorry to disturb you, Philip, so early in the day," he said to his lodger, "but this has just arrived for you." The envelope in his hand looked official. "It came by special delivery."

"I see," said Philip. Still in the process of wiping off the shaving soap from his chin, he tried to disguise his curiosity and excitement at receiving a letter at all, let alone one which had come by special delivery. "Special delivery, eh?"

"Thomas Allpress, it was!"

"I see," said Philip, giving nothing away, as he fingered the envelope, turning it over. "Thomas Allpress, eh?"

"Must be important legal business," suggested Mr Minns, for he knew that Thomas Allpress was the clerk to the most important solicitor in Ely. "At least it's not a subpoena," he added, chortling, "or he would have insisted on handing it to you in person!"

George Minns, who readily admitted to being "over the hill" and "the wrong side of fifty", was about to enter into one of his favourite stories from his college days in Cambridge, over thirty years ago, when his friend, a certain John Sellers, had been handed a subpoena and summoned to Cambridge Assizes for failing to repay a loan. Sellers was entirely innocent of the charge; it was all a ghastly mistake, for another John Sellers of Cambridge was the guilty party.

"Thank-you, Mr Minns," Philip, deftly and politely side-stepping the requirement to listen to one of his landlord's rambling stories from the past, which would be filled with clichés, maxims and quaint sayings, put an end to the conversation. "Much obliged to you."

Mr Minns felt obliged to leave, though he would have "given his eye-teeth" to know what was in this impressive missive, and allowed himself to be ushered out.

Philip looked at Caroline with raised eyebrows. "Now, I wonder what this is all about?" he said, curling the wire legs of his spectacles around the tops of his ears.

Caroline had just finished stoking the stove and was sitting enjoying the cosy warmth, which it gave out both night and day. More than a little intrigued, she was sitting on the edge of her seat, both literally and metaphorically.

She was excited and a little nervous too, for a letter was a rare commodity in their household. "Who is it from?" she asked, fearing it might even be some bad news.

Examining the imprint on the blue wax seal on the back of the envelope, he read, "Mr Joseph Rogers, Solicitor, Ely."

Using a knife from the parlour table set for breakfast, he broke the seal and carefully extracted the letter. There was a hushed reverence in the room before Philip read aloud the words of the communication: "Dear Mr Allen, you are requested to attend a meeting in my office on Thursday January 28th, 1894, at two o'clock in the afternoon, for the reading of the last Will and Testament of Richard Porter of Waddington Terrace, Ely, who died on January 21st, 1894. Yours faithfully, Joseph Rogers, Solicitor."

"What do you think it means?" Caroline was open-eyed with an inkling of expectation.

"It can mean only one thing. I must be a beneficiary. He must have left me some money."

"Oh, Philip!" Caroline's whole face lit up and she looked younger. Her eyes were sparkling, just like they had when she was a girl, when her youthful hopes for the future soared high. That was before she became worn down by the sheer weight of her humdrum existence as a clerk's wife, forced to make ends meet on only just enough money. Once again, she could imagine a bright new future, and she smiled radiantly with eager anticipation.

Philip thought how pretty she suddenly looked, and was reminded of the days when they were "walking out", before they were married. He could not help indulging in a grin, acknowledging past memories and present hopes.

"Wouldn't that be a nice little nest-egg, eh?" Then he checked himself. "Sorry he's gone though! Nice old soul. Always good to me, you know!"

"I know he was. Always good to you in life." She nodded in momentary agreement, trying to be respectful and sad about Mr Porter's demise, but unable to keep up the good intentions. "Good to you in death too! We can move out of here, get a place of our own." Caroline could see no bounds to what she would do with this bounty.

"Steady on, woman!" Philip was by nature a little more circumspect than his wife. "Let's wait till Thursday and see how much he's left us."

"Two whole days!" Caroline remarked, biting her bottom lip, "I don't think I can bear the suspense." Then she was off again, mentally spending her new-found fortune, "We'll be able to buy Annie some new frocks. I'll go and tell her the good news. It's about time she was awake."

"Say nothing to the child yet, dear. Not until we know for certain how much money is coming our way. We wouldn't want to disappoint her!"

"And we need a new sofa. A feather eiderdown would be lovely too." Then she was calling, "Annie, Annie, time to get up!" and disappeared, with a light and cheery step, into the small room which served as a bedroom for their daughter.

Philip was listening with only half an ear, as he sat on the uncomfortable, poorly sprung, horse-hair sofa, whose days seemed now to be numbered. How fortunate had been his decision to attend his employer's funeral! With this legacy now on the horizon, how very ungrateful and undeserving he would have appeared had he decided to stay away!

The Eagle Brewery had been closed for the afternoon as a mark of respect.

"Work finishes at twelve o'clock today," Mr Dawson, the head brewer, had informed the work-force of some thirty men and women, on the day of the funeral itself. "The funeral service is at two o'clock at Saint Mary's."

Philip had been so close to taking that time off as a holiday, like most of the other employees at the brewery did, rather than spend it in the driving rain in Saint Mary's graveyard, along with family mourners. Of course, Mr Dawson, as Head Brewer, had felt it befitted his position to attend the funeral, as representative of the brewery.

Also there was Susan Thom, who had been one of the first people to be employed in the Eagle Brewery by Mr Porter, when it opened in 1869.

"Nothing will keep me away." She had spoken up against the general opinion that they would all catch pneumonia in such appalling weather. "He was a real gent, and I want to see him sent off proper."

So it was that Mr Dawson, Susan Thom and Philip Allen were the only mourners who were not family members. These three unlikely companions huddled together, an odd picture of gloom, under Mr Dawson's black umbrella.

"From dust to dust…"

Reverend Cooper was reciting these well-worn words, when Philip had looked across the coffin as it was being lowered into the grave. He had suddenly become aware of the little figure in a black lace-fringed hooded cloak, which swirled about in the driving wind and rain.

A little girl in a black taffeta dress.

Philip was consumed with compassion for this orphaned child, who had stood motionlessly, with dry eyes, at the graveside. He had wondered at the time what would become of her. Despite the presence of her uncles and aunts, she was very much a lone figure. Even her Uncle Charles seemed to be too old to offer much comfort to his little niece, and her Uncle Henry John looked too preoccupied and sad to consider the little girl who had spent a few weeks in his house only the previous spring.

But now, as he sat with Mr Rogers's letter in his hand, Philip knew with certainty that Richard Porter would have made good provision for his daughter. After all, hadn't he left even his lowly clerk some money! Philip had no doubt that Ada would be adequately and even handsomely provided for.

Now, as he thought about the fortune which would soon be his, Thursday could not come soon enough.

Part 2

Philip was shown into the anteroom of Mr Roger's chambers in High Street, to find that Alfred and Frank Porter were already there. Seated beside them was another gentleman whom he only vaguely recognised.

"Good to see you again, Philip!" Alfred's polite address disguised his genuine surprise to see his father's brewery clerk at this time, in this place. He knew that Philip Allen was no longer an executor of the will and therefore his presence today was perplexing. Shaking him by the hand, Alfred added, "It's been a long time."

"Must be at least nine years." Philip remembered very well the last time he had seen Alfred.

It was in April 1884, two months before Richard and Matilda were due to marry. It was a memorable occasion for Alfred, then employed as Head Brewer of Wakefield and Leeds Brewery, had come to see his father, to try to change his mind about a certain matrimonial matter, which Richard had communicated to him and to Frank by letter. In the directors' quarters there had been a heated exchange between Richard and his son, words which Philip could not help but overhear through the thin partition between the main office and his adjoining clerk's cubicle.

"I cannot believe, Father, that you persist in this mad notion of taking Matilda as your wife! Why, she's half your age, a woman of no means."

"Opinion, I say. It's a matter of opinion!" Richard was incensed that his own son should interfere in his affairs, at his time of life. "What is it to you whether I marry or not?"

When Alfred had hesitated in his reply, Richard had seized the opportunity to be scathing to his son. "Oh, I see. You're still concerned about your inheritance, I take it. Terrified that it will all go to Matilda, eh?"

"Concerned, father. That's all."

Richard, remembering the hurt and disappointment he had suffered with his own father changing his will, now relented. He said more gently, "You and Frank will be well looked after. Half the Eagle Brewery, half Ricard's Carrier business and half of Waddington Terrace apiece, as was decided years ago. An annuity for Matilda will be set up, just the same as the one set up for your mother, had she been the survivor. You will be no worse off."

Alfred, astute enough to consider all possibilities, then asked, "And if there is any issue from this marriage? What arrangements then?"

Richard had laughed outright. "Issue! Issue! Children, at my age?" and that had seemed an end to the discussion.

Philip now wondered if Richard had changed his will after all, when Ada had been born, and genuinely worried for the little orphaned girl.

"You remember my brother Frank?" Alfred continued the formalities.

"Yes, indeed. How do you do, sir?" Philip had only met Alfred's younger brother once, and that was back in 1880, when Frank had called in to the Eagle with his new wife, Nina, to show her the extensive brewery premises and the newly purchased, modern vats. Although he now wore gold-rimmed glasses, time had treated him well, for he still had a full head of reddish-brown hair and there was hardly a wrinkle on his face. He was of a more easy-going disposition than his older brother, yet shared his views about the ill-considered past decisions made by their father.

Alfred now introduced the other gentleman who was present. "May I introduce Mr William Sayer from Holt."

Philip Allen and William Sayer exchanged bows.

"Holt in Norfolk, I presume?" Philip was making polite conversation. He wondered who this man was and whether or not he was a relative of Mr Richard Porter.

"That is correct. Though I used to live in Ely back in the early Eighties."

"We never met, sir, as I remember," Philip was trying desperately to put two and two together. "Were you in the brewery business?"

"I worked as a clerk at Foster's Bank."

Now it was making sense. This William Sayer, a banker no less, was obviously an executor of the will.

It was now two o'clock, and on the second stroke of the grandfather clock standing in the corner, Thomas Allpress, Mr Rogers's clerk, came through to them, with a sense of his own importance.

"Good afternoon, gentlemen. Mr Rogers will see you now. Please come this way."

Joseph Rogers was a dapper little man who was highly esteemed as a solicitor. He had only had offices in Ely for five years, but already his reputation was made, with a sizeable annual income from his clients. Not least of his talents was the ability to smooth over awkward situations.

Philip was immediately in awe of this man, who gave the impression that he was scrutinising them, categorising them, and deliberating as to what he should say. The tension was almost palpable.

Now seated on studded, brown leather chairs before a highly polished table, the heavy oak panelled door closed behind them. Mr Rogers gave instructions to his clerk. "Mr Allpress, be so good as to bring me the last will and testament of Richard Porter, deceased."

From one of the recessed pigeon-holes in the roll-top desk in the corner of the chamber, Thomas Allpress produced the said document and presented it to Mr Rogers to open and spread on the table top

"Gentlemen. As executors and interested parties, you are here for the reading of the last will and testament of Richard Porter, deceased. This will be duly read by me, Joseph Rogers, solicitor in Ely in the county of Cambridgeshire, in the presence of the following persons: Mr Alfred Edward Porter of Chertsey in the county of Surrey, son of Richard Porter and co-executor of the last will and testament of the said Richard Porter; Mr Henry Francis Porter of Clapton in the county of Middlesex, son of Richard Porter and co-executor of the last will and testament of the said Richard Porter; Mr William Thomas Sayer of Holt in the county of Norfolk; Mr Philip Spellman Allen of Ely in the county of Cambridgeshire; and Mr Thomas Allpress, solicitor's clerk."

So, Mr Sayers was not an executor! Philip wondered now whether he too was to be a beneficiary like himself. He found it all excessively interesting and full of suspense.

As Mr Rogers broke the seal, Alfred and Frank exchanged glances, two worried men, for although they had agreed to be co-executors of their father's will, they had absolutely no idea what was written in it. Philip noted this eye-contact, aware that they might be resentful that someone outside of the family should benefit from their father's will. He also saw a bemused expression on Mr Sayer's face. Clearly he had not the slightest inkling as to why he was here, but entertained the notion that he might inherit something of value, something perhaps in recognition of his wife's friendship with Matilda all those years ago.

Mr Rogers read from an original will of 1884, confirming that the Eagle Brewery, Ricard's Carriers, Number 1 Waddington Terrace, household effects and all the personal estate should be divided equally between Alfred and Frank. Philip Allen and William Sayer shared the same deflated demeanour, with disappointment etched on their hitherto blithe faces.

"The next part relates to you, Mr Allen." Mr Rogers tapped the document with his forefinger. Both Alfred and Frank appeared curious and quizzical at the same time, Alfred raising his eyebrows and Frank peering over his spectacles. It was becoming clear to Philip that Richard might not have discussed his intentions with his sons.

Rogers continued reading. "'I appoint Philip Spellman Allen to be the guardian of my infant daughter Ada Porter.'"

Here he was interrupted by Alfred, Frank and Philip, speaking one after the other in quick succession. In his domain in the corner, Thomas Allpress looked up at the commotion, which disturbed the usual quiet of the chamber.

"We are taking care of that."

"Are you sure you have read that correctly?"

"There must be some mistake!" Philip's heart had sunk to his boots. This was an unexpected turn-up for the books. How would he be able to face his wife later that afternoon? It must be a mistake, he fervently hoped. Of course, he liked Ada, and heaven knows he felt sorry for the poor child, but this must be some dreadful error.

"No mistake," assured Mr Rogers. "I drew this up myself!"

"Well you must be an ass, sir!" Alfred was enraged. "No offence to you, Mr Allen, but I cannot believe that my father would have appointed an employee as a guardian to his only daughter."

"Nor me, sir, I assure you," piped Philip, not taking offence, but trying desperately to make this intolerable situation disappear.

Frank was now making a final point, or so he thought, "Ada will live with either Alfred or myself. We always knew that we should look after her. Our father gave us one hundred pounds each to invest in our businesses to provide for Ada. Provision has been made! The decision has been made! So there's an end of the matter."

Joseph Rogers was smarting from being called an ass in his own office. His voice was terse. "I'm afraid that is not an end to the matter. This is a legal and binding document, according to the wishes of your late father. Now, gentlemen, if you would allow me to continue.

"'I give and bequeath the sum of two hundred pounds unto my said executors upon trust to invest the same in such manner as they may think proper for the benefit of my said infant daughter Ada Porter.'"

Here he was interrupted by Alfred. "Is this an additional two hundred pounds, or the original two hundred pounds?"

Mr Rogers was on slippery ground now, for there did appear to be some hitherto unnoticed ambiguity in the question of how much money was to be invested. Having already done his calculations on the assumption that it was just a single sum of two hundred pounds, he quickly and decisively asserted,

"Just the original two hundred pounds already given to you."

"There you are," rejoined Frank. "If our father made no change in the money provision, it's unlikely that he would have made any change in the arrangements for looking after Ada either."

"If I may continue," Mr Rogers sounded pained and affronted. "'And I declare that my executors or the survivor or survivors of them may at their own discretion apply the whole or part of the said sum of two hundred pounds for the advancement, maintenance, education, preferment or benefit of my said daughter during her minority.'"

"Wait a minute!" Frank was on his feet. "Are you saying that our father entrusts his daughter to a man whom he cannot trust with the money?

"That is not what is written here."

"It may not be written, but that's what it damn well means!"

Philip felt all the weight of insult. Frank's words cut him to the quick. But they did seem to ring true, for why had Richard not left it to his discretion to apply the two hundred pounds for bringing up Ada?

"And what's more, I refuse to believe that our father could not trust either of his own sons to care for Ada. We are her half-brothers, for God's sake, man! Did you not point that out at the time?"

Mr Rogers was getting irritated. His usual calm exterior was beginning to crumble. "Indeed I did sir, but he refused point-blank."

"On what grounds?"

Mr Rogers clearly recalled the interview with Richard and continued with assurance. He broke a confidence, in order to save face, taking delight in the upset it would cause. "He said that any sons of his who disliked the child's mother to such an extent that they refused to come to the wedding, were no fit guardians for the issue of the consummation of that union."

Joseph Rogers did not admit, however, that it would have been a most complex issue to have appointed either of these two siblings as guardians, if not an impossibility, when there were uncles and aunts living who had a clearer legal right of guardianship over Ada. Yet old Richard Porter had rejected any such uncles and aunts. Having made the acquaintance of Charles Porter, the retired veterinary surgeon, he was not surprised that he had been scratched off Richard Porter's list of possibles, for he was an old and decrepit man in his seventies. His daughter and son-in-law, the Graingers, would have been much more suitable, but the relationship was too distant for Mr Rogers to effect any such guardianship order.

But he was not going to divulge any of this information to these two men who were disrespectful of his professionalism. He would let them suffer, feel guilty perhaps.

It was Alfred's turn now. For past family friction to be thrown in their faces by a solicitor was bad enough, but to have it aired before two comparative strangers was insupportable. He was livid. "As a stranger to the town, sir, you may be forgiven for not knowing all the members of the Porter family, but surely you would have been aware of their standing! It must have been clear that any member of the family would have been better than an employee!" Then he looked at Philip, apologetic, "No offence to you once again, sir."

"I have nothing further to say. I do not wish to breach my client's confidentiality." The words sounded as hollow as they were untrue.

Frank and Alfred scoffed in unison. "Too late for that!"

Mr Rogers tried desperately to look inscrutable, a stony Sphynx expression to mask his inner turmoil. He held out his hand with applomb. "Mr Allpress, the first codicil, if you please."

The general intake of breath in the room suggested that the four men present at the reading of Richard Porter's last will and testament were now on tenterhooks. What can of worms would be opened in the codicil? And if this was a first codicil, how many more were there to be?

As Philip was wondering if the situation would get better or worse, he heard Mr Rogers reading, "'Now I hereby also appoint my friend William Thomas Sayer of Holt in the county of Norfolk, Bank Manager, joint guardian of my said infant daughter Ada Porter with the said Philip Spellman Allen during her minority.'"

Another uproar ensued with Frank in the lead. "Worse and worse!"

"You should be debarred, sir!"

"But where will she live?" Philip was considering practicalities: two guardians, living in different counties! "Has anyone considered that?"

"I refuse to act." This was William Sayer, who had remained relatively impassive and silent during the proceedings up to this point. There was an unmistakable note of finality in his delivery of these few words. He knew enough about the law to know that he was entitled to refuse to act. Richard Porter had never asked him if he would be guardian to Ada, he had never met the child, and although his wife Marie and Matilda had become friends when Matilda had lodged with them for a year, he could not say that he had been anything else but a business acquaintance of Richard Porter, certainly not a "good friend". He had no hesitation in refusing to carry out this ridiculous wish.

"I am surprised, sir," he was looking sternly at Mr Rogers, "that you did not seek to enquire of Mr Allen and myself of our wishes or willingness in this matter of Ada's guardianship. Negligence on your part, sir."

Mr Rogers had had enough of this interview and desired to conclude the proceedings without much further ado, but there was another codicil. He snapped his fingers impatiently at Mr Allpress to bring it over to him.

The contents were brief and to the effect that Alfred and Frank, in addition to administering monies for Ada's education and maintenance, also had to pay her "ten pounds per annum upon the twenty-fifth day of March in each year until she shall reach the age of twenty-one years."

Alfred had endured all he was going to endure for one day. The bounds of Mr Rogers' inefficiency were limitless. "Another unchallenged notion of my father's, we may assume?" he sneered tartly.

"On the contrary, sir. Your brother was party to the decision. You will vouch for that, Mr Porter, sir?" He looked earnestly at Frank, who it may be said was in the process of loosening his fly collar, which was suddenly tight and uncomfortable.

"Ah, yes." Frank had to agree, but only to a certain extent.

"When?" Alfred, as the older brother, felt that he should also have been party to any codicil of his father's will.

"On that last day."

Frank had arrived by train the day after Richard's birthday, in response to an urgent request from Doctor Tulk, via Maud Harrison. Alfred had been too late. His father was dead by the time he arrived.

Frank was explaining, trying to pacify his brother, exonerating himself from blame. "Father was bothered about Ada. I did everything I could to assure him that all would be well, but he refused to listen."

In the brief conversation he had had at his father's bedside on that day, he had deemed it prudent to advise him to make better provision for Ada. It had obviously been troubling the frail old man, and Frank had done what he thought best in the circumstances to allay the fears and worries of his ailing father. Mr Rogers had been sent for in order to write a codicil, and Richard's unmarried sister Ann had arrived at Waddington Terrace, just in time to be a witness, along with Nurse Willson who was attending Richard in what were to be his last hours.

Mr Rogers was sitting back in his chair, a smug expression on his face. He was glad that the flack was being directed at someone else.

"However, I was not given any information by any party," Frank spat out the words, looking aggressively at Mr Rogers, "as to the exact revised provision for Ada. Let that be understood."

For all his denials and excuses, Frank realised now just what his own kindly advice to his father had brought in financial terms. With a wife and three young children to support, he knew it would be hard to come up with the five pounds for Ada each year, without careful money management. It had also caused a discernable rift between him and his brother. He was not sure where to direct his annoyance.

Alfred exhaled a dejected sigh. Five pounds each year was money he would have gladly spent on Ada within his own household budget, as part of his family, but in cold money terms, it appeared a great amount to pay out as a lump sum each year.

William Sayer sat back with his thumbs in his waistcoat pocket, satisfied that he had made the right decision. He did not need money; the bank paid him a handsome salary. He did not want a small child in his house, now that his own family had flown the nest. His initial disappointment had quickly given way to relief.

To Philip, ten pounds was a handsome enough legacy to put in his family coffers, and would do very nicely indeed.

A new sofa looked more and more probable.

Part 3

In his office at the brewery, Philip sat brooding on this Saint Valentine's Day over the cleft stick in which he had been unwittingly caught. Richard Porter's last will and testament had been proved and registered in the District Probate Registry of Her Majesty's High Court of Justice at Peterborough the day before.

On the one hand, ten pounds extra per annum would be coming into his household, but on the other, an extra child would need to be fed, clothed and looked after. He would have the responsibility of bringing up Ada Porter as his own child, while Alfred and Frank Porter, as executors of their father's will and responsible for the administering of monies, would be breathing down his neck, ensuring that he was doing right by his new ward and spending the money on her, as was her right.

There was also the problem of his own daughter, Annie. Was she to be kept in serge skirts, pinafores and workaday boots in her own house, while Ada swanned about in fancy frocks and delicate, patent pumps? Were the two girls to leave for different schools each morning: Annie to walk down to the corner of Ship Lane to Broad Street School whose motto carved into the school wall was "Obey them that have rule over you"; Ada to return to Waddington Terrace to the private Preparatory School run by the Misses Bird, gentlewomen of grace and virtue?

Caroline had no such worries. She could see no further than the few little luxuries she would at last be able to purchase. She was out on a spending spree at the moment, tempted by the advertisement for "Ceylindo Tea" in the shop window of the International Stores at the top of Forehill. The slogan "Hurry to Tea-time" and a picture of a little boy on a chair changing the hands on a large clock-face had caught her eye each time she passed the shop. Now she was able to afford to buy such a rare tea, like a real lady. She enjoyed the sense of grandeur she experienced when she asked for a pound and a half, saying, with assumed panache, that she would pay just as soon as their "legacy" came through.

All the shopkeepers that day smiled, impressed that Caroline had money to spend. Perhaps they may even have been a little envious that the Allens had been singled out for such good fortune in the form of a legacy, but their commercial sensibility overruled any personal feelings, and they gladly gave her goods on the slate.

Philip knew he could have said no to the whole business, refused to act, as William Sayer had done, but there was the money to consider. Ten pounds almost matched his annual salary: too tempting to discard. And Caroline would never have forgiven him had he said no.

Mr Dawson entered with a piece of news. "The valuers will be here in the morning. We'll have to get everything ready for them."

"Valuers?" Philip was not a man to get over-anxious, but this did not augur well.

"The sons are going to sell the brewery to the highest bidder."

"What!" Philip was more than a little surprised. Both Alfred and Frank were head brewers, and it seemed logical that both men would want nothing better than to be their own bosses in the Eagle Brewery, which was now their property.

"I know," agreed Mr Dawson. "Madness, if you ask me, but there it is in black and white." He brandished a letter to the effect that the brewery was to be sold and that valuers would be arriving on the fifteenth.

"So, it didn't take them long to make the decision to sell!"

"No, more's the pity!" Mr Dawson's future as Head Brewer no longer looked a certainty, and his voice betrayed his inner anxieties.

"And the carrier business?" Philip asked, half-knowing what the answer would be. If the old established brewery was to be sold, with Alfred and Frank in the brewing business, then what would they want with a haulage firm?

Mr Dawson nodded his head sadly. He did not approve of old established family firms being sold off to the highest bidder. He highly valued family tradition, and admired old Mr Porter for what he had built up in his lifetime. If he had been Richard Porter's son, he would have been proud to have carried on either business. And there were others to consider too: what would happen to Mr Stokes and his team of ostlers and drivers?

"What about the house?" Philip wanted to know.

"That too. The auctioneer has been notified."

Philip felt a surge of disappointment. He had been secretly playing with the idea that Alfred and Frank Porter would come to him with a proposition which he could not refuse: that for minimal rent he would take on the tenancy of Number 1 Waddington Terrace, thereby enabling Ada to remain in her home. Alas, this was a stupid pipe-dream, he now realised. How could he have been so foolish as to think that he might live in such a magnificent house?

Above everything else, Philip was sad for the little girl who, the very next day, was to be summarily evicted from her home, that last bastion of security in her dismal life.

He called at the house on his way home from work that evening. Maud opened the door to him. He could see that she had been crying, for her face was blotched and her eyes were red.

"Oh, Mr Allen," she half whispered, unable to say any more before sobbing into her handkerchief.

"There, there," Philip put his arm round the poor woman's shoulders. Her master was dead, her position as housekeeper was about to be terminated, for the house was to be sold, and the little girl whom she cared for was to go and live with someone else. Would she go back to Coveney, the village where she was born? Would she seek employment in Cambridge? Philip inwardly sighed. There was something wrong with society, he thought, if someone as good and kind as Maud Harrison could not even have been considered as a guardian for Ada. As a spinster of the parish, no matter how upright and Christian she had proved herself to be, she was, after all, a single person. Unmarried, widowed and divorced women had very few rights and little independence. An annuity, or a kind male relative, was the best they could hope for. He wondered what would become of her.

Philip had read lately of some very politically-minded ladies who were demanding equal voting rights with men. Although initially sceptical about these females with such avant-garde notions, he was coming round to the view that their ideas did merit some consideration from fair-minded citizens. Maud was a victim of society. Ada, it was evident, was another.

"Maud?" Her little voice could now be heard coming from upstairs.

"She's in the nursery," Maud said. "Poor little thing!"

"Has she taken it in that she's coming to live with us?" Philip was concerned for this youngster.

Maud nodded, remembering the misery etched on the child's strained face when the news had finally sunk in. Maud now looked very unhappy about the whole business. How she wished to care for Ada herself! If wishes were horses, then beggars would ride, she thought cheerlessly.

"You mustn't fret. She'll have a good home with us," he continued, hearing the hollow dissembling of his words as he spoke, "and you'll come and visit her every day, and…" His voice trailed off, for there at the top of the stairs was Ada.

"Maud?" Again the plaintive call.

Maud collected herself. "Come down, my pretty one. Here is someone to see you. Say good-day to Mr Allen, child."

Now this was another problem, which Philip had not quite solved. What was Ada to call him and his wife? Clearly "Mr Allen" and "Mrs Allen" would be inappropriate, and "Philip" and "Caroline" would be disrespectful. He made a rapid decision there and then.

"You are to call me 'Uncle Philip'," he insisted. "And

tomorrow when you come to live with us, you are to call Mrs Allen 'Aunt Caroline'."

"Good-day, Uncle Philip," Ada dutifully responded to his directive, but Philip noted her puzzled expression, which betrayed her knowledge that he was not her uncle at all. Her uncles were Uncle Charles and Uncle Henry John.

Philip could understand that Richard would have deemed Uncle Charles and Aunt Mary too old to become guardians to Ada, for they had celebrated their golden wedding in 1891. But why had he not considered Henry John as a suitable guardian? Philip was unaware of the animosity between Richard and Henry John. Ah well! he thought. He would do the best he could.

"Show me all the things you are to bring with you tomorrow," he encouraged.

Before he knew it, he had been led up the stairs and introduced to these "things". There was a trunk full of the fine clothes which Miss Sneed had so painstakingly fashioned for her rich customer. Next Ada patted a box of books which she said were her favourites, including *Treasure Island* and *David Copperfield*, the ironic inappropriateness of both choices unremarked by Philip, for he was no avid reader of novels. The fact that Charles Dickens had signed this first edition of *David Copperfield* would go unnoticed for many a year!

With professional interest, he liked the look of Ada's fancy, mahogany writing desk and determined to encourage her to keep in contact with as many of her old friends and relations as time would allow.

"Do you like writing letters to people?" he enquired.

"Oh yes!" Ada fairly bubbled over. "I write to my cousins, Hilda and Olive and sometimes Florence. I write thank-you letters to everyone who gives me a present at Christmas time. And I want to write to Maud every day, because I'll miss her terribly." A lost look crept over Ada's face.

Not wanting to be the instigator of unnecessary pain, Philip changed the subject. "What's in here?" he asked, patting her dove-grey, velvety vanity case, which was brimming with all kind of precious keepsakes.

"This is my special birthday book," she confided, extracting The Glad Year Round book from the case.

Heaven knows there's nothing to be glad about in her past year, Philip thought ruefully as he read the title. "Special, eh?"

"It's got our birthdays in it."

"I see. Birthdays, eh?"

Ada turned to the July page where her own birthday had been penned by her father. She pointed to it. "That's my birthday."

"Ah yes!" Philip was remembering the previous July when Richard and Ada had called at his house. Thinking back, he now realised why Richard had made a point of visiting him. At the time, it never occurred to him that his guardianship of Ada was the ulterior motive for the frequent visits to his home.

"And this one is Mama's," Ada said, turning to the first wintry December page and pointing at the first day.

Philip found himself repeating himself. "Ah yes!" he murmured, not knowing what else to say.

Carefully returning to January she ran her fingers gently over the copperplate writing in the space for January 19th. "Rich. Porter. That's Papa."

There was a brief pause. Here in the Waddington Terrace nursery, Philip felt the vastness of the deep loss in Ada's young life. He put a comforting arm round her shoulders, prepared for her tears.

"Was Papa very rich, Uncle Philip?" she cheerfully asked.

The question took Philip quite off-guard. "Rich?"

"It says 'Rich Porter' here," Ada simply explained.

"Ah yes," he found himself saying, yet again. "Yes, he was!" He was thinking that Ada was to see precious little of the old man's fortune. Alfred and Frank, as males, had benefited, whereas Ada as a female in this unfair world had very little in comparison.

"Uncle Philip, when is your birthday?"

"April 4th."

"Will you write your name in my book, please."

"Of course, my dear," he replied, a warm feeling of privilege permeating his mind and body.

Across the faint imprint of primroses in the space for April 4th, he wrote "Philip Spellman Allen", using Ada's very own special fountain pen with its shiny gold nib.

Part 4

Thinking back over the past two months since Ada had come to live with them, Philip now sat back on the comfortable new horse-hair and flock-filled sofa, with its gold and purple brocade loose-cover, satisfied that the transition for all of them had worked extremely well. With his head resting on the finely embroidered antimacassar, he puffed his pipe contentedly. Yes, everything had worked out very well indeed.

Caroline was seated at her new Singer sewing machine, beside the new paraffin lamp, which gave out a bright working light. There was a faint sporadic whirring from the machine as she moved her right foot up and down on the ornate wrought iron treadle, putting the finishing touches to a white cotton pinafore she was making for Ada.

Ada had grown considerably and the pretty clothes, which Miss Sneed had made for her the previous spring, were now far too tight and far too short. With no extra material available in the seams to let out the frocks, there was no alternative but to make the child some new clothes. Of course, Ada was delighted with the prospect of a new array of clothes, especially when Aunt Caroline allowed her to choose some colourful printed cottons in Harvey's ladies' department at the corner of High Street. As she pointed at this and that roll of Lancashire cotton, she felt like a real lady.

Annie, who was slighter and shorter in stature than Ada, despite being a year older, was able to fit into all the creations which Miss Sneed had hand-crafted for Ada. How delighted Annie was to be able to wear that white organza frock with the rainbow smocking, and the dress with the sailor's collar, which she admired so much! As she twirled round and round in the parlour, she too felt like a real lady.

Annie and Ada were now asleep. They both shared the bed which had once been Annie's alone. Philip was genuinely relieved that they had managed to become friends in such a short time. He supposed that his decision to send Annie to the Misses Bird's Preparatory School along with Ada had gone some way to bringing the two girls closer together.

The closeness had its beginnings on the evening of Annie's first day at her new school: as she sat at the parlour table laid for supper, Philip could not help but notice how subdued she was. Even her lips were pursed.

"You're unusually quiet, Annie," Philip had remarked. "Are you unwell?"

"There's nothing wrong with her that a good dose of salts won't cure," Caroline answered sharply for her daughter. "She's put out because she couldn't do some of her schoolwork today, and the others made fun of her." Caroline was not unkind, but did not offer sympathy and affection readily.

"First day of a new school, my dear, is always a trial." Philip had tried to cheer his daughter, "Why, I remember mine. I could do nothing the other boys could do, but look at me now."

"There's no talking to her. She's as cross as two sticks!"

"But they pointed at me and laughed and called me 'a big stupid girl'!" moaned Annie.

"What was it all about?" Philip had looked at both Annie and Ada, for he knew that they were taught in the same classroom, as was the norm, along with the other six-to-ten year olds.

"Sums!" pouted Annie. "And I hate them! I can't do them. They're too hard." Here she folded her arms with a look of defiant resignation.

"I'll help you if you like," Ada had offered. "Papa taught me how to do sums. He was very clever with numbers."

Now Annie had been warned that above all else she was to be kind and pleasant to this orphan who had come to live with them, and not make her cry. Philip and Caroline both gave their daughter a hard look as if to say, "Remember what we told you!"

"Will you? Thank-you," Annie had politely said with natural eagerness, for she was an ambitious young girl, and really did want to learn. She also liked this new, quiet friend. Her parents need not have worried that she would even consider upsetting Ada.

"There you are now, Annie. A remedy is at hand." Satisfied that the problem was solved, the smell of lamb stew was becoming too tempting to resist. "Now, Caroline, be so good as to serve the supper, and then afterwards the addition and subtraction can be tackled."

"Oh no, Father, it's much more complicated than that. We're doing long division, aren't we, Ada?"

And so Ada and Annie had become friends, and could be heard each night chattering and giggling before they snuggled down to sleep. Ada still wrote to her cousins every week, keeping up her old friendships, but she settled down well to life with the Allens because of her new-found friendship with Annie.

Philip now began to feel sleepy. It was that drowsy feeling of inner peace and contentment. He was sure and happy in the knowledge that everything had been well taken care of.

"Things are looking up, eh, Caroline?" he smiled at his wife. She looked remarkably pretty in the light of the new lamp. "There will be fine times ahead."

Part 5

Caroline started, stifling a scream. She had not expected Philip to be home at this time of day, and there he was huddled in the corner of the sofa, in the gloom of this dark and dreary October mid-afternoon. The only light, which emanated from the newly installed gaslight outside in the street, cast eerie shadows in the parlour.

"Oh, you gave me such a start!" she said, putting her hand over her heart in alarm.

"Sorry, my dear. I didn't mean to." Philip offered only this brief apology, but no explanation.

"But what are you doing here at this time of day? It's the middle of the afternoon!" Caroline's initial fright was giving way to alarm.

"Where are the girls?" he asked, ignoring his wife's concerns.

Caroline was surprised at this non sequitur, but she responded to his question. "In Mr Minns's parlour, having their usual Thursday afternoon tête-a-tête, as he calls it."

"Good! Sit down, Caroline. I need to speak to you." The worry lines on Philip's face became more pronounced, so that he looked as if he had prematurely and precipitously aged.

Caroline put down her latest purchases from Harveys and sat down, upright and tense, on her sewing machine seat. Her husband's tone of voice demanded serious attentiveness.

"I have bad news, my dear. Best brace yourself for the worst." Here Philip took a deep breath, before launching into a resumé of the day's events.

"The worst?" Caroline faintly repeated his words.

"Today I've been handed my notice to quit the Eagle."

"I don't understand. Quit the Eagle?" Poor Caroline had a beleaguered look, mixed with the half-expectation that what her husband was telling her was some kind of mistake, which would be rectified in the morning.

"Mr Cutlack doesn't need any of us," Philip fairly spat out the name of the new owner of the Eagle Brewery. "He calls it 'amalgamation'."

"What does that mean?"

"It's some fancy word for cutting down on the employees."

"But who's going to run the brewery?" Caroline did not understand the financial and practical implications of an amalgamation.

"He's closing it down, woman. The whole damn works. Transferring all the business and brewing to the premises down by the quay, near The Cutter's Inn. There'll be no work for the likes of me before long."

Philip looked morosely at his feet as he thought about The Cutter's Inn and their advertised sales of "Eyre's Celebrated Lynn Ales" emblazoned across the front of the building. There would be no custom now for local brews, with ale from rival firms already on sale in local public houses. The future in the brewing trade in Ely looked bleak. It would even take the three remaining big breweries, Halls, Cutlacks and Harlocks, to join forces if they were to stay in existence. He could see the way things were going in the future, and his place in that future was far from assured.

Caroline cut in to his thoughts, "But they can't do without you, Philip."

"They don't need a chief brewer's clerk... they've got one already down at the quay brewery. They don't even need Mr Dawson!"

"But he's the head brewer!"

"I know, but they don't need him."

"What's to be done? What will we do?"

"They've offered me some work as a junior clerk."

"A junior clerk!" Caroline was disbelieving, after all that her husband had done to better himself. She enjoyed the kudos of being the wife of the head clerk at the Eagle Brewery. She stared at him, her incredulity diminishing as the stark reality of this inevitable situation began to sink in. If it had to be, then it had to be! Jobs did not grow on trees, she knew. "I suppose it will have to do."

"Have to do?" Philip was angry. "I'm not working as a junior clerk, for anyone!" How could his wife think that he would stoop so low? He did have some self-respect.

Caroline opened her mouth to argue the point.

"Not ever!" he shouted, adding the next piece of information to silence his wife, "Do you expect me to work for half the salary?"

"Half?" Caroline's voice began to waver. "They can't only offer you half! Have you told them that?"

"No!" He was not going to work as a junior clerk, and that was final. There would have been no point in negotiating a salary. It would have been hopeless.

Caroline's gaze was all too penetrating. He even thought it was accusatory, and heaven knows he had nothing to be ashamed of. He was a victim of circumstance. She began to wring her hands in frustration.

"What's to be done?" She was worried. The money, which she had grown accustomed to and enjoyed spending, was to dry up. She could sit still no longer and began to busy herself with lighting the oil lamp beside her.

Philip felt for her in her agitation and dismay. He tried to lessen the impact of their blighted future with a cheap comparison, another story of a good man's career wasted. "Mr Dawson hasn't even been offered a job, junior or otherwise. They have enough brewers."

"It's a sinful disgrace!" Caroline sat for a time saying nothing. Then she began to think of practicalities. "What's he going to do?" Perhaps Mr Dawson had some idea how to put things right and they could follow suit.

"He's talking about going to America."

Caroline looked away, shaking her head. Well, there was no way she was going to America! Philip would have to sink his pride and take the job at Cutlacks. What else was there to do?

Philip was not quite so glum. He had worked out a reasonable solution to the problem of money and household expenditure. On his way home from what was his last day in his office at the Eagle Brewery, he had walked past Smock Hill Alley, down the tree-lined road leading to Cambridge, which some of the older residents still called Bugg's Hill, and he had even looked at "The Spike" workhouse in the distance, thinking how man continually walked a knife edge. "There but for the grace of God go I," he had even muttered as he walked on home.

"We can manage, money-wise," he asserted, taking the upper hand, now that Caroline's anger and frustration had subsided. "I've worked it all out." He had done his sums on that last journey from the Eagle.

"You'd best tell me," she said simply.

"We'll have to take the girls away from the Birds' private school. So that will release the money spent on school fees. They'll both go to Broad Street School." His own ambitions for his intelligent and well-disposed daughter were evaporating fast. Philip also knew that this was not what old Mr Porter had wanted for Ada, just as he would not have wanted the Eagle Brewery to have been sold off, but what other alternative was there now? He concluded, "It means that, with Ada's money, we shall be about the same as we were before, except we'll have an extra mouth to feed."

There was an admission which Caroline would now have to share with her husband.

"Ada's money is all but spent already," she murmured, dreading what her husband would say.

"How come: spent already? It's only October. What have you spent it on?" Philip was growing fearful. It was true that, when the money for Ada had been paid to them on the twenty-fifth of March, as per Richard's instructions in that final codicil of his last will and testament, he had entrusted the total amount to the safe-keeping and sensible spending of his wife. He had not discussed the prices of all the luxuries which had systematically graced their home over the past six months.

Caroline was on the defensive. "Well, there's the sofa you're sitting on, the eiderdowns, the treadle sewing machine, the lamps, your new suit from Taylor's men's outfitters and the Ceylindo tea and the bonnet for Ada and Annie's new shoes and your new pipe. I didn't hear you complaining before."

Philip was annoyed at himself. This unwanted state of affairs was not Caroline's fault, after all. "Please, please, Caroline," he tried to appease her, "I'm not blaming you. It's just come upon me with no warning. I had such high hopes for the future. And now look at us. Back at square one, even worse off than before."

Husband and wife sat in miserable silence. The solid joys, which had been theirs for the taking only this morning, were running through their fingers like sand in an hour-glass.

The clatter of feet brought them both back to the disappointment of the present. Annie and Ada burst into the parlour.

"Uncle Philip, did you know it's a small world?" Ada was looking very wise, nodding her head as she asked this question, a broad smile on her flushed face.

"Small, eh?" To Philip no truer description could have been made. It was getting smaller by the minute, caving in on him. "Who told you that?"

"Mr Minns told us. In our tettitet." In the absence of a response from either Uncle Philip or Aunt Caroline, Ada sought some support. "Didn't he, Annie?"

Annie nodded.

Trying to put a brave face on the whole situation, so that the girls would be spared the pain of the unpleasant news until the following morning, Philip asked, "So why did he say it was a small world?"

"He says he went to music college in Cambridge with my Uncle John."

"I never heard tell of your Uncle Henry John going to college, my dear," Philip gently contradicted her. "After his schooling at

King's here in Ely, he went straight into his father's business in Haddenham."

"Not Uncle Henry John, but Uncle John!" corrected Ada.

"Uncle John, eh?"

"The one who lives in the north of England," Ada patiently explained.

Philip was none the wiser. He looked at Caroline for help in identifying this hitherto unheard of relation, but she just shook her head. Her mind was dwelling on more important issues than distant and probably fictitious uncles fished out of Mr Minns's imagination. She did not hold much store by his stories of the people he said he'd known in days gone by.

"Perhaps he's your mother's brother," Philip suggested.

"He's not," Ada insisted. "He's married to my auntie."

Philip was trying to be as even-tempered as possible. "Which auntie, my dear?"

"Aunt Priscilla."

"Aunt Priscilla, eh?" Now where had he seen that name? He remembered distinctly seeing it written down somewhere.

Ada solved the problem, "You know, the auntie who gave me The Glad Year Round birthday book."

Yes, that was it. The inscription inside the birthday book.

"Glad Year Round, eh?" Philip repeated.

The irony of the title once again was not lost on him. Only this time it seemed to apply as much to him and his family as to Ada herself. He sighed inwardly.

For most of that night in bed, he lay beside Caroline, unable to sleep. His mind was a turmoil of rhetorical questions. How could he hold his head high in the town, after years as a chief clerk? How could he suffer the indignity of taking back his new suit to Mr Taylor? How would he and Caroline manage with an extra mouth to feed, on slightly less money than they'd had before Ada came into their lives? What were they to do between now and March? How could he tell Annie and Ada about their leaving the Misses Birds' Preparatory School? How could he tell Caroline to sell the sofa and her treasured new sewing machine? How could he broach the subject of Ada's spent annuity to Alfred and Frank Porter, for it would now appear to be misspent?

As the morning light dawned in the sky outside, he got up and stood dejectedly looking out of the small, lattice parlour window into the street. The first signs of daily routines were stirring: the gasman was about his business of turning out the street lights; Jacob, the baker's boy, was running down Forehill, late for work; Mr Stapely was opening up the International Stores at the corner ready to catch the early shoppers. It was the same diurnal, rigorous hustle and bustle of Ely, except Philip was no longer a cog in the city's wheel. The future looked darkly sullen as he thought of the days and months ahead.

"What's wrong, Uncle Philip?" a little voice broke his silent thoughts. Ada slipped her hand into his.

"Oh, I was just thinking of things," he answered, looking down at the little figure in her nightgown.

"What things?"

"Oh, grown-up things."

"You look very sad."

"Sad, eh?"

"Mr Minns always says 'every cloud has a silver lining'." Ada tried, in her own gentle way, to soothe away her Uncle Philip's worry-lines.

"Yes, he has quite a store of those sayings. A saying for all occasions, eh!" Inwardly he thought that 'It never rains but it pours' would be a saying to more adequately sum up the situation, but he kept this to himself. Instead he squeezed Ada's hand to give her some assurance. "Well, I'll have to put a smile on my face, especially for you."

He would try to put a brave face on everything from now on.

CHAPTER 4
ADA

Part 1

"Don't cry, Annie!" Ada was valiantly trying to comfort her friend and companion. "My dear sister, don't cry."

"It's all your fault!" Annie sobbed. These were no crocodile tears, but angry drops of frustration. "And I'm not your sister!" she snapped emphatically, folding her arms and turning away.

Ada sat down on the bed beside her. Now here was a predicament: no matter how much she wanted to be sympathetic and share in Annie's bitter disappointment; she had this hysterical urge to shout with joy and a limitless sense of relief. The news which Uncle Philip had imparted to them that evening at supper-time was the root cause of these conflicting emotions.

When they all sat down at the table at the customary hour of six o'clock, Uncle Philip had looked so stern that Ada thought the world had come to an end. Mr Minns was always telling her, in their Thursday afternoon tête-a-têtes, to mark his words, for the end of the world was nigh.

She remembered when Uncle Philip used to be so kind and approachable, but over the past week he had been morose and very cross. She longed to make him smile again, like he had early that morning when they'd stood hand in hand watching the dawn come up. He and Aunt Caroline had barely spoken pleasantly to one another since the day of the shouting-match when he had insisted that she sell her sewing-machine and the new oil-lamps.

"We need money to pay the rent. We need money to put food on the table. Where else is it to come from?" Uncle Philip had demanded.

"Sink your pride and go to Mr Cutlack!" Aunt Caroline had

snapped back, though Ada was not sure how this Mr Cutlack fitted in.

"Never!"

What a dreadful episode that had been! Annie and Ada had crept out of the parlour into their bedroom, not daring to even light a candle, for fear the light would somehow direct Uncle Philip's ire in their direction.

Tonight, Aunt Caroline had placed the pot of scrag-end stew on the table, with a carefully manufactured expression of accusation and apology: accusation directed squarely at her husband, for he was the one who had refused to work for Mr Cutlack as a junior clerk and was making life so difficult for them; and a look of apology mixed with a martyred smile to the two girls, to show that there used to be better times, when the food on the table was more nourishing and appetising.

Uncle Philip had suddenly stood up at his end of the table, knocking his chair over in the process. Everyone eyed him with a certain degree of trepidation.

"Something had to be done, and it's been done today," he said solemnly.

Caroline looked expectantly at her husband, a hint of optimism in her eye. Perhaps he had decided to work at Cutlack's Brewery after all. Annie and Ada were more wary, not daring to breathe.

He spoke to the upturned faces around the table. "Money is short. It doesn't grow on trees. I've come to a decision." He took a deep breath, and grasped the edge of the table. "It's not been an easy decision, but it has had to be made. Annie, Ada, as from tomorrow, you will be going to Broad Street School."

"What?" Annie had grown pale. Even in the candle-light she looked wan. "Why, Father, why?" Her bottom lip was trembling. This was the end of all her dreams and ambitions.

"The prep school costs too much money. The Bird ladies do not come cheap." It was an unintended pun, and no-one smiled.

"But I want to be educated!" Annie's colour was returning.

"There's nothing wrong with the education you'll get in Broad Street. And anyway, what do you want with an education at your station in life?" Philip looked as if he would have taken those words back, if it were humanly possible. He remembered not long ago how proud he had been about the prospect of his daughter going up in the world, and becoming an independent woman. He was beginning to feel shabby and ashamed.

"I want to become a teacher."

Ada piped up, with a smile on her face. "I don't mind, Uncle Philip. I'm glad I'll never ever have to go to that school again!"

Annie regarded Ada as some kind of traitor in the midst. Caroline was astonished that the child should want to leave the security of the school she had always attended.

"That seems a strange thing to say, dear," she said. "Why are you glad?"

"Don't press the child!" Philip stepped in to save Ada having to explain her reasons, and save her the pain of putting them into words.

On the way to school one morning, when Ada had become more and more agitated the further they walked down St Mary's Street towards the school premises, he had asked her why she was so reluctant. She had confided in Philip. She hated going to Waddington Terrace: looking at what used to be her house at the end of the terrace; seeing strangers coming and going up and down the gracious steps up to her front door; being reminded of her Papa and Mama, both now dead and gone; and thinking about dearest Maud, wondering where she was and if she looked after another little girl now.

"There's my girl!" Philip smiled at Ada, his ally amongst strong opposition. "You'd best take a leaf out of her book, Annie."

Now at bed-time there was no consoling Annie. Ada quietly took off her pinafore and skirt and crept into bed wearing her blouse and shift. It was very cold under the bed-clothes in almost sub-zero temperatures. It was already promising to be as cold a winter as the previous one, but there would be no skating this year, no fun with Papa. As she shivered in bed, she longed for the warmth of Annie's body close to hers.

"Annie, I'm sorry," she said. "I'll hate going to Broad Street, just to please you." After a few seconds' silence in the darkness she tried to sound encouraging, "Annie, you will be a teacher one day, I promise."

"You don't know." Annie still sounded defiant, but her sobs and her anger were subsiding.

"Yes I do. Mr Minns told me. He said, 'Your sister's got a good head on her shoulders. She is a regular brain-box'."

"That doesn't mean I'll be a good teacher."

"Yes it does! He said all teachers are brain-boxes." Putting on a funny voice to sound like Mr Minns, she intoned, "'So you mark my words, your sister will be a good teacher'."

"Honest?" A hint of a smile crossed Annie's face.

"Cross my heart and hope to die!"

Annie sounded more content now as she got into bed beside Ada, though a trace of belligerence could be heard as she warned, "But I'm not your sister."

"I know," said Ada. Then, after a pause, she added wistfully, "I wish you were."

The two girls cuddled up together and snuggled down to sleep.

Part 2

Ada sat quietly at her usual place in the Broad Street School classroom assigned to the six-to-nine year olds. The bench was hard with a plethora of splinters on the edges, which had a habit of catching stockings when least expected. There was nothing particularly notable about Ada's silence as she waited for Miss Cartwright to begin the afternoon lessons, for she was by nature a quiet and polite seven-year-old.

The rest of the children had a respectful affection for her resilience and stoicism. Even Robert Tucker and Ben Bodkin, the two nine-year-old tearaways of the class, had left her alone since her first day in school when she had withstood their taunts with a cool, steadfast look in those dark brown eyes of hers. Though these two classroom tyrants tormented and bullied most of the other pupils in the class, given half the chance, there was something too imperturbable about this new pupil for their liking.

Miss Felicity Cartwright, a sweet and well-bred young woman from Lynn, was their new teacher. Just out of the Jessop Ladies' Seminary, where she had acquitted herself with honours in academic subjects, Miss Cartwright wore her inexperience on her cuff. Robert and Ben saw a victim from a mile away and plagued this poor woman unmercifully.

"What am I to do with you young rascals?" she would lamely ask at least twenty times a day, but never found a satisfactory answer.

"Put us head-first into the waste-paper basket!" Robert shouted out on this January afternoon. The bold insolence of this scruffy boy was difficult for a lady such as Miss Cartwright to handle. She had never encountered such behaviour and stood rigid, not knowing which way to turn.

"Stick us up the chimney!" Ben cheekily sneered, looking round at the rest of the class with a smirk on his face.

"You'll be the death of me!" Miss Cartwright sat down, deflated and miserable, on her high stool behind her tall desk. Neither the imposing desk, nor her elevated position above the rows of pupils made a whit of difference. She had no control over these boys and that was that. The burning coals in the grate beside her did little to cheer her spirits. She would have to ask Mr Sparks to help her out, eat humble pie once again. She dispatched Annie Allen, known to be a sensible and trustworthy girl, and academically superior to the rest of the older pupils, to the headmaster's study, clutching a desperate note, which asked for his assistance in disciplining these impossible boys.

The headmaster, the indomitable Mr Reginald Sparks, self-confessed "graduate of the school of life and proud of it", was under no illusions regarding young Robert and Ben. He knew them for what they were. And he knew how to deal with them effectively. He stormed into Miss Cartwright's classroom.

"Tucker, Bodkin!" he roared, flexing a cane. "To my study! At the double!"

Robert and Ben were cowed, for the present at least, at the thought of the six of the best they were about to receive, but their vengeful backwards glance at Miss Cartwright left her feeling cold and fearful of what the rest of the day would bring.

Once they had returned to the schoolroom, watery-eyed and red-faced, knowing that it would be a day or two before Miss Cartwright would dare to summon Mr Sparks again, Robert and Ben began a hissing undercurrent of chanting – not loud enough to bring upon them the wrath of the said fiery headmaster himself, but quiet, insidious and threatening. Over and over again, like some tribal rhythm, the chant gathered momentum:

"Sparks a-flying
Rears a-frying
But we stay happy and strong.
No shrieks or blubbing

During the drubbing,

For we ain't done nothing wrong."

Other boys, eye-balled by Robert and Ben, were afraid of being deemed cowardly. In no time they joined in and soon the boys became a pulsating circle around the solitary, helpless, weeping figure of Miss Cartwright.

The girls felt a degree of sympathy for their teacher but, beyond refusing to join in with this nasty, diabolical chant, they did nothing. Annie, our up-and-coming teacher, put herself in Miss Cartwright's shoes and felt for her with all her heart, yet did not know what to do.

But Ada had listened to the silly boys long enough. Into the midst of the circle she stepped, a tall, quiet girl with light brown curled hair, tied back with a blue and white checked ribbon. She stood beside Miss Cartwright, her hand resting lightly on her shoulder. She regarded the offending boys with a stony expression of disapproval and disappointment. The more sensitive children began to stop chanting, feeling rather small under the gaze of this slim and willowy figure. She was very nice to look at, one of the prettiest girls in the class. Some of the older lads entertained many a fancy regarding her. Young Tim Thompson, for example, was secretly making a Valentine's card especially for her.

"Leave her alone, do you hear!" she commanded. Ada's inner strength was so awe-inspiring that all but Robert and Ben began to fall back. Tim and his mate Basil Williamson were the first to return to their places on their benches, and the others followed suit.

"Listen to Miss Hoity-Toity!" sneered Robert, looking to Ben and the rest of the pupils for support. But all he heard was an unco-operative silence and not one of the class would make eye-contact with him. Even Ben looked uncertain as to which side he should take.

"Leave Miss Cartwright alone," Ada's quiet, unwavering voice sounded clear and authoritative.

"Yes, leave her alone!" the rest of the girls chorused, not

wanting to be left out of the general censure of Robert and Ben's confrontational behaviour to their teacher.

The girls had had as much as they could take from these two boys. Marion and Jemima had had enough of being tripped up in the playground. Therese and Beatrice were fed up having their pigtails pulled. Susan and Gwendolyn were furious each time their hop-scotch slate was stolen and chucked over the red brick wall surrounding the quadrangle in which they played. Jenny, Ruth and the twins, Lilian and Rachel, would never forgive Robert for illicitly bringing to school one of his father's butcher's knives and conspiring with Ben to cut their thirty-foot long rope in two, thereby spoiling their break-time skipping games. The accompanying chant, "Salt, vinegar, mustard, pepper", was never again repeated more than twenty-one times, once their skipping rope was knotted and distorted. In the past, they had managed to reach fifty-three uninterrupted skipping sequences.

These girls were glad at last to stand up against Robert and Ben.

Some of the boys began to silently summon Robert and Ben to their seats with a quick sideways turn of their heads. Tim actually called out, "Sit down, you warts!" which was followed by derisive laughter directed at Robert and Ben.

"Ah, they're just two bully-boys!" This was Pauline Gotobed addressing the class. Her great grandfather's photograph had recently appeared in the "Ely Gazette": Paul Gotobed was one of the last remaining and indeed the oldest eel-trap maker in the whole region. Pauline had felt a certain superiority and reflected glory through this notoriety, and now she was able to make good use of it. "My great grand-father says you're only cowards. And he should know, because he met many a French coward in Napoleon's army, when they was running scared!"

Ada continued to hold her ground.

"Come on, Rob. Let's sit down," Ben muttered, beginning to feel embarrassed under Ada's scrutiny. He found her condemnatory gaze too much to withstand. "Come on." He sat down, red-faced and impotent.

With his last ally gone, Robert was beginning to feel very foolish: that this willowy girl, two years younger than he was, with her posh accent, should get the better of him, was humiliating. Ada looked at him with unflinching eyes, and the more he tried to stare her out, the more he found himself being sucked under her spell. His eyes began to tingle, they began to water, until he had no alternative but to blink and give in.

"Just you wait!" He spat out this empty threat as he flumped down onto his seat. "Just you wait!"

Miss Cartwright dabbed her eyes on her lace handkerchief, saying, "Thank-you, Ada." Then, as if the whole episode had been engineered by her, she pertly and coolly announced, "You may go back to your seat." But in her heart she felt eternally grateful to this quiet, orphaned girl who had spoken out on her behalf, and made a mental note that she would bring in some of her own special books for Ada the very next day.

At the end of the afternoon, when the pupils were filing out of the schoolroom, she called Ada back.

"Teacher's pet!" Robert snarled, jostling and shoving Ada, deliberately trying to stamp on her toes, as she stood back to let everyone past her. Naturally, like all defeated bullies, and subversive cowards, he made sure that no-one else would see what he was intending.

"Ask Aunt Caroline to wait, please," Ada called to Annie, who was making her way out through the door with the rest of the boys and girls.

With her back to the dying embers in the grate, Miss Cartwright stood with her hands clasped in front of her. Ada waited for her to speak, with a sinking feeling that she was about to be chastised, for hadn't she overstepped the mark by telling the class what to do?

"That was a very brave thing you did today, Ada."

Ada stood immobile with her head down.

Then Miss Cartwright asked the question which had been revolving in her head since the incident. "Why did you do that for me?"

"It's a special day," Ada said simply. Slowly raising her eyes to meet Miss Cartwright's, she added, "I wanted to keep it special and nice and peaceful."

"What's special about today?"

"It's the day Papa died. One year ago. It's his special day." Tears welled up in Ada's eyes, and began to fall freely and unbidden down her soft, pale cheeks. She wept for her dear, dead Papa.

"Oh, my child," Felicity Cartwright compassionately whispered, "this is indeed a very special day!"

Unaware of the significance that this was the first day Ada had succumbed to a show of tears, she added, "Your father would be very proud of you."

Ada was not so sure that he would be, and longed for the spring when the crocuses would be in bloom.

Part 3

Ada was feeling excited, favoured and special on this Valentine's day, for she had received a card from "TT", whom she knew to be Tim Thompson, the flaxen-haired boy whom she often caught looking admiringly across the schoolroom in her direction. It was enough to make her dance with joy.

She wanted to show the little card to Annie, to point at the letters AMP and TT which had been written across a very prettily drawn and coloured red heart, and to read out the traditional little verse inside the card:

"Roses are red, violets are blue,

Sugar is sweet, and so are you."

However, she could not give voice to her happy thoughts on this particular morning, for everyone in the Allens' lodgings was remarkably ill-at-ease.

"You could cut the atmosphere with a knife," Mr Minns would have said, had he been there.

Annie sat at the breakfast table eating her piece of bread, which was spread thinly with some new, inexpensive foodstuff called "margarine". She was looking exceedingly unhappy, on the verge of tears, but whether this misery was because she had not been a recipient of a Valentine's message, or because her father was packing his threadbare carpet-bag to go away to Cambridge to find work, was not altogether clear. Aunt Caroline was sitting on one of the two wooden chairs, which had replaced the new sofa, at the window. She was stony-faced, not knowing if she was more annoyed with her husband for refusing to get work in Ely, or for his sudden decision to leave her on her own with the two children while he earned the money they so desperately needed.

Over the past winter weeks, Ada and Annie had not been able to help but overhear a series of arguments, all about money, with Uncle Philip's refusal to work for "a pittance" in Ely the main underlying cause. Aunt Caroline had verbally bludgeoned her obstinate husband time and again, only to be met with a mulish look. She had wrung her hands pitifully at Christmas time. "It's a crying shame when the only Christmas boxes for the children have to come from Ada's aunt."

"It's very kind of her," Philip had muttered, meeting his wife's eye, daring her to say more. Then to Ada he had gently said, "She's always been a very kind lady, eh, Ada, as I recall."

"Yes, well, I would also like to have the money to be kind," Caroline had hissed at him, "to give our own daughter a Christmas box, and something nice for Ada too."

In the New Year, when there was hardly more than three weeks' coal left in the coal cellar, Caroline had faced Philip accusingly. "And when it's all finished, how are we going to keep ourselves warm? They say it'll be even colder than last year. We can't go on like this, Philip."

His reply of "I'll have to think it through" was hardly adequate, and was met with a tart rejoinder: "There's no money to pay Mr Minns his rent. I can hardly look the man in the face! I wouldn't be surprised if he puts us out on the street, and what then?"

"All right! All right!" Philip was finally being worn down.

Caroline pressed home her advantage. "Do you think I should be reduced to taking in washing to keep the family clothed and fed?"

Finally Uncle Philip had relented, but on his own terms. "Peace, woman!" he had stormed at her, after a meagre supper of bread and dripping. "I'll pack my bag and go in the morning. Nothing will please you better, eh?"

"Go where?" Aunt Caroline had suddenly looked fearful, for might she not have driven him out of the house for good with all her badgering? At bottom, although he had not fulfilled his role of sole breadwinner in recent months and the last of

Ada's annuity was at an end, she could not imagine life without him.

"There's work in Cambridge. I'll find employment there. Experienced clerks are always wanted, always in short supply." He spoke confidently enough, though his eyes betrayed some misgivings. After all, he was a homely man at heart and his departure to Cambridge would mean the break-up of the basic social unit of the family.

"Very well. Go then!" Aunt Caroline had sounded subdued at last, though it was not clear to Ada whether she looked more relieved or worried about this sudden turn of events.

Uncle Philip, looking strained and saddened, left the lodgings in Forehill on this bitter February morning, his heavy carpet-bag in his hand. He had to hurry to catch the nine o'clock train. Still feeling the sense of injustice and grievance of a man who fights and loses a lone battle, he gave his wife only a summary farewell peck on the cheek.

"Now don't fret, Caroline, and wipe away those tears. It's what you wanted, after all!" Then he became more practical. "When the money is right, I'll send for you."

Then he kissed Annie, saying, "Now, be good while I'm away, and work hard at school."

"Yes, Father." Annie's voice was no more than a whisper.

Ada received a hug. "Look after your aunt, d'you hear, and be a good girl."

"Yes, Uncle Philip." Ada voice wavered, aware now of the full import of his departure. Her Uncle Philip was leaving them!

She waved him goodbye, still clutching the Valentine's card in her hand. TT's avowal of love for her did nothing to fill her sense of loss as Uncle Philip disappeared into the frosty mist at the far end of Forehill.

Part 4

True to his word, Uncle Philip did find employment as an office clerk in Cambridge, with the Simon Armitage Haulage Company, but the rate of pay was the same as that which he would have earned at Cutlacks back in Ely. With rent for lodgings in Cambridge to be paid, Philip Allen found himself financially worse off, once again. To be fair, Mr Cutlack would have employed a reliable man like Philip Allen with not a moment's hesitation, but nothing would ever induce Philip to sink his pride and work for Cutlack, nor anyone else in Ely. He sent as much money as he could to Caroline, who scrimped and saved to make ends meet. She eagerly awaited the twenty-fifth of March, when Ada's annuity would be paid as a lump sum into Philip's bank account.

With the departure of Uncle Philip, Ada turned to Mr Minns for adult company. There was now a regular Monday tête-a-tête, as well as the usual Thursday tête-a-tête.

At the beginning of March, Mr Minns opened his parlour door late one afternoon just as Aunt Caroline and the two girls came into the house.

"Good-day to you, Mrs Allen. Blustery outside!" He greeted her with his usual commentary of the weather.

"Yes indeed, Mr Minns," Aunt Caroline looked apprehensive. Although the January arrears had been cleared, the rent had not been paid for February and for this month, and dear knows where the money would be found. "I need to get in and stoke up the stove."

"March winds and April showers will bring forth May flowers," he suddenly announced, as if sensing her anxiety.

Ada nodded thoughtfully in agreement, fleeting pictures of snowdrops and crocuses flitting through her mind.

"Perhaps." Aunt Caroline sounded doubtful. Mr Minns and his maxims were of little comfort. "Good-day to you, Mr Minns."

"Before you go," Mr Minns quickly said, "I wonder if it would be possible to speak with Ada for a few minutes?" Aunt Caroline had barely taken a breath to answer when he continued, "I know it's not one of our tête-a-tête days, but I have something I'd like to show her."

"There will be no pleasure talking to her today," retorted Aunt Caroline, looking disapprovingly at Ada. "She's like a bear with a sore head! And all over a piece of string."

"A piece of string?" Mr Minns asked Ada. "That sounds intriguing! You must tell me all about it."

"It's all stuff and nonsense, if you ask me!" Aunt Caroline dismissed the school episode which had so annoyed Ada.

"Ada will be cheered in a trice," the gentle Mr Minns assured Aunt Caroline, "when she sees the letter I received in the afternoon post."

Ada and Annie looked at one another with raised eyebrows. This sounded very exciting to two girls whose lives had become dull.

"Very well!" agreed Aunt Caroline, too immersed in her own troubles to show any interest in a letter, as she and Annie went into their own apartments. "Now, Ada, make sure you don't make a nuisance of yourself!"

This instruction was quite superfluous. Ada was not given to being a nuisance. Although she was still cross at being likened to a piece of string by Robert Tucker, she was itching to know whom the letter was from and why it should concern her.

"Now tell me all about the string saga," Mr Minns encouraged Ada, as he indicated her favourite russet velvet armchair for her to sit in. He wanted to clear Ada's mind of all horrid thoughts before he told her his news.

"Miss Cartwright, she's our teacher..." began Ada.

"Yes, I know Miss Cartwright. A first-rate teacher by all accounts."

"She got a ball of string and measured everyone in feet and inches and then in metres and centimetres."

Mr Minns waited patiently for this story to unfold. "Yes, go on, my dear."

"Everyone had their own bit of string, and we had to pin them up on the wall and see whose bit of string was the longest."

"I see."

"And mine was, but I'm not the oldest, and Robert Tucker… he's a hateful, hateful boy… said I looked just like my bit of string on the wall."

"I'm sure he didn't mean anything particularly hurtful."

"He did, he did! He said I was like the string, all yellow and straggly and too long for a girl."

"There's only one thing I can say to those remarks, my dear. They are all balderdash! Why, I never heard of anything so silly! Have you regarded yourself in the looking-glass of late?"

"Yes. No. I don't know." Ada was not sure when she had last seen herself in a mirror. Aunt Caroline had sold her cheval mirror just before last Christmas. "December, maybe."

"Come with me!" directed Mr Minns. He took her through to his dining quarters where he had a full-length mirror at the far end of the room. "Now, in answer to the descriptions made by young Master Tucker: first, are you yellow?"

"No, sir."

"Exactly. Secondly, are you straggly?"

"My hair is."

"Perhaps there are one or two wisps out of place, but your person is far from straggly. You're not like the gypsies in our song are you?

"No, sir." Ada loved singing *The Raggle Taggle Gypsies-o* to Mr Minns's accompaniment. On the front cover of the sheet music there was an etched drawing of these bedraggled women of misfortune, with their hair flying in the wind and their clothes all tattered and torn. She certainly did not look at all straggly, compared with them. "I am not!" she said emphatically.

"Exactly. And finally, Master Tucker thought you were 'too

long for a girl'. Did he suggest what was the right height for the female of the human race?" In answer to what was really a rhetorical question, he said, "Of course not."

"But, Mr Minns, I am taller than everyone else in the class, and I'm only seven and a half." Ada looked unhappy with this state of affairs.

Mr Minns now decided to broach a subject which he had never dared to before. "Do you remember your dear Mama?" he asked gently.

"Of course," replied Ada stoutly; she remembered Matilda lying on her death-bed. She looked at the head and shoulders portrait photograph of her mother every night when she said her prayers, asking God to look after her Mama and Papa in heaven. Of course she remembered her Mama!

"Did you know that your Mama was a tall lady? She stood taller than all the other ladies in the town. She even stood shoulder to shoulder with your dear Papa. She was one of the most beautiful and graceful ladies I ever beheld, and you should feel very proud to be tall just like she was."

"Yes, sir." Ada was fit to burst with pride. Mr Minns could not have chosen anything better to have said to this troubled child. She now stood tall and looked at herself in the mirror, with new understanding and a little admiration.

"That's right, Ada. You stand tall and see just what a lovely and graceful lady you are becoming. Just like your Mama. And remember the saying: 'Sticks and stones may break my bones, but words can never hurt me.' Now, let us return to the parlour where I have this important letter to read to you."

Back in the parlour, Mr Minns rang a small, brass hand-bell to summon Sophie Morris, his maid.

"The afternoon tea and muffins, please, Sophie."

"Yes, sir, Mr Minns, sir." Sophie, a local fifteen-year old lass in her first month of employment, dropped a curtsy before leaving the room, just as Mr Minns had taught her to do "if she wanted to get on in the world and learn how to become a lady's maid or even a housekeeper one day". Poor Sophie was such a plain girl that it was more than certain that her lot in life would be to remain in service, for no likely lad on the look-out for a mate would glance twice at her.

"We mustn't forget our afternoon tea and muffins, Ada, must we?"

Ada could have dispensed with this regular twice-weekly treat on this day. Normally she loved drinking tea from the adorable Crown Derby china teacups, which Mr Minns had told her were his mother's heirloom, though she was not sure what an heirloom actually was. She vaguely remembered her dear Papa saying that her Penny Black in her Mama's little purse was an heirloom. There did not seem to be much similarity between a china tea-set and a stamp!

Today, however, heirlooms, stamps and china teacups were of no interest to Ada: she was filled with curiosity about Mr Minns's letter. Who was it from? What did it say? And why should it be of interest to her?

After what seemed like an age, Mr Minns finally walked over to his bureau, a fine light oak piece of furniture with many pigeon-holes, drawers and even secret compartments. From the small drawer below the desk he produced a small, cream, vellum envelope, of the type usually used by ladies, and regularly used by Ada in the past when she would write each week to her cousin Hilda at boarding school and to her cousin Olive at Vine House. That was before Aunt Caroline had put her foot down and told Ada that, at a penny a time, stamps were too expensive and Ada would write no more letters, with the exception of a thank-you letter to her Aunt Priscilla who had sent her a blouse and a straw hat for Christmas. Ada's lap escritoire was now hidden away, unused, under the bed.

"Now, my dear, this is a letter from your aunt," Mr Minns began to explain.

"Which aunt?" Ada had a number of aunts. Aunt Mary Ann at Vine House might write to her. Aunt Mary lived in Ely, so she and Uncle Charles could visit, only they never called to see her any more. Old Aunt Ann in Haddenham was dead now. "Is it Aunt Priscilla?"

"Correctly deduced or guessed. It is from your Aunt Priscilla."

"And Uncle John?"

"Ah, now that's where there is a problem. Your Uncle John is no more." Mr Minns looked serious.

"Dead?"

"Good gracious me, no! Not dead. Gone to America. Mind you, he might as well be dead in that God-forsaken country!" Mr Minns did not rate the United States of America very highly, not since his cousin had been killed in a skirmish in Carolina during the Civil War.

"Has he gone to America to make money for my aunt, just like Uncle Philip has gone away to Cambridge to make money for us?" Ada was trying to equate the behaviour of these pairs of aunts and uncles.

"Not like your Uncle Philip." Here Mr Minns heaved a big sigh. "No, your Aunt Priscilla and Uncle John are divorced." He did not approve of divorce. A devout Christian, he believed marriage vows made before God were not to be broken. Had he known that Priscilla and John Sellers had broken their vows, he would never have written to them in the first place. However, the deed was done, and Aunt Priscilla had written back to Mr Minns. "Now, to the letter." Here he unfolded the page and began to read:

"'My dear Mr Minns,

'As you rightly assumed, I was most surprised to receive your communication, addressed to my husband and me. First, I must tell you that my husband and I divorced ten years ago, and he is now living in America with a new wife and family. He makes only moderate provision for me but I endeavour to live comfortably enough here in Preston with my son and daughter. John and I regularly keep in touch. There was no acrimony involved in our agreement to part.

'As you say, it is indeed a small world. Imagine you and John being students together, and now my niece is living under the same roof as you.

'I was pleased to hear of your continued enjoyment of your musical profession. Before John took up accountancy in America, which suited him

105

well with his own first-hand experience of business here in Lancashire, he went back to giving piano lessons and did some piano-tuning from time to time. His love of music never left him either, you see.

'Thank-you for giving me news of Ada. Apart from an annual letter from Ada herself at Christmas, your communication has been the only information about my niece that I have received since her father died over a year ago. All the more welcome for that, I assure you, as I must admit to having concerns regarding her. I would like to put you right about one issue. You have credited me with generosity which regrettably I do not deserve: I did not send a Christmas present to Annie Allen. The blouse you mentioned was in fact a present intended for Ada along with a straw hat'."

"The blouse was too small for me, Mr Minns, so Annie had to have it." Ada interrupted here, telling a white lie. She did not tell Mr Minns about the sorry state of affairs at Christmas when Aunt Priscilla's gifts had to be shared.

"My apologies, Ada. I obviously gave incorrect information to your aunt. I shall make amends when I see her." Mr Minns suddenly clapped his hand over his mouth. "Oh dear, now I've spoilt the surprise."

"Surprise? Is Aunt Priscilla coming here?" Ada could hardly believe her ears.

"Hold your horses, young miss," laughed Mr Minns holding up his hand. "Let me continue the letter, and all will be revealed. She goes on to say: *'I am planning a trip to Cambridgeshire at Easter. I have been too long away. It will be a trip down memory lane, the opportunity to place flowers on family graves, and make visits to family and old friends. Perhaps my niece would like to join me for a few days' holiday. I shall, of course, be writing to the Allens on this matter. As an old friend of my former husband, and a friend to Ada, perhaps you would do me the honour of joining me for dinner at The Bell Hotel on Easter Sunday'."*

Here Mr Minns broke off. It had been many years since he had been out to dinner with a lady. He was already considering his attire for the evening.

"How very kind! I shall accept the invitation to dinner, and you, my dear," he said nodding sagely, "may be assured that Mrs Allen will have no objections to your going on a holiday with your aunt." He would see to that!

"When is Easter?" Ada wanted to know.

"In exactly four weeks time!"

Part 5

Ada was sitting on the floor beside the grate in the Allens' parlour. She was hugging her knees, looking disconsolately at the flames. It seemed that the knife in the wound of fate was about to be twisted yet again. The scar kept opening up time and time again. Would it never be healed? Just when she'd been looking forward to a holiday with her Aunt Priscilla, Uncle Philip had unexpectedly come home late one afternoon in the middle of the week and destroyed it all.

In the flickering firelight glow, Ada's mind was in turmoil as she recalled snatches of the moribund discussion which had ended in Annie sobbing on her bed, Caroline dejectedly staring out of the window, and Philip walking out of the house muttering that he'd be better off in The Ship Inn with a jug of Eyre's ale in his grasp.

The key words of "America", "money", "Ada", "guardian", "annuity", "arrears", "prospects", "brothers" and "future" jangled in her brain, like broken horseshoes in an empty bucket.

"I will have to refuse to continue to act!" Although Ada did not fully comprehend the intention in this jargon, it sounded ominous. Uncle Philip had spoken like a man driven to desperate remedies.

"After all this time?" Aunt Caroline had shaken her head as she looked sadly at Ada. "What's going to happen to her if you do?"

"It's not our responsibility. She's not a relation!" Philip had tried to distance himself from the rejection he was asserting.

"But she can't just be shoved onto someone else at the drop of a hat!" For all Aunt Caroline's cold exterior, she was a good woman who cared for their ward.

The awful truth was beginning to dawn on Ada. She was not wanted any more.

"I know that," Philip had sighed, but he knew when he was beaten. Even with Ada's annuity recently placed in his bank account, try as he might, he could not get the books to balance, and he knew it would be impossible to make ends meet in the coming twelve months. With two sets of rent to pay and four mouths to feed, the time had come for decisions. "I'll write to the brothers. After all, they hold the purse-strings. They should sort it out between them."

Ada hardly dared breathe for fear she would cry. Was she to leave her home with the Allens? Was she to go and live with Alfred and Frank? Where did they live? She never saw them! They never visited her! She didn't know them! Panic was not far from the surface.

Then Uncle Philip had suddenly and bluntly proposed that he, Caroline and Annie might even uproot and go to live in America. Caroline sat rigid, Ada clamped her jaw together, desperately trying not to cry, and Annie was belligerent. "I don't want to go!" she complained emphatically.

"You'll do as you're bid, young lady."

"I hate America!" Annie countered, undaunted.

"Don't be ridiculous! You know nothing about it. Now keep quiet!"

Here Philip took out of his pocket a letter sent to him by Mr Dawson, who had been appointed Head Brewer at the Jeffers Brewery in Boston. He spoke to Caroline, nodding to encourage her approbation. "There's money to be made out there. Mr Dawson has offered me a job at Jeffers in Boston."

"But I don't want to leave Ada behind!" interjected Annie.

"I've told you to keep quiet. Now leave the room if you can't do as you're told. Now!" he shouted, ordering his daughter out of the parlour.

Annie fled sobbing to her bedroom, flinging herself on the bed, convulsed with uncontrollable, angry tears which soaked the pillow. This future in America without Ada was as unwanted as it was unattractive to her young mind.

Trying to soften Caroline's hardened facial features, Philip shrugged. "Needs must when the devil drives."

Caroline had sat quietly long enough. Now she spoke up, defiant, "You'll be going without me!"

"I hardly think so, woman!" Philip was taken aback by his wife's adamant rejection of his decision.

"I've no intention of setting foot in Boston or any other part of America for that matter. Let me tell you that!" This sounded so final.

"Consider this. I would earn three times the salary I'm earning here. Think on that." Philip knew this trump card would win the day. Money was almost a by-word with his wife, a dangling carrot, a guiding star. "Before you snap at me that you're not going, think on that!" he repeated.

Caroline sat still, coolly eyeing her husband. She was suddenly controlled and dignified as she thought of all the financial implications of what her husband had proposed for her family's future. She pragmatically understood and accepted the fact that Ada could not be part of that future, whatever decision was made. If they stayed where they were, they would not be able to continue to look after Ada without seriously damaging their own daughter's prospects and running into serious debt. So it would be better for Ada to live with someone else. It had always been such a daft idea to appoint Philip, a comparative stranger, as Ada's guardian anyway.

If Philip insisted that they move to Boston, she would have to accompany him, for she was ill-equipped to deal with a life on her own should she refuse, and what would happen to Annie? She thought the authorities would never allow them to take Ada with them to America, as she was not their adopted daughter, only their ward. She looked down at the silent Ada, who was a vulnerable, solitary little huddle by the fire.

"Very well," she said. "Perhaps you're right."

"Perhaps," was all Philip could say. Despite his enthusiasm, his thoughts were focused more on the fate of his ward, Ada.

Caroline stroked Ada's hair, fondly pushing back some of the wisps of hair which had fallen over the child's forehead.

"It'll all turn out for the best," Caroline said. "You'll like living with your brothers or someone…" Here she trailed off, unable to finish the sentence which sounded such a hollow promise, and looked out of the lattice window as the lamp-lighter did his rounds, his lamps bringing a warm glow to the street outside, but unable to penetrate the cheerless atmosphere of uncertainty within.

Ada spoke not a word. Philip felt the weight of this silence. It was the weight of censure, betrayal, disappointment and misery. He felt he was letting this little girl down. How he wished things had turned out differently for her! He put on his coat and hat. Before leaving the house, he listened to Annie sobbing in the small bedroom, watched Caroline sitting morosely looking out of the window, and felt the sharp arrow of Ada's stoicism pierce his heart. There must surely be another way out of this sorry mess.

Angry with no-one but himself, he left the house muttering and made his way down Forehill towards The Ship Inn to think things through.

Part 6

Ada knew the holiday would soon be over. This was the last day of their grand tour round Cambridgeshire. How she wished that this special time with her Aunt Priscilla would last forever! They had set off from Ely on Good Friday, taken the train to Soham and Newmarket where they had stayed in The Crown Hotel.

On Easter Saturday they had visited Devil's Dyke, that ancient linear earthwork, known as the "best and biggest area of chalk grassland", famed for its rare pasque-flower growing wild. Ada had picked some of these purple, anemone type flowers to add to her collection of pressed flowers.

She became aware that her aunt was staring at her, and felt mildly embarrassed. Perhaps Aunt Priscilla wanted to get on with the journey.

"I'm sorry, Aunt Priscilla," she said, though not sure what she was apologising for.

"Whatever for, my dear?"

"I don't know!" Ada simply replied. "You were looking at me very hard."

Aunt Priscilla breathed out a sad, nostalgic smile. "You remind me of Jessie and Ida."

Ada looked puzzled. These were new names to her. "I don't think I know them, do I?"

"No. You don't know them. They were my two little girls. They died just before you were born, on the same day as each other."

Ada saw the calm, wistful look on her aunt's face. She said nothing, but gently stroked her aunt's hand to show that she understood the pain of such loss.

They had spent a couple of days seeing the sights of Cambridge, the highlight of which for Ada was the wobbly trip in the punt on the Backs.

Mr Minns was always telling her, "All good things must come to an end", and in her young life she had certainly found this adage to be too true. But wouldn't it be wonderful if, just for once, one of his sayings could be proved wrong? Here they were on the last day of her holiday, on their way back to Ely, breaking their train journey from Cambridge at Haddenham Halt.

"Allow me, madam." A familiar voice could be heard over the groaning and hissing and squealing of metal as "Old Grunty", the local name for the Grunty Fen train of the Great Eastern Railway, pulled out of Haddenham Station behind them.

"Thank-you, driver." Aunt Priscilla accepted the assistance of their coachman, who helped her into the waiting landau. Despite the mid-morning sunshine of this Easter Tuesday, it was not yet warm enough to put back the adjustable covering hood of this stately German carriage.

"Why, Miss Porter! I can hardly believe my eyes!" It was Mr Stokes, no longer sporting his forest-green livery, but nonetheless the same Mr Stokes who had once been her friend.

"Mr Stokes!" Ada was so excited that she was about to give him a hug, until she recollected that she should remember her manners. "Good-day! How are you?"

Mr Stokes could have swept this little girl up into his arms, he was so pleased to see her. She was as pretty as a picture. Ever since his summary dismissal as chief ostler of the Eagle Brewery and Ricard's Carriers, at the time of old Mr Porter's death, he had often wondered how Ada was faring with Philip Allen. Although he liked Philip and had worked with him for a number of years at the brewery, he had thought at the time that it was a most peculiar arrangement to appoint a comparative stranger as guardian to such a sweet daughter like Ada, but it was none of his business.

"I'm well, miss, thank you, and all the better for seeing what a fine young lady you're growing up into. Your father would have been proud of you. Now let me help you up. It's quite like old times!" he said, chuckling.

"Thank-you, Mr Stokes!"

"Excuse me, madam," he apologised. His passenger, attired in a two-piece couturier costume in light beige velvet, had been sitting patiently in the landau. "I used to work for Miss Porter's father before he died."

"It's Mr Stokes," Ada buoyantly and proudly announced.

"Ah, I see," replied Aunt Priscilla, trying to sound impressed for her niece's sake, but also retaining an acceptable distance between herself and this man who was in her employ for the day. "I'm Mr Porter's sister-in-law, from Lancashire. Mrs Porter was my sister."

"I knew Mrs Porter well, ma'am." Mr Stokes was offering his condolences in his own quiet and inoffensive way, lowering his head deferentially as he spoke. "She was a very gracious lady, if you will permit me saying."

"Yes, she was!" said Aunt Priscilla, the weight of his words hitting her like a blow. Here in Haddenham the full impact of her loss and Ada's loss stared her in the face. She nodded and then patted Ada on the knee. "Thank you."

She felt acute pangs of guilt that she had not been here when her own mother Ann needed her, then when her sister Ada was dying, and latterly to bring comfort to her orphaned niece. Trying to avoid a show of emotion, she abruptly said, "Now, let's get on. You have the itinerary, I presume, Mr Stokes?"

"I have indeed, ma'am. Your old house down at Linden End first, it says." Then he closed the door, placed the luggage at the back, jumped aboard, shook the reins of the stalwart Suffolk Punch, and they were off on their tour round Hadddenham.

Aunt Priscilla had made arrangements with the Great Eastern Railway company for a means of transport for the day. Within a week of losing his job in Ely, Mr Stokes had managed to secure himself employment in Haddenham as a driver for the railway company, finding temporary accommodation with his ailing grandmother. When she died just before Christmas, she had favoured this kind-hearted grandson of hers in her will. What had begun as temporary was to become permanent, and he now enjoyed the ownership and comforts of a cosy cottage in Haddenham, out towards Hillrow.

For Priscilla, it was a poignant trip down memory lane. This was the village where she had been born and raised; she had married John Sellers in the temporary church here twenty years before; her sister Ada had died in their cottage at Linden End in that same year. Her father, Marshall, had disappeared the year before that, amidst all the scandal of divorce. She thought now how odd it was that John and she should have followed in her parents' footsteps along the path of divorce, for her John had walked out on her ten years ago, in search of a better life and a better wife in America. There had been rumours that Marshall too had gone to Florida and married again.

As the thoughts thus revolved in Priscilla's mind, the carriage made its way up Station Road, past Vine House, and Ada was calling out, "Look, Aunt, there's Vine House!"

"I know, dear, that will be our last port of call today. We are to have afternoon tea there! Remember?" Aunt Priscilla's voice sounded distant, as her mind was whisked back from the past to the present. To Ada, who knew nothing of her aunt's thoughts, it sounded irritable.

As they passed Holy Trinity Church on the right, Ada did not speak, did not ask when they were to visit the graveyard. Their holiday had included so many wonderful places and so many itineraries that her brain was fairly swimming with different names, times and places. She did not want to annoy Aunt Priscilla again. She did not want the magic of this holiday to end; she did not want to be cut on the knife-edge of happiness.

Then they were passing the old finger signpost at the crossroads in the centre of the village, pointing towards Earith and Hillrow Fen in the west, towards Cambridge in the south, towards Wilburton and Ely in the east. Then down Main Street, past Setchell's bakery on the left, and the old school-house on the right.

"That's your great-aunts' house," Priscilla indicated a large but dilapidated town-house further down on the right of Main Street. "We'll be in good time to see them for lunch, as arranged."

Finally, at the other end of the village, at Linden End, where the houses give way to orchards of cherry trees, now ablaze with pink blossom, there, set back from the road in an overgrown plot, with an unruly and ancient climbing rose round the door, was the cottage where Aunt Priscilla had been born, and where she had spent her childhood.

As Ada alighted from the landau, she went and stood beside Aunt Priscilla who was motionless as a statue. Sensing that this was a time "for little girls to be seen and not heard", as Mr Minns would say, she simply took her aunt's hand in hers. Together they regarded the exterior of this old family cottage, whose windows were all boarded up. Ada, for all her seven years, really did empathise with her aunt, for she too knew what it was to look at a place which was once your home, when all the loved ones therein were dead and gone. Both stood side-by-side, suddenly linked by a moment in time and a single thought, thinking of Matilda: the dear sister departed, and dear dead Mama.

The atmosphere surrounding Ada here was that of measured calm in the face of adversity. She felt a pervasive sense of belonging, a suffused oneness with the Haddenham Porters who had come before her. Ada could know nothing of the forebearance of her grandmother Ann Porter, who had been left to bring up a family on her own and had died of consumption; she could know nothing of the patient suffering and shattered hopes of her mother's sister, Ada, who had also died of consumption, in her teenage years; she could know nothing of her mother's own stoicism and selfless devotion as she nursed her dying sister and mother.

But she felt it all nonetheless.

"I remember my mother planting that rose by the door!" Aunt Priscilla suddenly broke the silent spell. "And look at it now! It'll have thousands of blooms on it this year. And no-one to pick them!"

"Can we look into the house?" Ada was eager to look through the cracks in the rough boards at the windows.

Priscilla called back to Mr Stokes, who was standing by the gate. "Mr Stokes, would anyone mind if we had a peep through the windows, do you think?"

"I shouldn't think so, ma'am. The place has been deserted for about ten years, as I understand it! It won't bother anyone. You have a good wander round, and if anyone comes by, I'll explain who you are – about the trip down memory lane and all that!"

For Ada it was a disappointing wander round, for there was nothing much to see – just boarded up windows, and the ground round about all overgrown and unattractive. The place abounded in nettles and, although she had heard that nettles were not supposed to do any harm to human flesh until the middle of April, these were obviously the vanguard with poisoned sharp spears. Now her bare legs between the new boots and the new red velvet travelling dress, which Aunt Priscilla had bought for her, were stinging horribly. She was glad when she and her aunt had come full circle to the front of the house and were leaving.

"You need to rub some dockens on them," remarked Mr Stokes, when Ada complained about all the itchy white lumps on her legs. "Hang on a tick and I'll get you some."

In a couple of minutes he was back, armed with a bunch of juicy, broad-leafed dock leaves. He gave instructions to Ada on how to apply this ancient and efficacious herbal remedy, which she duly did as they made their way to Main Street to visit the great aunts.

Aunts Mary and Rachel – or was it Rachel and Mary? – were spinster ladies who lived in what had been the family home, with limited financial resources. Their father, William, had left them money, but not enough to live on and to maintain the grand, double-fronted home. As a house, it was not more than fifty years old, but it was showing considerable signs of wear and tear from the unopposed buffeting of the raging winds, which sweep the fenlands in the winter months each year.

Aunt Priscilla had said to Ada on the way to their house, "I haven't seen either of these aunts for twenty years. I don't imagine we have much in common, but they are family. After all, you and I both share the same second name as your Great Aunt Mary. And she was called after her grandmother, Mary Clay. And my daughter Mabel was christened Mary Victoria. Mabel is just a nickname!"

Ada loved all these family ties. "I really belong."

"Of course you do, my dear!"

"I love my name. Ada! Ada after my Aunt Ada, Mary after you, and a cousin Mary, and my great aunt Mary, and my great, great grandmother Mary!" She was as happy as Larry.

Mary Porter and her younger sister, Rachel, were in their sixties, but they gave the impression that they were much older. Gentle souls! How they had admired and adored Matilda! In their own way they had helped to secure this favourite niece a position with Richard, which had led to marriage. Destined to remain spinsters themselves, they had patted themselves on the back at their success as match-makers.

They were not so forthcoming in affection for this older niece, Priscilla, for hadn't she and her older brother, George, left home, leaving Matilda to look after the ailing family? Hadn't she only come home to get married, when Ada was hardly cold in the grave in that summer of seventy-four! But for dear Matilda's sake and for their great-niece Ada, they would be courteous and hospitable.

"Welcome! Welcome! My dear niece, how wonderful to see you!" cried Mary, a little too loudly for sincerity. "Heavens! It must be twenty years since you set foot in the place!"

Ada stood by, waiting her turn, thinking that twenty years was a very long time.

"Welcome, Ada! My, my! How like your dear mother you

look! Why, I could swear that it was she standing before me! Mary, couldn't this be Matilda?"

Ada generally enjoyed being likened to her mother, but she did not like being referred to as "this". Mr Minns had always told her, "Never ever refer to anyone present in the third person. It shows a want of real feeling!"

Rachel enveloped Ada in her mauve and muslin-clad arms before anyone else could even begin to think of the insensitivity of such remarks. Of course, both these ladies meant well, but they saw so little of society nowadays that they hardly knew the difference between polite and politic conversation.

Lunch was a strained affair, the goodbyes a relief.

Mr Stokes all but overturned the landau at the crossroads, as he turned abruptly to the right in the direction of Wilburton. "Beg pardon, ma'am," he called back to Aunt Priscilla. "The road is full of pot-holes. Something will have to be done before someone gets killed."

"No harm done, Mr Stokes." Aunt Priscilla was made of sterner stuff than Mr Stokes might imagine.

Even when she entered the graveyard in Wilburton to stand before her mother's grave and her sister Ada's grave, there was no betrayal of emotion on her face. She was not a beautiful woman, did not have her sister Matilda's soft and pretty looks: but there was something very attractive in her finely-chiselled, classical features and her high cheekbones; something imposing and majestic in her high, marmoreal forehead.

"This is where my mother, your grandmother, lies," Priscilla said in a sombre tone befitting the occasion. Then she read aloud the inscription written on the gravestone. "'When the snowdrops fade, the spring flowers will bloom again.' What a lovely epitaph, don't you think?"

Ada did not know what to say.

Priscilla now said, "And this is where Ada lies. Poor Ada! Only seventeen when she died!"

But Ada was not listening. She was thinking of Mama and Papa and snowdrops. Then her eyes focused on a haze of colour beneath the yew tree at the far end of the graveyard. It was a magic carpet of colour: hundreds of crocuses in bloom, yellow, purple, mauve and white.

"Look, Aunt Priscilla, crocuses! Hundreds and thousands of crocuses!"

Priscilla did not comprehend and stood silent, a bemused expression on her face, as Ada pointed at the bonny flowers whose delicate heads were bobbing in the gentle breeze.

"Spring flowers!" Ada explained. "Now we can be happy!"

Ada fairly skipped across the grass, and through the gate towards Mr Stokes. Priscilla's visit to her mother and sister's final resting place was no longer dismal. Ada had strangely cheered her and she walked to the waiting landau with a lighter step. She wondered what unexpected reactions the next graveyard visitation would yield.

At Holy Trinity all was different. The old overhanging oak trees were just beginning to produce new, wrinkled shoots of dull umber and yellow ochre leaves, the ancient yews stood still and darkly awesome, and the leaning gravestones gave the graveyard a surreal, or unreal, ambience. Ada did not like this place at all. Standing in the dark shadows before the joint gravestones of her great-grandparents, William and Catherine, the brightness of the happy crocuses diminished and, when the great bell sounded in the newly replaced church spire, she was ready to run as fast as her legs would carry her.

"Aunt, please let's go!" she begged. "I don't like this place at all."

"This is where your grandparents lie," Aunt Priscilla was saying. "Child, stop tugging my hand! Look, there are their names: Henry and Alice."

But Ada could not look at any more graves. Had she looked around the graveyard she would have felt that she truly belonged to a great and wide family, for there were Porter graves wherever you looked: Henry and Alice, her great grandparents; Henry and Elizabeth, her great-great-grandparents; John and Martha, born two hundred years before; and finally the grave of her earliest forbear here in Haddenham, the master brewer, John Porter, who had built Vine House in the late sixteen-hundreds.

"All right, Ada, we'll go now. I've seen what I wanted to see." Priscilla had a warm feeling inside. It had been a long time since she'd felt so close to family. "And I hope you have too!"

Although Vine House was easily within walking distance, just a short way down Station Road, Mr Stokes drove Aunt Priscilla and Ada there, just in time for afternoon tea.

The house was just as Ada remembered it. The spacious vestibule, the front room bedecked with family portraits, and there was her dear Papa smiling down at her, with his white hair and his fob-watch. It was nice to see him again.

Uncle Henry John was standing imperiously with his back to the fire and Aunt Mary Ann was fussing round her saying, "How you've grown, my dear! Well, I declare! You must be taller than Olive now. Come here, Olive, and stand back to back, till I see for myself."

Aunt Priscilla was talking to Hilda, who was on Easter vacation from Miss Michael's Seminary in Cambridge. "I believe you and Ada used to correspond. You'll have to start that up again, you know. I always think that letters are so important in keeping family ties together."

As Ada stood like a ram-rod, shoulder-blades touching Olive's, she wanted to say, "I'm sorry, Hilda, but Aunt Caroline wouldn't let me spend money on stamps any more. I'm so sorry!" But she could not say anything without incriminating Aunt Caroline and, being a steadfast, loyal child, she was not going to make anyone think ill of her Aunt Caroline. She liked her too much to incur anyone's censure, no matter how deserved it might be.

Afternoon tea was a rushed affair, for time was running out and trains wait for no man, although the converse may be true.

No sooner had they sat down to sipping tea from Spode china teacups and eating hot-buttered scones and delicious Simnel cake, baked specially as an Easter treat, than Ada and Aunt Priscilla were saying their goodbyes and were on their way. Hilda gave Ada a special hug as if to say, "I understand" and Ada left Vine House feeling good inside. Friendships were not so easily broken, it seemed.

"Goodbye, miss," Mr Stokes was saying now, as he handed her down from the landau. "I hope to see you again soon!"

As the train pulled out of Haddenham station that evening towards Ely, when the skies in the west were turning the yellow gorse bushes to orange, Ada and her aunt sat in their first-class carriage, both thinking of the day that had passed, both thinking about the goodbyes which would have to be said at the end of this short journey.

Priscilla would spend the last night of her holiday in Ely in The Bell Hotel. She would have an early dinner with George Minns that evening, as arranged, and would take the first train the following morning, on her long northwards journey home.

Ada would face her uncertain future.

CHAPTER 5
PRISCILLA

Part 1

Priscilla was "not without a penny or two", as the good northern folks in the well-to-do Preston suburb of Ashton would say, but she was wary of spending money unnecessarily, and a second journey to Cambridgeshire within the one year stretched her budget. However, what had to be had to be: it was imperative now that she went to Ely to try and sort out this sorry business with Ada.

George Minns had written to her. When she saw his handwriting on the envelope, she pursed her lips with apprehension, for her meeting with him in Ely was not one she would like to repeat. He had been simply too forward during their Easter dinner engagement at The Bell Inn. He was a pleasant enough man, she supposed, for Ada had spoken most enthusiastically about him and his quaint sayings. Judging by the smell of mothballs, he had obviously taken great care to bring his best suit of clothes out of the closet for the occasion, so he was doing his best to impress her. But he had spoken to her in rather familiar terms, almost as if he had some matrimonial designs on her.

"It must be excessively difficult for you to manage on your own, now that your husband has left," he had said, even before the landlady, the veritable Harriet Charlotte Davis, had presented them with the dinner menu.

"I manage well, thank you, with money from my lodgers," was all Priscilla would say, not wishing to tell Mr Minns anything of the five lodgers currently living in Oundle Villas, two adjoining semi-detached houses, one of the villas owned by her mother-in-law and the other her own.

"Ah yes," said he, "but they hardly pay us enough, do they?"

Priscilla did not like his use of "us": it was as if she were being paired off with this fellow landlord, so she just smiled and cast her eye over the menu.

"I'm considering increasing the rent for my lodgers. Decent folks, the Allens, but the original agreement was rent for three lodgers, and now there are four."

Before Priscilla's inward eye was the indelible imprint of the near poverty evidenced in the Allens' lodgings. This did not bode well for her niece's future. But still she said nothing.

"Is rent from your lodgers your only source of income?" George Minns inquired, sensing that his companion was deliberately unforthcoming. Although she seemed to him to be a surprisingly genteel personality, he still adhered to the opinion that a divorced lady should be viewed with some suspicion. She had broken her solemn marriage vows, perhaps had even driven away her husband, and her worldly independence made him feel vulnerable. He put her reticence down to the fact that she was playing at being coy. Maybe she considered him a suitable match. She had even flattered him by inviting him to dinner.

"A little music tuition too." Priscilla had not been going to elucidate, for it was becoming evident from the way her companion leaned forward that he was itching to know more about her. The fact that she had spent the past ten years earning money as a pianoforte and violin instructress was not really any of his concern.

"My, my! We are alike as two pins!" Mr Minns had enthused. "Which instrument do you specialise in?"

"Pianoforte and violin," she replied curtly but politely, keeping the information to a minimum.

"My, my!" he repeated. Leaning even further forward, he whispered, "It's as if destiny has played a hand: a little duet!" Here he began to chuckle at his musical metaphors. "For here we are together: we play the same tune!"

Priscilla restrained herself from raising her eyes heavenwards, but enjoyed delivering her non-sequitur: "I think I shall try the asparagus soup."

Now, on this bright August morning of 1895, she sat in her front parlour in Oundle Villa with Mr Minns's letter in her hand. Upon opening it, she was immediately struck by the presumptuous informality of the greeting "My dear Priscilla", and was about to throw the letter away when she glimpsed the words "bad tidings". Her heart lurched and she quickly read on.

"Far from being a scandalmonger and a harbinger of bad tidings," Mr Minns had written, with a preponderance of spidery curlicues on his lettering, *"I felt it was only right that you should be made aware of information regarding your niece, Ada."*

At this point, Priscilla nervously bit her lower lip, for she had hardly had a day's respite from worrying about the child since her visit to Ely at Easter. She had even gone so far as to write to the Probate Office in York to obtain a copy of Richard's last will and testament, because she could not fully accept that the Allens had been named by her brother-in-law as suitable guardians for Ada, a gentleman's daughter.

Years ago, although it was only a pipe-dream, Priscilla and Matilda had entertained the notion that, if anything happened to either of them, the other would look after their orphaned nieces and nephews. They knew that it was a silly idea in reality, for women, even natural mothers, had no rights over their children, but there was always the possibility that one day attitudes would change.

This medieval, legal anomaly never failed to incense Priscilla. In her estimation and in her experience, it was the women who were the more responsible of the two sexes; and their own monarch was a woman, now in her diamond jubilee year as the revered figurehead of the greatest nation in the world!

She often thought about how her own father, Marshall, had renegued on the family, how he had divorced her mother and left her to bring up George, herself, Matilda and Ada, thus abandoning all claim to his children. She remembered with pride how her mother had fought the system of prejudice by giving music lessons in Haddenham, and how finally she had been appointed a school mistress – almost unthinkable for a divorcee in those days.

She considered the plight of Matilda, who had spent much of her life nursing their sister, Ada, and then their mother, missing out on opportunities to be educated or to marry. With hardly a penny to her name, Matilda had systematically forged a spinster life for herself, first as a bank clerk and later as a housekeeper. Only in her late thirties had she finally gained a secure future as the wife of her elderly second cousin, Richard, incurring much disapproval from his sons in the process.

Priscilla's mother-in-law, old Mrs Sellers, another Matilda, who lived in the adjoining house, was an indomitable lady, widowed many years before. She had never succumbed to scrounging from male relatives.

"I am no-one's parasite!" she had announced, steadfastly rejecting the charity of her brother-in-law. "I own Oundle Villa and I shall take in lodgers." As she grew in independence, so she became more austere and forthright. In the early days, when Priscilla had first come to Ashton, she had found her mother-in-law to be very repressive, but over the years she came to regard her highly for her courage and will-power. Priscilla had learned much from this tough old lady.

Now she thought also of her own situation: how she had been left to manage her family in the absence of her husband, John. She had dealt single-handedly with the deaths of her two daughters, had managed her own financial affairs, had become a music teacher, like her mother before her, and had taken in lodgers, like her mother-in-law beside her. How the law could deem women unable to take responsibility for their children and their lives was incomprehensible to her. Lately, her own daughter Mabel was following family tradition and becoming a woman with an independent streak, with her sights set high. Educated and ambitious, Mabel was ready to challenge the world.

As a pragmatist, Priscilla could understand that, in the antiquated, stultifying social and legal climate in which they lived, Richard would not have wished his daughter to be looked after by a woman, a divorcee with only a modest income. But the Allens were a very poor substitute. Richard, she well remembered from the day he had married her sister Matilda in Preston, was indeed a gentleman, and a most kind man too. It was odd and ill-conceived that he would have entrusted his only daughter to the care of the Allens, who were so obviously socially and financially inferior to the Porter family. The will, however, proved the point, and no-one but the Allens or the Sayers, who had refused to act, it appeared, had any say in the matter.

Ada's half-brothers, Alfred and Frank, the co-executors of their father's will and controllers of her money, could not be happy with the situation. She concluded that they must be unaware of what was happening. But if so, how could that be? Surely they would want to keep in touch with their little sister. It was all very perplexing and disturbing.

Apart from all that, Priscilla was suffering from a gnawing sense of guilt that she had let her family down. Her mother had scrimped and saved to send her to school in Cambridge, where she had received a first-rate education at Miss Michael's Seminary. With hardly a word of thanks, she had briefly visited her native village of Haddenham simply to get married to her dashing, northern hero and had not returned, even when her own mother was dying. She had not gone to her mother's funeral, nor her sister Ada's. She had happily accepted Matilda's help as housekeeper in her own time of need, when the children were small, but in Matilda's time of need, she had done nothing. She had not even gone to her funeral. Worst of all, she had not even supported little Ada when Richard had died.

Oh yes, there were always excuses: she had a young family to look after, she had suffered when her husband upped and left her to rear the family on her own, she'd had her share of grief with the death of her two pretty daughters, ten-year old Jessie and six-year-old Ida. But now she felt that none of that exonerated her from her responsibility to little Ada. How could she have thought that sending an annual Christmas present was enough?

As she continued reading the following words of Mr Minns's missive – *"I received a letter from her today. I presume you've heard the gossip that the Allens have flitted to Boston..."* – she put her hand up to her heart. This news was all so sudden. Why were the Allens in Boston? Where was Ada? The Allens could not have taken her to Boston, surely? The Law would not have allowed that! Priscilla's mind was racing. And if Ada was not with the Allens, it would be the Parish's responsibility to care for her in the absence of her guardians.

"...and that Ada is living, for the time being, with her brother Alfred in Chertsey."

Priscilla thought she should have been relieved that Ada was now living with her half-brother and his family, enjoying a more appropriate standard of living, but Mr Minns's expression "bad tidings" told of another interpretation of the emerging facts.

"She writes, and here I quote her very words: 'I miss our tettitets, I miss my sister Annie, and I miss school, especially Miss Cartwright. My brother wants me to call him 'Papa' like Basil, Frances, Elsie and Ethel call him. But I don't want to. He's not my Papa. He's my brother. I want to call him Alfred. Ethel and Elsie are quite nice. It's very strange. Elsie is older than me, but I'm her aunt! They laugh when they call me Aunt Ada'.

Priscilla hoped that the laughter was mutual enjoyment. There was no way of knowing, but the description of Ethel and Elsie as "quite nice" suggested that there was no nastiness. She continued reading.

"Now the next part of her letter is most important and relates directly to you. She writes, 'I really wish I could live with my Aunt Priscilla. She is a very kind lady, and bought me a lovely red dress and took me visiting with her. She could look after me. But I don't know her address. She could be my mother'."

Priscilla sighed a long, deep, regretful breath. If only things could be different! She read the final part of the letter: *"Being the 'kind lady' you are, I trust that you will be able to do something to help Ada, for she is a very special little girl. When you come to Ely, I look forward to continuing our acquaintance. We must meet again for dinner. Yours ever, George Minns."*

Priscilla sat back in her comfortable armchair with its chintz loose covers and shut her eyes, her brow furrowed with troubled thoughts. "Well," she thought, tackling the easiest issue first, "one thing is absolutely certain: when I go to Ely, I will not be having dinner with George Minns."

Then she moved to her rosewood bureau, the one her husband John had bought for her thirtieth birthday, way back in 1876, when times had been good and money was plentiful. That was before his skip manufacturing business had gone bust and he had packed his bags and left for de Soto, Florida, selling off his diamond cuff-links to purchase his passage on the steam packet from Bristol.

Priscilla was far from happy, and even the brilliant August sunshine streaming in through the bay window failed to lift her spirits, as it would normally have done. She rummaged through some papers in the second drawer down and produced the copy of Richard Porter's last will and testament, which she had put away for safe-keeping. She was going to pen a letter to Mr Joseph Rogers, the solicitor who had signed his name at the bottom of the document. It seemed to her that he might be the very person who could be of assistance: he would know the intricacies of the case; he should be able to help her put into practice her plans, which were already beginning to form in her head, for Ada's future.

Of course she would have to pay for his services. She never expected any favours, was beholden to no-one and enjoyed her independence. She would advertise her availability as a music tutor and take on extra pupils. She would take in another lodger. Whatever it took, she would go to Ely.

It was more than a little fortuitous, therefore, that the following afternoon, Mrs Margaret Margerison, who had lived in the three-storey town-house opposite for the past ten years, visited her.

"Priscilla," Margaret suddenly said with her china teacup halfway to her mouth, "may I ask a big favour of you?"

Priscilla nodded expectantly. Margaret, seven years her junior, was normally of such an easy-going disposition that any kind of determined initiative came as a surprise.

"It's about Edith. Now I know she's only five, and probably far too young, you'll say…"

"Too young for what, before you put words in my mouth?" asked Priscilla.

"Piano lessons." Margaret preferred the shortened form of pianoforte, as it sounded more modern and avant-garde. Barely passable as a musician herself, she rather enjoyed indulging in her dream that her two daughters, five-year old Edith and little Bessie, would be proficient enough to play in polite society drawing-rooms one day. She never even considered that her two sons, Gilbert and Harry, aged nine and seven respectively, who both had a good ear for music, might also have benefited from early piano tuition.

"Never too young, you know," Priscilla advised her friend, in all seriousness. "Think about Mozart. He composed his first work when he was only three."

"Yes, I know all that," said Margaret, waving her empty cup impatiently and placing it with an unaccustomed, hurried clatter on the saucer, before adding, "but can you take her?"

"For lessons, you mean?"

"Yes." Margaret was grimacing, as if expecting her friend to answer in the negative. "Of course, no favours, you understand. All above board. Paid for in advance. Would ten lessons paid for in advance be acceptable? Now what do you charge?"

Unlike Priscilla, Margaret enjoyed a honeyed life in which money was no object. Her husband George was one of the directors of the Margerison soap works in Preston, a family firm that enjoyed prosperity to match its popularity.

Priscilla was not given to shows of emotion, but she would have jumped up and hugged Margaret there and then, had there not been an afternoon table with her silver tea service, cake-stand and china tea set on her favourite Belgian lace table-cloth between them. As it was, all she said to show her gratitude was, "You're an answer to a prayer, my dear Margaret!"

"Does that mean you'll take her?"

"Of course I will. When can she start?"

In the post the next day came more good news: a letter from Mr Joseph Rogers, agreeing to meet with her at two o'clock the following Tuesday afternoon, at his chambers in Ely.

Monday, the first day of September, was one of those halcyon days, which brought forth the usual round of meteorological prognostications from the old local Prestonians enjoying a mid-morning rest on benches on the bandstand in Avenham Park. As they predicted an Indian summer, a cold winter, a wet autumn and early snow, they looked across the park to the North Union railway bridge, with its wrought iron railings, spanning the River Ribble. A gleaming passenger train slowly rumbled across the bridge.

"That'll be the eleven o'clock, bound for London," commented old Michael Entwhistle as he puffed on his briar pipe.

"That it will," agreed Thomas Hinton, adjusting the minute hand on his fob-watch. "You can set the time by it, it's that regular!"

Priscilla was aboard the train, which now powerfully forged its way southwards, leaving a cotton wool stream of smoke behind. With money in her reticule and determination in her heart, she was on her way to change the world, or at least to try to put some of it right.

Part 2

As soon as she met Mr Rogers, Priscilla liked the man. Although quite small in stature, he had a good, solid hand-shake and clear, intelligent eyes. He was impeccably dressed in pin-stripe trousers and black morning coat, "well turned out" her mother would have said, and she knew immediately that she could trust him.

When all the polite formalities – the weather, her journey, whether or not she required some refreshments, the nature of her business with him – were complete, Priscilla and Joseph Rogers found that they could discuss the matter of Ada comfortably.

It was fortunate for Priscilla that Mr Rogers was a ladies' man, with an eye for an attractive face and a lively mind. On seeing her, with her handsome features, trim figure, smart mauve costume with puffed sleeves, and a lovely cameo brooch at the neck of her elegant lace blouse, he had immediately put aside all memories of the acrimony which had surrounded the Porter casebook two years earlier. It was also fortunate that there was an underlying resemblance between Priscilla and her sister Matilda, for Joseph Rogers had been captivated by the alluring looks of the late Mrs Porter, and was saddened at the turn of events for her little daughter, Ada.

"I am like putty in your hands, Mrs Sellers. I shall endeavour to assist you in whatever way I can. Now, tell me exactly what you want of me." He placed both hands on his large, impressive desk.

"Mainly advice, and some information regarding the guardianship of my niece, Ada, according to the interpretation of my brother-in-law's will."

"I'm sorry, I'm not really at liberty to divulge information relating to individual wills. Although they're in the public domain

132

and available from probate offices, I cannot personally assist you here."

Priscilla produced the copy of Richard's will from her vanity case. "You misunderstand. I have my own copy here. It's more a question of why my brother-in-law named Mr Sayers and Mr Allen as Ada's guardians. I'm very surprised that Richard should ignore the possibility of appointing one of his own family members as Ada's guardian. Are you at liberty to explain the circumstances?"

Here Mr Rogers could not keep at bay the memory of breaking a confidence when faced with almost the same question from Alfred and Frank Porter, and being called "an ass" here in this very office. But whereas the brothers' tone had been rude and accusatory, this lady's was polite and respectful of his professionalism. He would do his utmost to explain, though it would inevitably cause him some embarrassment, for it was a hotch-potch of a will, which he now judged should have been more carefully considered at the time it was drawn up. No use crying over spilt milk, he thought, but it would ease his conscience to try to put matters right, if things were now aglay.

"Richard Porter refused to nominate any of his brothers as guardians. It was as simple as that. They were rather advanced in years, you understand, with the exception of his youngest brother, Henry John. That had some bearing on the decision, as I remember: he believed them to be too old to take on a young girl as their ward. It's a long-term responsibility."

"I have two children, a daughter of seventeen and a son of fifteen, so I do know about the responsibility you speak of."

"I could not persuade your brother-in-law to even entertain the idea of his brother Henry John being guardian, though he should have been the most likely choice. There seems to have been some family feud. I never got to the bottom of it."

Priscilla had only a hazy idea of the disagreement between Richard and Henry John. She thought it was something to do with Vine House, but she was not sure.

"What about Ada's half brothers? It would have been a

simple matter of one of them taking her in. And they have children the same age."

"Same problem again. Old Mr Porter was adamant that neither of the sons would ever be guardians to Ada."

"At the time, was my name put forward at all?" Priscilla asked.

"It was mentioned, as it happens, but my client, Mr Porter…" Joseph Rogers was hesitating and beginning to look hot under the collar "…found your status to be a difficulty."

"My status?" Priscilla repeated. "Do you mean my divorced status, my single status, or the fact that I'm a woman?"

"It sounds blunt, but yes, your divorced status. Now, of course, I have nothing against divorced ladies, in fact I find them to be most delightful and capable…"

Priscilla accepted this show of charm, aware that it was intended to smooth over the problems which unattached women had to face. She thought back ten years to the time when she had had to ride the storm over her broken marriage. When John had gone to de Soto, he had wished to wash his hands of his wife and family, take on a new and exciting challenge in a young country. He did not want any millstones round his neck and relinquished his responsibilities. Priscilla and he had agreed that she was to tell everyone he was going to make his fortune and then send for her, but the reality was that she would remain in England with Mabel and Herbert. Oundle Villa would be hers and John would regularly send her money, while he would live a new and separate life in America.

His filing for divorce in 1888 had come as a shock. The annulment of their union was a sad affair, for Priscilla had loved her fun-loving and impetuous husband. He wrote to her regularly, keeping her informed about his different jobs, then his subsequent marriage to Mary Mizel and the birth of their daughters Zeulah and Carrie, but he never once fully appreciated the pain such letters caused her. There was never any likelihood that Mabel and Herbert would give their consent, according to the Poor Law Amendment Act, to be taken from their natural mother to emigrate and live with their father. And John, of all people, did not desire it. He was very happy with things as they were. Sending Priscilla a monthly money order was simple, and she presumed it had the added advantage of salving his conscience.

Priscilla's mind was brought back to the present. Joseph Rogers was continuing to ease her over any sense of personal affront or grievance: "…but old Mr Porter was of a different generation, you appreciate, and he could not accept a divorced lady, or any woman for that matter, as a fit guardian for his daughter."

"So he preferred two strangers?" Priscilla's voice had a cynical, sarcastic edge to it.

"Not strangers," Joseph Rogers quickly rejoined. "Mr Sayers was a close friend," he said, though recalling that the very same gentleman had failed to verify that friendship. He looked away.

"Mr Allen can't have been a friend," Priscilla said with the assurance of one who has knowledge.

"Have you met Mr Allen?" he inquired, beginning to feel that this lady might be made of sterner stuff than most ladies of his acquaintance.

"No, but I've been to his house and met his wife, Caroline, and his daughter, Annie. A man may be judged, I think, by the home he keeps. Have you been there, Mr Rogers?"

The question was asked innocently enough, but Joseph Rogers breathed an inaudible sigh of relief that he had not visited the Allens, for now, from her condemnatory tone, he knew he would have been in deep water, probably accused of negligence and failing in his duty. He said, "No. I've not had the pleasure."

"Pleasure, my foot!"

Joseph Rogers blinked. Priscilla looked at him keenly, her eyes wide, and a little too steely now for his liking.

"It's a pig-sty!" she exclaimed. "No comforts: cold, bare and utilitarian. Hardly a fitting place for my niece; hardly a fit place for any child to grow up in!"

"Well, I'm sure I can do something to help." Joseph Rogers

was going to do all he could to make Ada's stay with the Allens more comfortable. He felt responsible and negligent too.

Joseph Rogers was reacting nicely, Priscilla thought.

"I'll go round in the morning to discuss the matter with him," he continued.

"It appears you're as much in the dark as I was, Mr Rogers." Then she triumphantly delivered her bombshell: "The Allens are reputed to have gone!"

"Gone? Gone where?"

"Boston." Priscilla said the name, with precise pronunciation of the plosive sounds.

"Boston, Massachusetts?" Joseph Rogers knew his geography.

"Boston, Massachusetts," Priscilla repeated, waiting for the next predictable question.

"And Ada?" was all he could muster.

"No, she has not gone. That would not have been possible, according to the Poor Law Amendment Act, would it?"

He could see that she appeared to know something of the Law concerning minors and emigration. He shook his head. "It would have been difficult."

"Difficult or impossible?" Then she added, as if quoting from a well-remembered document: "No emigration of an orphaned minor can take place without the consent of that child before the justices, unless by express order from the Secretary of State. Is that not so?"

"You are well-versed in legal matters, Mrs Sellers." Joseph Rogers could not mask the open admiration in his voice.

"On emigration matters, yes, I believe I am. Thank you."

"But what of Ada's whereabouts?"

"She is living in Chertsey with Alfred, her half-brother. Presumably he is now her guardian?" Priscilla knew the answer to this arch question, and she also knew what the solicitor's reaction would be. "Unofficially, of course," she added.

"No, no, no, no, it cannot be, officially or unofficially. Richard Porter was absolutely adamant. I would be failing in my duty if I did not follow his wishes, and the law, to the letter. Leave this with me, Mrs Sellers. It will need immediate investigation."

"I also understand that my niece is unhappy living with Alfred and his family." Priscilla moved onto another pre-planned tack now, striking while the iron was hot. "I have a letter from her to that effect."

With a dramatic flourish, she fished Mr Minns's letter from her vanity case, but if her little deception were to be challenged and Joseph Rogers insisted on reading the actual letter for himself, she knew, if needs be, that she would have to run the gauntlet and go to Mr Minns's house on Forehill to procure it. Fortunately, he appeared to be satisfied.

She waited a few moments before saying, "From the frying pan into the fire, Mr Rogers." She knew it would have the desired effect, and it did.

"Children cannot simply be bandied about like shuttlecocks! That's the whole point about the new law."

"What new law?" Priscilla asked, quick-witted enough to realise that the answer might be to her advantage and help to further her plan.

"The Custody of Children Act," Joseph Rogers answered, adding, "passed four years ago."

"Ah yes, the Barnardo Relief Bill," Priscilla smiled, as she recalled the nick-name given to the new Act. She had read in the Lancashire Evening Post all about how Doctor John Barnardo, a key force in the campaign for children's rights, had fought for new legislation to protect the interests of orphaned children. A Standing Committee of the House of Lords had looked at the workings of the Poor Laws, and in particular at the plight of children at-risk, and the result was The Custody of Children Act, passed in 1891.

Joseph Rogers called over to Mr Allpress, his clerk, who was sitting in his customary corner at his work-desk. "Mr Allpress, be so good as to bring over the copy of The Custody of Children Act."

Joseph Rogers turned to the second page of the document and traced his finger down to the quotation he had in mind.

"Yes, here we are. I quote the exact words: 'It gives the courts power to consult the wishes of the child in considering what order ought to be made'."

"I see." Priscilla looked thoughtful, as she remembered Ada's wishes.

"The Act is designed to protect the interests of minors, for example, those left as orphans, abandoned or whose parents are in prison."

"Ada is surely included in one of the categories now." Priscilla held her breath, hopefully.

"I believe she now may be, if Mr Allen has renounced his guardianship. It is complex and detailed." Joseph Rogers sounded somewhat unsure of himself, for child protection was not normally within his remit. "As Richard stated categorically that he did not want his sons to have any jurisdiction over his infant daughter, and now neither of the two appointed guardians wish to look after Ada, it appears that she should be made a ward of court, looked after by the parish."

Priscilla was suddenly apprehensive. Her plan was slipping from her grasp. As a ward of court, Ada would be caught in a legal trap, and there might be no way out.

After a pause, during which Mr Joseph Rogers was thinking of the next move, Priscilla made up her mind. She had come to Ely with a plan, and nothing would shake her resolve, whatever the odds. She would have to act quickly before Ada was taken over by the court and the parish.

"So, if Mr Allen has emigrated and Ada is now legally an orphan, and the court is in a position to intervene in the interests of the child, would you care to act for me?"

"Act, Mrs Sellers, in what way?"

"I wish to apply for legal custody of my niece, Mr Rogers. Will you agree to be my legal representative?"

"In the Chancery Court?" he asked, with a surprised expression.

"Wherever these cases are dealt with."

"Impossible, I'm afraid," was his disappointing reply. "The

Official Solicitor is the only person who can deal with these cases. To protect the children, you understand, from unscrupulous guardians."

"I can hardly be called unscrupulous!" Priscilla was indignant.

"No indeed, madam, but some people will stop at nothing to get custody of children, simply to set them to hard labour. That is why only the Official Solicitor is permitted to bring the custody cases to court. He acts as a barrier between guardians or parents and vulnerable children."

"I am not giving up on my niece, I can assure you." Priscilla's measured voice was arresting in its determination and intensity. "How does one go about bringing this case to the Chancery Court?"

"A lawyer, like myself, presents the case to the Official Solicitor, who in turn brings it before the judge of the High Court of Chancery in London. Documentation is set up, the suitability of the applicant is checked and may even be backed by testimonial references from respected members of the community, then the case is brought before the judge, and the minor is asked whom he or she would like as guardian, or if the person being offered as guardian is acceptable."

"That seems straightforward," Priscilla smiled encouragingly at Joseph Rogers.

"I must advise you, Mrs Sellers, that your divorced status will be a stumbling-block. I see problems of great magnitude ahead."

"Mr Rogers," Priscilla said simply and peremptorily, "we shall succeed."

Joseph Rogers looked admiringly at the lady before him. Here was a highly intelligent woman, an independent and undaunted spirit. Although it was a clichéd expression, he really had been like putty in her hands. She had manipulated and moulded him till he wanted nothing better than to act on her behalf.

He would apply post-haste to the Official Solicitor of the High Court of Chancery. He wanted to arrange a secure future for Ada, and from what he had seen of this lady today, he was convinced that Mrs Priscilla Sellers could furnish the child with that security. Not everyone was given a second chance: few were given the opportunity to put things right. However, even as he felt this surge of gratitude towards Mrs Sellers, there was a gnawing sense that he was embarking on a hopeless mission.

After discussing fees, procedures and time-scales, Priscilla shook Joseph Rogers warmly by the hand.

"I'll keep you posted," he said, as they parted. "I mean to start straight away. I'll try my best."

As she said goodbye, she thought: so far so good.

Tomorrow she would go to see Ada in Chertsey, in the county of Surrey. If the child was to be asked in court with whom she would like to live, no wrong answers could be given. It therefore seemed expedient that Priscilla should spend time with her niece, so that they could build up a friendly rapport and an affectionate relationship.

There would be no second chances.

Part 3

Priscilla broke her homeward journey in Crewe, that half-way mark for so many rail travellers. The Station Hotel did its best to off-set the murky, industrial atmosphere of the urban surroundings, by offering its one-night residents a reasonable tariff for a comfortable room for the night and a hearty evening meal of midlands fare. She had eaten as well as anyone can when fatigued from four hours of the rhythmic cacophony of Pullman carriage wheels on iron tracks, and was now in her bedroom. It was cosy enough with the curtains closed, a coal fire brightly burning in the grate, but Priscilla's own spark was a mere flicker. She sat back in the modest fireside wicker chair, thinking back over how her intended two-day sojourn had turned into five.

On arrival at the Porters' house in Chertsey, Alfred had been more than a little taken aback when the housekeeper stepped into his study and announced the arrival of a Mrs Sellers.

"Why, cousin Priscilla," he said, "what a pleasant surprise!"

She had been ushered through to the friendly drawing room, decorated with homely, almost rustic artefacts. Alfred had married Ellen Milnethorpe, a woman of farming stock from near Doncaster, so Priscilla assumed that the ornaments were her choice. She liked the simple refinement of the room.

"I apologise for my unannounced visit..." she began.

"You're most welcome. Please, sit down." Alfred sounded gracious, but he was not a man to waste words and got straight to the point. "To what do we owe the pleasure? I assume it's on account of your niece?" The bald inquiry sounded rushed to the point of being unmannerly, so he added, "Ellen will be back shortly. She's gone into town with the children to spend some of my money!" He laughed magnanimously.

"Then Ada must be with her," Priscilla conjectured. "It's Ada I've come to see." Keeping mum about her real intentions, she added, "To keep in touch with her, you understand."

"That won't be possible, I'm afraid," he stated, bristling. He paused momentarily, looking her squarely in the face. Priscilla was taken off-guard by this threatening undercurrent. Undaunted, driven forward by her determination to succeed, her hackles were rising. She was preparing for a fight, if necessary. "As I already told that ass of a solicitor," Alfred snorted.

"Solicitor?"

"Yes, your Mr Rogers."

"Mr Rogers has been here?" Priscilla was incredulous. She remembered Joseph Rogers's last words to her: "I'll keep you posted. I mean to start straight away". She never for one moment thought that he would personally go in search of Ada and that she would be following in his footsteps. She was annoyed at such interference. She had meant for him, as her solicitor, to deal with the matter through normal legal procedures, not go traipsing around the country! She could see that Alfred was annoyed and if her plan was to succeed, she did not want to get on the wrong side of him: it did not augur well for the future. An outright court battle with him or his brother would be a major set-back.

"The man's a damned fool, you know!"

Priscilla did not like his language. "Go on," she said.

"Anyway, as I told him, Ada has gone to Clapton."

"Clapton?" Priscilla felt deflated. Her disappointment was discernable in her voice, and in her body language, as she leant her head back against the fine linen antimacassar.

"To live with brother Frank for a month," Alfred said. "It is all agreed between us."

Priscilla's dejection was turning to curiosity. Her raised eyebrows denoted someone waiting for some kind of explanation.

"We had to do something for the girl," Alfred reasoned.

"What about Philip Allen?" Priscilla asked, already knowing the answer. "Is he not her guardian?"

142

"Quite extraordinary! He simply turned up with Ada and, without a by-your-leave, said he washed his hands of the whole affair, that he was unable to fulfil his role as guardian, and left, literally depositing Ada on our doorstep."

"Where has he gone?"

"I have no idea, and quite frankly the less I know the better. He should never have been appointed her guardian in the first place. I told that ass of a solicitor just what I thought at the time, and I've been proved right. So Frank and I are to have Ada month about. She's been here for the month of August. Now she's with him."

Priscilla said nothing: it seemed the best policy. She hardly knew where to apportion blame in what was a most unsatisfactory situation.

Sensing his second cousin's disapproval, Alfred shrugged his shoulders in regretful accord. "Not perfect, I grant you, but it is the best solution we can devise."

Priscilla smiled politely. She did not agree with him, but was beginning to see that Alfred was at least trying to do something constructive and make the best of a bad job. "Then I shall have to go to Clapton, it seems, to catch up with my niece."

"As you wish, but it's too late in the day to travel and I insist you stay here until the morning." He put up his hand. "I won't take no for an answer."

Despite the prickly start, Priscilla liked the family. Alfred was brusque and down-to-earth, but he was a hard-working family man, a master brewer like his forefathers. He had moved on from his job as Chief Brewer at the Wakefield and Leeds Brewery early in his career, and now made good money here in his own lucrative Surrey brewery. Ellen, with just the slightest trace of a Yorkshire accent, displayed the kind of energy which is typical of women of farming backgrounds.

Their son Basil, an upright lad of fourteen who had been allowed to join his parents and Priscilla for dinner, had announced after the main course, "I'm joining the navy soon."

"Ah, to sail the seven seas!" she replied. "Such freedom and adventure!"

"Yes indeed, ma'am, but I think of it more as a serious career. I'm going to be a captain one day."

Priscilla hoped that his ambition would be realised.

Before their bedtime, Alfred and Ellen's three pretty daughters were full of stories about Ada. Ethel, in particular had struck up a good friendship with her.

"Don't you think it's hilarious that Ada is our aunt?" Elsie revelled in this strange relationship, just as Ada had done.

Priscilla had almost enjoyed the family's sedate hospitality, fine fare and a rare vintage port after dinner, but there was an undercurrent of mutual reserve and wariness. She had kept quiet about her real intentions regarding Ada and when the subject of Mr Rogers had been raised at dinner, she'd been glad that Alfred did most of the talking about the man, even though it was in terse, uncomplimentary terms.

It seemed to Priscilla that it would be inadvisable to give either Alfred or Frank advance warning which might put in jeopardy her hopes for the future of her little niece. She was a little concerned that Mr Rogers had intimated to Alfred that he was her solicitor, and hoped that he had not been indiscreet as to why, for she was paying him a handsome enough fee. With all this talk of him being an "ass" and a "fool", it was an additional worry.

The next day, after a short journey by train, on approaching Frank and Nina's house in Thistlethwaite Road, Clapton, north-east of London, Priscilla was excited at the prospect of meeting up with her niece again. She imagined the look on Ada's face, could almost feel the hugs. It would be a grand reunion.

It was just after midday when the hansom cab pulled up. Frank and his wife Nina and their strapping, teenage sons Harold and Cecil all stood in a belligerent row at the gate. The coachman had just opened the door of the shiny, black cabriolet which had brought Priscilla from the station, and she was about to step out onto the footpath when an accusatory finger was thrust in her face.

"It's all your doing!" Frank exclaimed. He recognised his father's cousin from many years earlier when they were all children. He had not liked her then, when they all lived in Haddenham, and he did not like her now.

Priscilla recoiled into the relative safety of the cab. She was not used to being intimidated in this ugly way. A distant, childhood image of a little boy rushing up behind her and pulling her hair flitted through her mind. So this was the grown-up Frank now, she thought. How people remained the same! She quickly gathered her thoughts, preparing for another fight.

The coachman asked, "Is everything all right, madam? Would you like to move on?"

"I would like an explanation," she coolly replied.

The coachman was impressed with this lady's fortitude.

Frank was breathing heavily, momentarily speechless. It was his wife Nina, a sensitive soul, who answered the question.

"They came and took her away!" she sobbed. "Just minutes ago!" She was suffering from delayed shock. The terrible scene of her husband's little half-sister being led away by a matronly court official, who looked as if she would have been more at home as a prison warder, was one she never wanted to see repeated. What made it all the more shocking was that Ada had uttered not a sound but had just looked straight ahead, like a martyr being led to the flames. Nina knew she would remember this to her dying day. She shuddered when she thought that her sister-in-law had spent less than twenty-four hours in her house before being so summarily and shamelessly removed.

"Who came?" It was clear that it would be fruitless to expect any introductions to this woman whom Priscilla presumed to be Frank's wife. Priscilla's voice was shrill and crisp. "Who came?" she repeated, demanding a response.

"A policeman wafting a court order in my face, and a damned court official! Aided and abetted by that infernal ass, Rogers, sent here, as per your instructions!" Frank shouted. He had found his voice again, as angry as his face was red.

Priscilla did not like his language. "Not by my instructions, I assure you," she objected.

"He mentioned your name," Frank argued.

"Not sent by my instructions," repeated Priscilla, so there would be no misunderstanding.

"All right then," apologised Frank, begrudgingly, "my mistake!"

Any prolonged conversation with Frank was as unlikely as it was unattractive, so Priscilla curtly asked, "Where have they taken her?"

Trying to make amends for his pugnacious behaviour, and take the heat out of the situation, he volunteered the bare essentials of information.

"Cambridge, they said. Going by rail. Two o'clock train."

"Then I shall follow. Driver, to the station if you please!" Priscilla commanded. "We may be just in time."

"But this whole sorry mess is none of your business," Frank advised, emphasising the word "your". He continued with the same patterned inflexion, "It's not even my business now, and I'm her brother, for God's sake! It's no-one's business now, it seems. Just the damned legal buffoons."

Priscilla was not inclined to submit at this juncture. "I have come all this way to see my niece and I shall not be disappointed!"

"I fear you may be." Frank looked hard at her. Then he added weightily, "I fear you may have a lot to answer for."

He put his arm solidly round his wife's shoulders, and they stood side-by-side, flanked by their broad-shouldered sons, saying no more. Three small, troubled faces peered through an upstairs window, counterpointing their father's rash bellicosity.

There was no waving goodbye, no acknowledgement at all. Priscilla was saddened and frustrated: her hopes were almost dashed. Frank's humiliation fanned his anger as he watched the hansom turn the corner and disappear from view. Nina was frightened and confused but, no matter what happened in the future, and no matter what the obstacles, she was determined to make amends. She would make it up to Ada somehow.

On reaching Platform two at Clapton Station, Priscilla found that the two o'clock train had already departed. All that could be seen in a haze of belching smoke and steam was the back of the guard's van rounding the distant corner. The next train to Cambridge was at four o'clock.

She sat patiently in the waiting room with her suitcase. To her fellow travellers, she must have looked demure and at ease with the world, but this smooth outer veneer belied the inner, sand-paper turmoil of her mind. At every turn she had encountered an obstacle. This grand plan of hers was turning into a nightmare of disappointment and suspense.

The next morning, at the Cambridge County offices in Shire Hall, she met an insurmountable bureaucratic wall which prevented her from seeing her niece. She did learn however that Ada was "comfortable" and residing temporarily as a ward of court with a lady who had once been a governess. Priscilla was not permitted access to the child, nor was she given any contact address.

"If you wish to write to your niece, you may send your mail here, and I will forward it to her court-appointed guardian," Mr Clement Nesbitt had whispered to her, feeling sorry for this woman who wore such an expression of concern on her face as he had rarely seen in all his thirty-one years as clerk in Shire Hall.

Then Priscilla returned to Ely to confront Mr Rogers, only to be told by Mr Allpress, "Mr Rogers is in London, madam, I believe, acting on your behalf."

"I sincerely hope he is," she muttered, for her trust in this man was no longer as sure as it had been a few days earlier when she had first met him in this office. She desperately hoped that he was not the " infernal ass" Frank had so disparagingly dubbed him. There was too much at stake.

"He will be contacting you in the near future, I feel sure," said Mr Allpress, trying to mollify his boss's client. "We have your address 'up north', as we say down here!"

Priscilla was in no mood to acknowledge this attempt at civil jocularity. "Good-day to you, sir!" she said curtly, and left.

That afternoon, as Priscilla stared out of the Pullman carriage window at the flat Cambridgeshire landscape on the first leg of her journey home, even the spotted crakes and red-shanks did little to lift her spirits. Normally she would have been straining to catch a glimpse of such beautiful fen-land birds, but now the snicker-snack rhythm of the wheels rushing over points and the white flashes of level-crossing barred gates had a soporifc effect, and she dozed fitfully as the flat countryside gave way to more undulating terrain. She awoke to glimpses of the midlands industrial wasteland, where factory smoke was belching unremittingly forth from soot-blackened, tall, red-brick chimneys. Finally, the train ground and squealed to a halt at Crewe station, letting out a sigh of relief.

"All change! All change!" intoned the station-master's unmistakable midland nasal tones, as he marched up and down the platform opening carriage doors and organising his team of porters, each with his own handcart, to assist passengers with their luggage.

As she now sat in her apartment in The Station Hotel, Priscilla wondered what the future would bring. These five days had been a wild goose chase. Things could only get better. She prayed that they would.

Part 4

It was quiet in the house now that Herbert had gone. The words which Priscilla's son had uttered before he left exuded all the confidence of a young man embarking on a new life. Like his mother, he valued independence of thought and spirit but, like his father, he craved the freedom to go where he pleased and do what he wanted in life. A humdrum existence was not for him.

"Life's too short, Mother," Herbert had argued. "I can't sit here, wasting my days, when there's a whole wonderful world out there waiting for me."

"Where will you go, son? You can't just set off. The world may not be as wonderful or as welcoming as you think."

"I'll go to Father first, in de Soto," he had said.

"Is that wise?" Priscilla had asked tentatively, for hadn't her husband left them in the lurch and didn't he have another family now?

"I've already written to him," Herbert had stated with a note of finality.

"I wouldn't visit him, even if he paid me," Mabel had offered, with a vehemence born of disappointment and hurt. Her father had left home when she was seven, and she remembered very well how unhappy she had been. That unhappiness had turned slowly to anger, and she now had no time for a man who would abandon his wife and his family to follow a dream.

Herbert dismissed her remark with a shrug of the shoulders, saying, "Let bygones be bygones, eh?"

Priscilla had tried another line of approach, claiming that at fifteen he was very young and inexperienced in the ways of the world.

"Mother, don't fret! I'll be right as rain. Why, boys younger than me are in the navy or the army, fighting for the country!"

So Herbert had left on October the fifteenth, on the first leg of a journey which was to take him round the world, he said. He would work his passage; he would be beholden to no-one. He was his mother's son, without a doubt!

"I'll return, Mother," he had said seriously, as he hugged Priscilla goodbye in the eeriness of the lucent green light which filtered through the glass roof of the station. "And then I'll marry a rare and beautiful maiden, and live happily ever after, here in Preston!" he remarked lightly. To Mabel he cheekily said, "I'll give Father your love." It was a feeble attempt to be jolly, to diffuse the solemnity of his leave-taking, for now that the moment to part had arrived, he felt strangely sad. Mabel stood immobile, torn between tears, anger and a playful riposte to his sarcasm. Before she knew it, he had kissed her awkwardly on the cheek, hopped on the train, and let down the carriage window with the central leather strap. The carriage door was slammed shut and, with a shrill blast of a whistle and a wave of the guard's green flag, he was off.

Through all the weeks of worry and preparation for Herbert's departure, Priscilla had kept up a regular flow of letters to Ada, via Mr Nesbitt at Shire Hall in Cambridge. However, not once did she receive a reply and, although Mr Nesbitt had made assurances that any mail would be directed to Ada, she grew more and more concerned about the welfare of her niece in the absence of any response.

This waiting game was beginning to grate. She complained bitterly one Wednesday afternoon to Margaret Margerison, after Edith's fourth piano lesson.

"Mr Rogers has deigned to reply to my letters!"

"Oh, that's good," Margaret began, but ended with a question, "isn't it?"

"He says that things are 'progressing satisfactorily' and that he will 'communicate further details in due course, when they became available'."

"That sounds promising, doesn't it?"

"No!" Priscilla was quite adamant. "Mr Rogers is vague to the point of being unhelpful. I simply don't know what's happening. It's like being in a dark tunnel with no light at the end, and time is ticking past." Like Herbert, she objected to any waste of God-given time on this earth. Life was indeed too short.

The following week, when Margaret came to collect Edith after her piano lesson, she noted that Priscilla was a little subdued.

"And you say there's been no letter at all from Ada?" she said, after Priscilla had told her the latest news. "It's certainly a most unsatisfactory state of affairs, to my way of thinking."

"But what's to do?" complained Priscilla outwardly, yet inwardly she was doggedly trying to devise an alternative plan of action if this present one failed. She would parry whatever slings and arrows outrageous fortune might thrust at her. "Another visit to Cambridgeshire would be fruitless. Brick walls, wild goose chases and so on and so on."

Margaret interrupted her, in an attempt to comfort her friend. "Now you mustn't worry, my dear, I'm sure it'll all turn out for the best." Her bland words were well meant, but of little value to Priscilla, whose frustration and irritation were not far from the surface. Margaret was always so generous and thoughtful in spirit, and provided a kind listening ear, but she was unskilled in the ways of the harsh world outside of her comfortable lifestyle. Although Priscilla liked Margaret, she knew that this friend was too easy-going and naïve to be able to offer practical solutions to problems.

However, Priscilla was soon proved wrong.

On the last Monday in October, a long-awaited communication from Mr Rogers arrived by the afternoon post. Priscilla's heart missed a beat when she recognised the neat handwriting on the envelope addressed to her, and her fingers were clammy as she broke the seal. She quickly skimmed the contents to discover if this was good news or bad news, or to be informed that things were still "progressing satisfactorily".

Joseph Rogers explained that they had now reached the next part of the legal process. He wrote, *"In answer to a demand by the Official Solicitor, please send him testimonials from three upstanding members of your community, who will vouch for your good name and reputation. Before any decisions can be made regarding your suitability as guardian to Ada, the court will have to take these into consideration."*

Over a cup of Earl Grey tea, it was Margaret who came up with the idea of asking her father-in-law, Joshua, to write a testimonial for Priscilla, and within two days she had arranged a dinner party for Priscilla and Mabel, Joshua, George and herself.

Joshua Margerison was a most remarkable man. At sixty-five, he still worked as owner and joint director of the soap-works which, by dint of unrelenting perseverance, he had founded. He had been strongly influenced by Mr Pilkinson, a pushy Mancunian, whom he had met as a young man.

"It's not doing what others can do that succeeds: it's doing what other folk cannot do that succeeds," Mr Pilkinson had asserted.

Now Joshua walked ten miles a day, down through Avenham Park, across the iron railway bridge, along the Ribble embankment to Penwortham and back. He claimed to be "as sound as a bell". That was his own recipe for continued success.

He had an eye for a smart woman, and a belief that marriage was a business arrangement and nothing more. The more intelligent and capable the woman, the more marriageable she was. He had been married twice and both his first wife Mary Croasdale and his second wife Margaret Cook were worthy, Methodist women, with good heads on their shoulders. After Mary had gone to the angels, who had stood at the end of her sick bed beckoning her to heaven, Joshua had selected a woman "who knew something of business and would not be ashamed of helping in a full and hearty way", as he had written only last week in his biography, entitled *My Life*, a book which he hoped to complete within the year.

He firmly believed that his own son George had let his heart rule his head when he chose Margaret for a wife, for she was little more than a pleasant adornment, in his estimation. From what he knew of Priscilla Sellers, whom he had met on a few occasions in the past, she was a more suitable kind of woman: hard-working, determined, with strength of character. He even went so far as to inwardly admit that he liked her, and regarded her thoughtfully across the dinner table.

"Mrs Sellers, I shall write you such a character reference as no judge worth his salt will be able to ignore," Joshua stated with assurance. He knew from his business dealings how to present a watertight case.

"Thank you, Mr Margerison. I'm much obliged to you."

"Where are you to find two others?" asked Margaret. She had already played her one and only trump card.

"Mr Braithwaite, for one," suggested George. "As your oldest and most respected lodger, and a man who has been acquainted with you for…?" Here George paused for an answer to an unasked question.

"It must be ten years, Mother," said Mabel, adding, "he came when Father left."

Priscilla looked quickly at Joshua to see if this reminder of her divorced state would produce an adverse reaction but, by his nodding smile, it seemed that he was even more resolved to sing her praises.

"Yes, a good choice," she said. "I hope he won't mind the inconvenience."

"Inconvenience! Nonsense! If he so much as hints at inconvenience, he'll have me to answer to!" interjected Joshua, who now had a proprietorial regard for Mrs Sellers.

"You could also ask Basil Wilson. As your bank-manager, he would be able to show that you manage your money carefully," George suggested after dinner in the drawing-room, as he sat down to a glass of Marsala wine. He himself found money matters too troublesome, and generally his personal accounts were a shambles.

"Now, if you manage your own financial affairs, it would certainly be to your advantage to get him to write something complimentary," advised Joshua. "What sort of finances would be involved?"

"Priscilla is a marvel!" piped Margaret, unable to hide her sheer amazement that Priscilla managed her own affairs.

Priscilla listed household accounts, annuity payments, lodgers' accounts, music tuition fees and so forth.

"Excellent!" Joshua believed that this woman had all the right qualities to make someone a very good wife, let alone a good guardian.

The following Wednesday afternoon, Edith failed to appear at the appointed time for her piano lesson. Priscilla waited for half an hour before determining to cross the road to ascertain what had happened. As she placed her finger on the china half globe of the bell-press, which George Margerison had recently had installed, she heard a loud commotion of raised voices and scurrying feet inside the house.

"Fetch Doctor Negus!" a male voice was shouting, and the cloaked figure of Stella, the housemaid, hurtled through the doorway, almost bowling Priscilla over in the rush.

"Ooh! Beg pardon ma'am. The mistress is took bad!"

Priscilla had no time to catch her breath before she found herself alone once again on the doorstep, but this time with the door open. She was in a quandary. If she turned tail and walked quietly to her own home, it might subsequently appear that she was cold-hearted and unfeeling, sloping off in the face of illness in the house; if she entered uninvited and unbidden, she would appear embarrassingly impertinent and nosy in a time of her neighbours' personal troubles.

"Oh, my dear Mrs Sellers! Come in, come in! Just the very person!" It was George Margerison, rushing through the vestibule, towel in hand, who spotted her standing on the doorstep. "It's Margaret. She's not at all well. I fear she may lose the child."

Priscilla tried hard to conceal her surprise, for Margaret had shown no signs of pregnancy. Or had she? Thinking back, Priscilla remembered a conversation only two weeks ago, which should have alerted her to her friend's condition. Perhaps she had been too preoccupied with her own concerns to have given enough thought to Margaret.

Priscilla had remarked to her friend, "My dear, you should eat more, you know. I fear you're getting exceedingly thin."

"I have little appetite these days," Margaret had replied. "I wake up feeling quite nauseous every morning and it stays with me all day."

"Have Doctor Negus call out and see you. He'll be able to prescribe one of his tonics to settle the stomach."

Now, looking back, it seemed clear that Margaret's nausea had only one cause. Priscilla remembered that the only time she herself had suffered from nausea in pregnancy was when she had had a miscarriage. They had named the dead foetus Sydney: it was John's wish that if his infant son could not travel through life, he would travel to the other side of the world in death.

"Would you like me to sit with her, Mr Margerison?" Priscilla was trying to be helpful.

"Yes, yes!" said George and then, "No, no."

Priscilla waited while George made up his mind. "Would you be good enough to go to the children instead?" he almost implored. "There's no-one with them."

The man was distraught, she could see that, and felt sorry for him. "Of course. Are they in the back parlour?"

He nodded and she made her way down the terrazzo hall to the parlour at the far end. On entering, she found the two boys engaged in entertaining a sister apiece. Gilbert and Edith were playing the board game of snakes and ladders on the floor, Gilbert sitting cross-legged and sombre, Edith lying prone with her chin propped up in her cupped hands. Harry was almost swallowed up in the huge soft leather armchair by the fire, with Bessie on his knee, and he was reading aloud from Rudyard Kipling's new volume of stories, about Mowgli and Sher Khan.

"Good-day, Mrs Sellers," Gilbert greeted Priscilla. His attempt to stand politely when she entered the room failed as his crossed feet upset the counters and dice on the snakes and ladders board.

"Now look what you've done, Gilbey!" exclaimed Edith crossly.

Priscilla could see that Gilbert flinched as Edith used this diminutive form of his name, but she also saw his look of determination to act like an adult. As the eldest, albeit only nine years of age, he was taking his responsibilities seriously on this day when his father depended on him.

"Now, Edith, don't let Mrs Sellers hear you being cross! That wouldn't do at all, would it?" he said.

Edith stood up and took Priscilla's hand. "Mama is in bed. Papa says we're to be very good, and stay here till he calls us. Is she going to die?"

Gilbert stood stock still, and Harry raised his eyes from the heavy volume of *The Jungle Books*. They all waited with bated breath for Priscilla's answer.

"Now what a silly question!" she lightly admonished. "Of course not!" She dearly hoped she would be right. "Now, what about setting up the board again, Gilbert, and I'll join you for a game of snakes and ladders. Good gracious! I haven't played this for many a year. Not since..." She faltered, for she remembered distinctly the last time her counter had slithered down the giant python near the home square at the top of the board to the bottom line near the start, like an omen. It was just before Jessie and Ida had died. "Not in your lifetime," she continued, and thus avoided detailing the exact episode – hardly appropriate in the present circumstances.

Two hours later it was all over. Doctor Negus had been and gone, his assistant, Nurse Allinson, had taken with her the brown paper parcel, which contained the dead three-month old foetus. It was for disposal, not for burial.

Margaret was dead. Cut down in her fortieth year.

Herbert was right: life was far too short.

CHAPTER 6
ADA

Part 1

Another nightmare! Only this time, Ada had been able to wake herself up before she fell over the edge of the cliff. It was always the same dream: she was escaping along a dark tunnel pursued by Tenniel's illustrations of *Alice's Adventures in Wonderland* and *Through the Looking-Glass*, grotesquely come to life.

"Off with her head! Off with her head!" the Queen of Hearts was shrieking, while Ada scrabbled with the brown earth to get free of the murky gloom which stank of moss and excrement.

Out into the sweet-smelling sunlight she was free to run. But which way?

"Which way? Please tell me?" she begged the White Rabbit, but he just sat there on a tuft of grass, singing an eerie tune, with the words "Tirra, lirra!" repeated over and over again.

"Across the snowdrop field!" goaded the Mad Hatter, doubling up with sinister laughter as he pointed to the lady in the white gown at the far side of a carpet of shimmering white flowers.

It was always the same. It was always her mother with hands folded delicately across her bosom, smiling and calling out. "Oh my child, come to me, come to me," the half-remembered voice was lilting.

And always Ada would run through the snowdrops, whose little heads bobbed up and down in encouragement as she passed. And then, before her very eyes, the lady in white would always grow thin and gaunt, with hollow eye-sockets and grinning teeth.

"Which way? Please tell me?" Ada would sob, and the spectre

would point a skeletal finger to a gilt-framed picture, at the far side of a meadow of purple and yellow crocuses.

Faster and faster her legs would carry her forwards, to see her dear Papa's face in the portrait, to touch those dear white whiskers. But just as she reached the distant horizon the picture would vanish.

"Come back! Come back!" she would implore. "Oh, please come back!"

She would be at a cliff edge, unable to stop.

Only now, Ada had learned how to wake herself up from a bad dream. There was no more falling, the wind in her hair; no more falling, desperately trying to fly; no more crying "Come back!"

She was in that half-world between sleep and wakefulness, a tall, slim, eight-year-old figure in a white cotton night-shift, rag tapers in her light-brown hair. Her hands were clammy and her heart was racing as she stood looking out of the bedroom window onto the street below.

A few thin shards of February sunlight filtered starkly through the crenellations of chimneys atop the terrace houses opposite. Lady Margaret Road, despite its grandiose name, was nothing more than a typical Cambridge cobbled street, steeply leading down from Castle Mound and Shire Hall at the top of the hill, to Madingley Road at the bottom.

"Another bad dream?" Alice Hawkins asked sleepily from the iron bedstead in the corner of the bedroom she shared with Ada.

"The same one," answered Ada dully, her mind still focused on the fears, which had seemed so real. "But I woke myself up, like you taught me to," she added with gratitude, for she had been spared the falling and the crying.

Alice Hawkins, respected spinster of the Parish of Ely, a huge diocese which extended across much of Cambridgeshire, had been engaged by the Parish to foster Ada while her future was being determined by the courts. Ada had been made a ward of court, and as such, she was in the care of the court.

Having been born in Ely, Ada was also the responsibility of the Parish of Ely, until such time as a suitable legal guardian for her could be found and officially appointed.

Miss Hawkins had lately been in the employ of The Reverend Geoffrey King, encumbant of Holy Trinity in Walsington, as governess to his children. That gentleman and man of the cloth had been so impressed with her capabilities that he had had no hesitation in recommending her for the position of foster parent to Ada.

"A capital young woman! A fine teacher!" he had assured Peter Troughton, who was a parish official engaged by the court to travel the length and breadth of the diocese to find suitable foster parents for cases such as Ada. "She is a good, upright Christian woman, a regular church-goer with high principles."

"A woman on her own is not what we are prepared to accept, I'm afraid, high principles or not."

"Now look here, you cannot let someone as dedicated as Alice Hawkins slip through your fingers. Besides," the vicar said with a note of worldly triumph in his voice, "she is not on her own. She has returned home and is now living with her father, a widower, in Cambridge."

"That sounds more promising." Peter Troughton scratched his chin thoughtfully. "And she has been governess to your family, you say?"

"It would be difficult to find a better teacher!"

"Good!" Peter was convinced. "So that would also take care of Ada's interim education."

It was therefore on the recommendation of Reverend King that Alice Hawkins became Ada's foster parent, along with her father. The whole business had been concluded swiftly to ensure the least upset to an already frightened child, who had been whisked away from relatives by a policeman with a court order for her removal. The system might not be perfect, but people like Reverend King and Peter Troughton, respected officials of the Parish of Ely, and others like Clement Nesbitt in Shire Hall, endeavoured to make up for any of its deficiencies.

Over the five months since Ada had come to live in the Hawkins' terrace house in Lady Margaret Road, Ada and Alice had developed a mutual trust and liking for one another, and were beginning to share some of their innermost hopes and fears.

"I have a recurrent nightmare too," Alice had confided one December night, in an attempt to comfort Ada who had woken in a cold sweat, screaming. "But I always wake myself up when the worst part comes."

"How can you do that?" Ada asked, still shivering from fright, wishing she too could make her nightmare stop.

"Before I go to sleep, I just say to myself, 'If I have that horrible dream, I shall wake myself up. God will help me.' And then when I do have a nightmare, I say, 'This is only a dream', and then I shout out loud to myself, 'Wake up, Alice! Wake up Alice!' and it always works. Then I thank God with all my heart for watching over me."

Ada was curious. "What happens in your bad dream?"

Alice simply said, "I'm trapped in a sinking boat and drowning. Then I wake myself up and everything is all right."

Except, in reality, everything had not been all right, and God had not been watching. Alice wanted to tell Ada that this recurrent nightmare was the reliving of a real event which had happened to her in her childhood, when she too was just eight years old, but the event was too shocking to tell a child who had suffered enough, and her own feelings were too raw.

In 1878, Alice's mother and father had taken her younger sister, Violet, and herself on a two-day outing to London. They had bought tickets, as a special treat, for a cruise up the River Thames from Tower Bridge as far as Windsor. They had been passengers on that ill-fated paddle steamer the Princess Alice. All had been going well until the paddle-steamer reached the bend of the river known as Gallion's Reach, when a collier heading downstream had smashed into the side of her, cutting her in two. It took less than five minutes for the Princess Alice to sink. No time to say prayers, no time to hold on to loved ones. Just a frantic search for the surface, with lungs ready to burst. Six hundred people perished on that day, Alice's mother and sister among the dead.

Yes, Alice knew all about the nightmares you have when you are asleep. She had learned how to deal with them, and she had taught Ada how to overcome hers. Alice had also learnt how to block out terrible memories by busily filling her day with religion, learning and altruistic activities, all of which brought her some measure of peace and tranquillity. She would ensure that Ada would be schooled in such a way that she too would be able to live at peace with herself, unfettered by unhappy memories.

To that end, each day began with a morning hymn and prayers. When the matin bell changes rang out from Great St Mary's belfry across the River Cam and the Bridge of Sighs at seven o'clock each morning, Alice would be seated at the spinet, which had been her mother's dearest possession, in the front parlour. Alice would play one of her repertoire of hymns on this eighteenth century harpsichord, while Ada and she would sing. Today was no exception.

Mr Hawkins never joined them for these morning sessions of praise to the Lord. Ada often wondered about his absence, but had never dared to ask, for it might have seemed impertinent. However, an answer to her query presented itself at the lunch table.

"You should join us, Father," Alice admonished her father for his refusal to take part in this solemn morning ritual, "as a good example to the child." Here she nodded towards Ada, who looked down at her plate, pretending not to hear what was being said less than a yard away from her!

"Give me one of the old-fashioned songs of praise, girl," he said to Alice. "All I ever hear you playing is this modern music."

"There's nothing modern about *Holy, Holy, Holy*," Alice protested.

"The tune is different to what it was in my day. I can't get my vocal chords round the notes. And it's not so religious to my way of thinking!"

"Religion is in your heart, Father, not in your vocal chords!" Alice looked at her father in triumph. He would have no answer to her comment.

"I suppose you like all these modern tunes, Ada?" Mr Hawkins looked over the upper rim of his spectacles as he spoke. His owlish expression reminded her of a funny picture called a cartoon, which she'd once seen in a magazine called *Punch*, and she wanted to laugh; but then, as she thought about the hymn she liked above all others, she wanted to cry.

"I like *I could not do without Thee* best of all. It was Mama's favourite hymn. You know, before she died."

"Now there's a sensible girl. A good, old-fashioned hymn. Sing me a verse, if you please."

"Father, this is hardly the time or place." Alice was indignant.

"Nonsense. There's always time for praising God." Mr Hawkins looked pleased with himself for outwitting his daughter at last. He knew that she was usually so much more superior in every way to himself, and was proud of her, until she managed to out-manoeuvre him in argument. "Now, Ada, a verse if you please."

Ada put down her knife and fork, wiped her mouth on her napkin and stood up to sing her favourite hymn to the tune usually associated with *The Church's One Foundation*.

"I could not do without Thee
Oh! Saviour of the lost!
Whose precious blood redeemed me
At such tremendous cost.
Thy righteousness Thy pardon
Thy precious blood must be
My only hope and comfort
My glory and my plea."

Ada sat down, blushing with embarrassment. This was the first time she had ever sung on her own for an audience, even though it was only Mr and Miss Hawkins. She had often sung songs with Mr Minns back in Ely, and joined in the songs of praise in church with the rest of the congregation at St Mary's in Ely. Lately she had sung on Sundays, morning service and evensong, in St Mary The Less, quaintly named so as to avoid confusion with Great St Mary's in the centre of Cambridge. St Mary the Less was a small, fourteenth century edifice steeped in tradition, with stained glass windows designed by Kempe. It had served the dual purpose of parish church and Peterhouse College chapel, until the seventeenth century when it reverted to being a separate parish church. Singing in church on Sundays with a hundred other parishioners, led by Reverend Andrew Allen and under the watchful eye of the Archangels Michael and Gabriel was one thing, but performing solo over the breakfast table was another! It was a new experience. However, she had such a sweet singing voice that, when she had finished, Mr Hawkins was engaged in wiping a tear or two away with the corner of his napkin.

"That's my girl!" he said, with emotion. "A good old-fashioned hymn, and a good old-fashioned tune."

In the afternoon, Alice and Ada donned cloaks, scarves and mittens and set off on their customary educational walk around Cambridge. Sometimes they would walk through the grounds of Queen's College and Alice would tell stories of Erasmus who stayed there, blotting his copybook by importing his own wine rather than drinking the local beer. Ada, as the daughter of a master brewer, always enjoyed this particular story. On very cold days they would visit the Fitzwilliam museum, taking delight in the Egyptian artefacts, Roman antiquities and paintings by famous Dutch artists. When they passed the chapel of Pembroke College, Ada was always given a lesson on English architecture, for it was Sir Christopher Wren's first completed design. Later, she would have to rhyme off the twenty-three London churches which Wren had designed.

On this February day, Alice decided to walk through the grounds of Gonville and Caius College, where countless generations of undergraduates in their gowns and academic garb had laughed together, swapped stories and discussed important academic concepts for over five hundred years. Stopping in front of the gate leading into Caius' Court, Ada noticed a wistful expression on Alice's face.

"What are you thinking?" she inquired. "You look very sad."

"Not sad, my dear. Yearning for something unattainable. Look at this inscription. What does it say?"

"It says 'Virtue'."

"That's what you need when you enter university life through this gate. Now let's see what's written on the gate leading out of the court."

When they reached the exit gate, Ada saw the word 'Honour'.

"The honour of success!" sighed Alice. "How grand it would be to be a university student: to have all that learning at your fingertips!"

"But you know so much," Ada honestly praised her teacher.

"Not by university standards, I fear."

They walked home along the sloping lawns of the Backs, stopping near the Bridge of Sighs, modelled on its Venetian namesake, to watch the ducks skating and skidding on the ice of the frozen Cam river.

"Now you're looking sad," observed Alice. "What are you thinking?"

Ada sighed. "I was thinking about Aunt Priscilla." She was remembering that spring day last year, when she and Aunt Priscilla had gone boating in a punt on this very stretch of the river. How they had laughed! "Do you think I shall ever see her again?"

"I'm sure you will, when the court case is over," Alice answered, though no-one knew for sure when the case to appoint Ada's guardian would be heard. The Official Solicitor had written to Alice on several occasions inquiring about Ada's general and mental health, and her preferences regarding potential guardians. She herself had talked with Ada, preparing her for the court case.

"I would like to live with her," Ada solemnly declared.

"No-one can guarantee that."

"Then why can I not go on living here?" Ada asked balefully.

"You know why not! I'm only a foster parent." Alice tried to sound stern and business-like, but her heart went out to this girl who had been flotsam and jetsam for too long. "This was always only a temporary arrangement."

Ada was becoming agitated. Her future was so uncertain. Nevertheless, she tried to sound optimistic and cheerful. "I have lots of relations. I could live with them."

Alice was in no position to comment. In the continued absence of Mr Philip Allen, it would be up to the Official Solicitor to make his recommendations on Ada's behalf to the judge in the Chancery Court, as to who might be appointed her guardian.

There were two ladies who wrote regularly to Ada, but it seemed improbable that her future would lie with either of them. Mrs Priscilla Sellers, Ada's aunt from Preston, was one of the ladies. Secretly, Alice hoped that this aunt would be appointed as Ada's guardian, because she had shown much kindness and interest in her niece for many a year, and just two months ago had sent her a set of scented note-paper for Christmas. In addition, Ada spoke enthusiastically about her. However, as a divorcee, Mrs Sellers was an unlikely choice for any judge to deem suitable as a guardian for Ada. The other lady was Mrs Nina Porter, Ada's sister-in-law, who seemed to be genuinely trying to put right the wrongs of that September afternoon. However, Ada had intimated that neither Nina nor Frank had shown interest in her hitherto, and the judge might deem their guardianship unsuitable on account of that lack of concern.

Ada continued, "Aunt Priscilla is my favourite aunt, you know, but I like Uncle Charles and Aunt Mary in Ely too. They're very old though. I have a lot of other aunts and uncles," she bragged, as if to give herself assurance. "There's Aunt Suzanna and Uncle Edward in Soham, and Uncle Henry John and Aunt Mary Ann in Vine House, but my favourite is Aunt Priscilla. I used to have an Uncle John too, but he left Aunt Priscilla and went to America."

"You're a very lucky girl," lied Alice.

"Also Uncle Philip and Aunt Caroline." Ada bit her lip and the trace of a frown crossed her brow. "I wonder where they are? And Annie?"

Alice linked arms with Ada and together they continued their homeward journey, across Magdalen bridge, past the Tudor gateway leading to St John's College on the left, and up Castle Street with Castle Mound on the right.

"I have two brothers, Alfred and Frank. And I have two sisters-in-law, Nina and Ellen, and lots of nieces and nephews. Then there's cousin Hilda: we used to write letters to each other."

To any outsider listening to Ada listing this catalogue of relations, it was sad. Alice considered it more than a little strange that a child with such a number of apparently responsible family members should be in a foster home. It cast serious aspersions on those people, and on the arrangements put in place by the child's father.

As the light was beginning to fade, Ada and Alice walked the last half-mile homewards at a brisk pace. Ada's mind was a kaleidoscope of half-remembered faces of brothers, cousins, uncles and aunts, nieces and nephews. It troubled her more than she could say that her Mama and Papa's faces had also joined that blurred melee.

Ada was feeling lonely and lost all over again in a recurrent daytime nightmare from which there was no waking.

Part 2

On Saint George's Day of 1896, Ada, Alice and Mr Hawkins were on their way from St Pancras to the Royal Courts of Justice in the Strand. Mr Hawkins had stood in the rain for a full five minutes outside this intimidating Gothic red-brick edifice, to hail a hansom cabriolet. Now the cabby drove his horse forwards with a series of well-worn cries, jostling for space on the roadway and dodging other cabs and carriages. As a horse-drawn omnibus trundled noisily past on the square sets, a sheet of spray splashed up against their vehicle.

"Why, it's raining cats and dogs! I've never seen rain like it!" exclaimed Alice, as she tried to peer through the side window of the cab, now streaming with spray turned to muddy rivulets.

"It's raining, it's pouring, the old man is snoring!" sang Ada. Even though there was little resemblance between the sunny, colourful picture of The Strand which Ada had seen in *The London Illustrated News*, and this dismal, dirty London road down which they now travelled, she felt buoyant.

"You sound very cheerful, my dear," observed Mr Hawkins. He was disappointed to be in London in such foul weather; cold under the uncomfortably damp, woollen weight of his double-breasted frockcoat; and sad to be on such an errand.

"Today is the day," Ada said excitedly.

Mr Hawkins and Alice exchanged glances, for neither of them could share in Ada's enthusiastic optimism. When they had embarked on their mission of mercy to look after Ada, they had always known it was only a temporary arrangement of six months, but now that the time had come, they were both very sorry to be saying goodbye to their foster child, who had brought such joy to their household. They themselves had brought happiness, comfort, security and benefits to Ada, but as good Christians, they were not given to self-congratulation. This would have amounted to pride, which Alice always referred to as "that deadliest of sins". Ada had come to them as a disorientated, homeless and frightened child, with only her dogged stoicism keeping body and soul together; and now she was leaving them as an educated, confident young girl, ready to embrace a new life with a new guardian.

"I hope it's Aunt Priscilla," Ada earnestly said, her yearning almost palpable.

"You mustn't build up your hopes too high, Ada," warned Alice. "I've told you how the courts view divorced women."

"Will your Aunt Priscilla even be considered?" queried Mr Hawkins. Answering his own question, he shook his head from side to side. "I doubt it. Alice is right: don't build up your hopes."

Ada was beginning to feel a tinge of unease, and she pursed her lips. She was growing fearful of the day's outcome. With Alice and Mr Hawkins putting a dampener on her excitement, she was beginning to lose faith in her own hopes and vision of an ideal future. Alice had done her best to allay any fears about the legal proceedings that Ada might have. She had taken time to prepare her for the event, to ease her through what would inevitably be a traumatic experience, by giving her information about the judge, the Official Solicitor, the court usher, the lawyers and their jargon. She had even taken Ada to the library at Caius College, by special appointment, where they had been admitted to the Reading Room where past editions of *The Times* newspaper could be read. In the edition of 5th December 1882, they were able to find out much information about the new Royal Courts of Justice, which had been officially opened the previous day by Queen Victoria. The Chancery Courts, where cases of guardianship were heard, were located in the Royal Courts of Justice. They were part of the High Court of Justice, which in turn was part of the wider Supreme Court of Judicature.

Such factual information as this was important, for it gave Ada a foothold on an otherwise slippery slope of the many possible outcomes of her case, when the applicants were as yet unknown. Alice had explained that each applicant would be scrutinised to ascertain his or her suitability to be Ada's guardian.

"But Aunt Priscilla is a kind person and she would look after me well," argued Ada.

"I have no doubt about that, my dear," agreed Alice patiently and honestly.

"And Papa told me that she looked after Mama too, in the old days, before I was born!"

"We're not the ones who need to be persuaded," countered Mr Hawkins, who could see that this conversation was leading to false hopes, "it's the Judge in the Chancery Court!"

Ada bit her lip, defeated. She knew that legal cases were won by logical argument, illustrated with facts. Her arguments were simple girlish hopes and wishes, illustrated with opinion and hearsay.

Alice came to the rescue. "Don't worry! It will all work out for the best." Trying to sound as cheery as possible, this kindly woman continued, "And as you have told me time and again, you have many relatives. I imagine they'll all be there, trying to persuade the Judge to let them be your guardian."

"Suppose no-one's there?" Ada was suddenly scared. "What happens to me then?"

Alice patted her on the hand. "There will be someone there, otherwise they would not have summoned us to the court, would they?"

This was indeed logical, giving Ada some feeling of relief, and renewed optimism. "I hope it's Aunt Priscilla!"

Alice could not help but feel glad that the hansom was pulling up outside the Royal Courts of Justice, as the conversation had gone full circle.

Rain or no rain, once Ada, Alice and Mr Hawkins had alighted from the cab and stood on the pavement beside their steaming cab-horse, they were in amazement at the sheer grandeur and massive proportions of the building. It was awe-inspiring, more impressive than they had ever imagined.

"The spire has almost disappeared!" Mr Hawkins remarked as he squinted upwards, blinking the drizzle out of his eyes. The pointed flèche, which rose over two hundred and forty-five feet from the Strand level, was touching the rain clouds above.

Shaking the droplets of rain from their outdoor garments, our trio entered through two arched porches, each with its own unique carvings.

"Look, Ada!" Alice was pointing to the three carved figures in the upper arch.

"Who are the two at the sides?" asked Mr Hawkins, for it was obvious to all who passed through this portal that the one at the highest point was that of the Saviour.

"Solomon and Alfred!" Ada remembered the details from her visit to Caius College library, though she was sorry not to see the sculptures of the cat and the dog, which represented fighting litigants in court, at the judges' entrance. They would have been much more interesting, she thought.

They then entered the imposing, oak-panelled Great Hall, two hundred and thirty-eight feet in length. The members of The Incorporated Law Society of the United Kingdom certainly were justified in their choice of architect. Eleven eminent architects of the day, including Mr Street and Mr Barry, had entered a competition run by the Law Society, each submitting his individual plans for consideration. The Law Society had finally selected Mr George Edmund Street's designs for the new Royal Courts of Justice over the ten other architects.

Feeling dwarfed in this eighty-foot high entrance hall, Ada and her two foster parents were very unsure of themselves. A porter directed them to the Cause List cabinet, situated at the bottom of the staircase, for information. As Mr Hawkins ran his finger down the list of all the cases being heard on this April day, Alice was admiring the three huge statues which sat in state above them: a bust of Queen Victoria at one end; a statue of Lord Russell, the first Roman Catholic judge to be appointed after the Reformation, at the other; and a statue of William Blackstone, the famous legal expert of the previous century, opposite the sweeping red-carpeted flight of stairs.

However, Ada was more interested in where her feet were standing. Knowing that each mosaic piece of the Great Hall's floor had been individually and painstakingly laid by craftsmen, she considered it almost sacrilege that her little brown boots, still damp from the puddles in the street outside, should be walking over such a work of art.

Mr Hawkins broke into her thoughts by announcing, "Court Number Seven on the first floor, at the far end of the corridor."

As Alice took Ada by the hand and led the way up the stairs, along the said corridor, where courts three to nine were located, they left behind the portraits of the Fire Judges, Masters of the Rolls, Lord Chief Baron and the Attorney General who had drafted the 1832 Reform Bill, which looked down imperiously on all the assortment of people who still milled about below.

Mr Hawkins held open the heavy, oak-panelled courtroom door, whose brass plate was engraved with "Seven", as his daughter and Ada entered into this Chancery Court where Ada's case was to be heard. They were directed by a court official to seats near the front to the right hand side of the court. As they made their way down the gently graded steps to their places, Ada looked at the group of eight people seated on the other side of Chancery Court Number Seven and caught a fleeting glimpse of one profile in particular.

Ada slipped her cloak from her shoulders and sat very still on her seat in the courtroom, hardly daring to breathe, for it was the profile of her Aunt Priscilla's face which she had seen.

"Do you recognise anyone?" Alice could feel her voice trembling, the imposing weight of the pomp and ceremony of the occasion getting the better of her.

"Aunt Priscilla!" Ada whispered. "She's the lady in the tall, maroon hat." She was at once elated and at the same time dismayed. She could not understand why Aunt Priscilla should be seated just behind that horrid Mr Rogers and, what's more, talking to him. The same Mr Rogers who had come with a policeman and taken her away from her brother's house in Clapton!

"That's good," smiled Alice, whispering too and looking in admiration at Priscilla Sellers's respectable attire. She was relieved that the application by Ada's aunt had at least got this far. When she noted Ada's worry lines, she asked, "Isn't it?"

"Mr Rogers is there with her," Ada answered flatly. "I wouldn't be here now if it wasn't for him."

"Surely that's a good sign?" Alice suggested, tentatively, for she could not determine whether Mr Rogers's presence would help or hinder Ada's case. He had been responsible for Ada being a foster child, yet by his position in front of Priscilla Sellers, he appeared to be acting on her behalf.

"I don't believe it is," answered Ada simply, trying to mask her apprehension.

"I see," said Alice, who did not really see what was going through Ada's mind. To change the subject, she asked, "And the other people? Do you know them too?"

"My Uncle Henry John is the man closest to the aisle." His clean-shaven face set him apart from the rest of the men in the courtroom. Alice could see a family resemblance between him and Ada.

"He's a fine-looking man!" said Alice, and, when her father looked askance at her for such a seemingly unseemly remark – a spinster's admiration of a married man, though innocently enough meant – she distracted him by asking, "That must be his lawyer in the seat in front of him, I suppose."

"On the other side of Aunt Priscilla is my brother Frank and Nina; and then my other brother Alfred is at the far end," Ada informed Mr Hawkins and Alice.

"How very popular you must be!" smiled Alice.

Ada considered the veracity of this observation. If she was popular, why was everyone looking so serious? No one had smiled over at her. Perhaps this was another nightmare, some ghastly conspiracy to show that they did not want her, or perhaps she had grown so small like Alice in her strange Wonderland that no one could even see her. She pinched herself to see if she was awake, then inwardly indulged in a wry smile at her stupidity. She shook her head.

"Why are they all here then?" Alice tried to reason with her.

"I don't know, and I wish they weren't here. I wish I wasn't popular! I only want my Aunt Priscilla here!" Ada petulantly blurted out her feelings.

Both she and Alice knew that the presence of Uncle Henry John, Frank and Alfred, three men of considerable means and importance, made Aunt Priscilla's claim seem more and more impossible, no matter how tall her maroon hat.

"Sshh!" Mr Hawkins ordered, because the door at the front of Chancery Court Number Seven had opened and two figures in black and wearing wigs were entering. One of the men, in a black silk gown with a lustrous sheen and wearing a full bottomed wig, walked majestically straight across the courtroom to take up position in front of Ada. Before being seated, he gravely looked down at the little figure in her pale blue frock with a pleated bodice and rounded lace collar, and shook her by the hand. He said in a rich and sonorous voice, "How do you do? I am the Official Solicitor, appointed by the court to represent you today." And he flamboyantly swirled his robes round as he sat down.

The other figure was the court usher, whose black robes were of a more humble material than those of the Official Solicitor, and whose wig was made of white horse hair, curled at the sides and tied back.

"All rise!" he suddenly commanded from the front of the courtroom in an imposing voice, which loudly reverberated off the oak-panelled walls, bounced off the arched stained glass windows, and finally fragmented into whispering echoes in the oak cross-beams of the ceiling high above.

Ada stood, flanked by Alice and Mr Hawkins with the Official Solicitor in front of her, and waited for something important to happen.

Part 3

The Honourable Mr Justice Theobald Davies, the presiding judge in Chancery Court Number Seven, enjoyed the stir which his grand entrance always created in his court, and liked to allow himself the added benefit of delaying his appearance for a few extra seconds to achieve maximum effect. As he came in, Ada and Alice momentarily shot a glance at one another, for Mr Justice Davies, in his scarlet and ermine robes and his crimped Friz Tye wig, cut an identical likeness to George III, whose portrait they had been studying only the previous week in the Fitzwilliam Museum in Cambridge. They had learnt that this third King George was a great head of state who had won the hearts of his people. Not only had he been a figurehead and symbol of national pride when war broke out against the French in 1793, but he had also been nicknamed "Farmer George" because of his interest in rural areas and the ordinary country folk. As Ada now looked at this important judge, all she could think of was the King's silly sobriquet, and wonder if the judge's name was George too.

Mr Justice Davies sat on his dais presiding admirably, the Royal Coat of Arms emblazoned on the panelled wall behind him. From his judge's bench, which was illuminated from above by an impressive gilt and crystal chandelier powered by the innovative system of electricity, he listened attentively. His body language indicated that he exuded authority from every pore. There would be no disagreeing with his deliberations and verdict, after he had heard the advantages and disadvantages of those who had allowed their names to be put forward as Ada's guardian.

A strong case was put by a Mr Popple, the thin Norfolk lawyer acting on behalf of Ada's half brothers, Frank and Alfred. As Mr Popple spoke, Mr Justice Davies looked first at Alfred, then at Frank, then back to Alfred again. It was as if he were trying to ascertain the truth by thoughtfully regarding each of them in turn. They were both undoubtedly upstanding middle-aged citizens, well-dressed, stolid, carrying the weight of their own success on their shoulders. Yet just how wholehearted they were in their resolution to be guardians of Miss A. M. Porter was unclear. The woman between them was an enigma: a well-to-do lady in dress, yet her countenance resembled that of one of the medieval, poor penitents desiring to be shriven by the eponymous Pardoner in Chaucer's Canterbury Tales. He supposed that she might have had some influence over the two men seated beside her.

Then Mr Justice Davies peered through his monocle at Ada. Her expressionless face did not assist him in drawing conclusions.

Mr Popple was now carefully summarising his clients' claim. "The Messrs Porter are both respectable, wealthy family men, who, as her half-brothers, have a strong blood tie with the minor in question, Miss Ada Porter. I submit that they would have the strongest claim to be her joint guardians."

Then it was the Official Solicitor's turn. He looked smugly dismissive. "Your Honour," he said, "Messrs Alfred and Frank Porter have applied to be joint guardians, sharing Ada, as it were." Ada liked the sound of his resonant voice, with its note of censure. She knew that he was on her side and listened intently to what he had to say. "Six months with Mr Frank Porter," he continued, fully extending his left arm, "and six months with Mr Alfred Porter," now fully extending his right arm, "effectively pulling her in half. This is totally unacceptable for Miss Porter's long-term education, security and emotional well-being."

However strong Alfred's and Frank's claim had appeared a few minutes before, their application was effectively dismissed by the Official Solicitor. He awaited confirmation from the judge.

Mr Justice Davies noted the mixed reactions of the two brothers: outrage and relief. It would have been difficult to decide which of the two was the stronger emotion. Ada herself had perked up, and was sitting a little more straight than she had been during Mr Popple's diatribe. This change in mien and posture, albeit very slight, did not go unnoticed by the judge.

He nodded sagely. Mr Popple's clients were unsuccessful in their bid. The Official Solicitor looked satisfied.

Mr Rogers looked satisfied too. He would also have found it totally unacceptable, as old Mr Porter had expressly stated that he did not want Alfred and Frank to be their half sister's guardians. He wanted to tell the judge that, there and then, but it would have to wait.

Ada thought about being pulled in half, and was reminded of the story in the Bible, when two people fought over the ownership of a baby.

Next, the other gentleman beside Mr Rogers stood up. He was a heavily-whiskered Mr Bradshaw, representing Henry John's application. He advocated that his client, Mr Henry John Porter, as Ada's natural uncle and father of ten living children, the youngest almost of an age with Ada, would be the best guardian. He explained that Ada had formed a strong attachment with the three youngest daughters, and would enjoy their company. As a finishing touch he said, "Mr Henry John Porter is a successful farmer and lives in Vine House in Haddenham, the Porter family house where Ada's own father lived as a boy."

It was a master stroke, worthy of the finest portrait painter. Henry John was justly proud of his standing in Haddenham and his success as a father, yet he was niggled by misgivings about his ownership of Vine House. He too was seeking absolution and, as Ada's guardian, his conscience would be forever clear.

Mr Rogers was looking grave. Mr Bradshaw, whose name in the legal profession was highly respected, had presented a solid case. It was very plausible, and Mr Rogers could recognise that Ada would be given a good home and upbringing under the care of this uncle. Yet he remembered that old Mr Porter had not had an easy relationship with his youngest brother, Henry John, and had distinctly rejected the idea that he be appointed guardian to Ada. He also wanted to inform the judge of this right away, but had to wait.

The Official Solicitor stood, saying nothing for half a minute while he deliberated on Mr Bradshaw's watertight case. He gently massaged his chin with his right thumb and forefinger, focusing first on the ceiling, then on the floor. Justice Davies was on the verge of urging the Official Solicitor to speak: this was time-wasting. If anyone was going to waste time in his courtroom, it would be him, and not the Official Solicitor. In the judge's opinion, the Official Solicitor often regarded himself too highly.

"This is indeed a worthy application, and one which this office finds acceptable," the Official Solicitor stated, with no reservations whatsoever.

An expression of irritation and frustration passed over Mr Rogers's physiognomy. This was bad news indeed, but this time he had not expected any less.

Ada looked at Alice and Mr Hawkins for some assurance, for surely the Official Solicitor was supposed to be on her side. Supporting Uncle Henry John was not being on her side at all. Alice was looking tense, and was of no help to Ada in her moment of doubt, nor was Mr Hawkins. But Mr Justice Davies noted the look of anxiety on Ada's pretty young face, and felt a sense of helplessness, for all his high powers. He twisted his monocle, as if to see things more clearly, in the physical sense as well as the metaphorical sense. It was clear to him that it would be difficult for any judge, or even the Official Solicitor, to dislodge Ada's uncle, Henry John Porter, as a strong contender for guardianship.

Then it was Mr Rogers's turn. When he stood to present his case to Mr Justice Davies, both he and the judge could not help but notice Ada's look of tight-lipped disapproval. The judge presumed that Ada did not approve of the elegant lady in the tall hat, a Mrs Priscilla Sellers according to his notes, who was being represented by this Mr Rogers.

Mr Rogers, on the other hand, supposed that Ada was remembering that ugly incident in Clapton at Frank Porter's house.

Or perhaps she preferred to live with Henry John Porter and the cousins with whom she had such affectionate ties. He suddenly felt a lack of conviction. He was in a quandary. Was he right to keep old Mr Porter's strongly held views uppermost in his mind, when the choice of Mr Allen as Ada's guardian had gone so disastrously wrong? Was he right to champion the cause of an aunt, a divorced woman living in another county, which would necessitate yet another upheaval in Ada's young life, moving completely away from the land of her forefathers? He knew that the Porter family could trace their Cambridgeshire roots back to the sixteenth century. Was he right to pursue this application by his client, Mrs Priscilla Sellers, when Ada looked so crossly at him? It was enough to fill the dapper Mr Rogers with a self-doubt never experienced before.

Just then, from the corner of his eye, he noticed a smile of encouragement from the serene woman who sat at Ada's elbow. It was meant only for him, a tiny spark, but quite sufficient to rekindle his self-esteem and his resolve.

"Your Honour, my client, Mrs Priscilla Sellers, is a divorcee!" he heard himself boldly announce.

Mr Justice Davies looked through his gold-rimmed monocle at this undersized lawyer. He was interested in how such a negative introductory statement could be made to sound so positive and aggressive. "Continue, er…" Here he looked down at his notes to discover the name of this smart lawyer "…Mr Rogers, if you please."

Mr Hawkins and Alice could not believe their ears. What had possessed Mr Rogers to present his client's weakest aspect first, or even at all?

"We have been presented today with three upstanding men, all well-respected and successful men, needing no approbation, no proof, other than the fact that they are 'men'. We do not doubt their success.

"Mr Alfred Porter of Chertsey is an eminent master brewer, following in family tradition, in that his father, Richard, was a master brewer. He is a solid citizen, a family man. We know that he took pity on his half-sister, Ada, and that she lived with him for all of a month, before being dispatched to his younger brother, Frank."

Joseph Rogers paused for a few moments, assessing the situation, hoping for the intended effect of his innuendoes. Ada still looked stern but her companion, that good-looking woman at her side, was smiling and nodding to him to continue.

"Mr Frank Porter of Clapton, Ada's other half brother and also a successful master brewer, took Ada in, presumably out of kindness, but did not have the opportunity to get to know the girl before she was made a ward of court." Mr Rogers momentarily looked down, the memory of that day, when he had come with a large female court official and a policeman to seize Ada, too fresh and incriminating to his sensibilities.

"Neither of these brothers showed much interest in Ada after their father's death. Neither man visited or contacted Ada in Ely, during those eighteen months when she was living with the Allens, her appointed guardians."

Alfred looked down, contrite. His previous lack of concern for Ada was painfully and publicly apparent. When this was all over, he resolved to show kindness to his hapless half-sister. He and Ellen and the children would keep in contact, somehow.

Nina had turned to her husband, mouthing his name in accusation. It was all his fault: Ada was his sister; he should have been kinder to her. Frank blamed his father's eccentricity, equally confirmed in his opinion that Mr Rogers was "an ass", and stared stonily ahead.

Mr Rogers himself turned the knife in the wound. "Oh yes, they are the executors of their father's will, and to that end they send, from the monies allocated to Ada under the terms of the will, her entitlement in the form of an annuity each March. But that is the sum total, if you forgive the poor pun, your Honour," he apologised, repeating, "the sum total of their interest in their sister.

"In addition, let it be said that their father, Richard Porter, according to his last will and testament, which I drew up and which I have here," Joseph Rogers continued, producing the said document, "categorically refused to appoint his sons, her brothers, Alfred and Frank, as Ada's guardians."

Ada looked at Mr Rogers with new appreciation, and the beginnings of shy liking. This augured well: she did not wish to live with either of her two half-brothers, and to learn that her dear, dead Papa did not wish it was a comfort to her now, at this time when her destiny was in the balance.

Mr Rogers, having dispensed with the brothers, now turned his attention to the more difficult contender, Henry John.

"We have learnt of the undisputed suitability of Ada's uncle, Mr Henry John Porter," he began. "Another upstanding man. A pillar of strength! A successful farmer in the Cambridgeshire village of Haddenham. He chose not to follow in the family tradition of brewing, despite living in Vine House, the family home of Porter master brewers for over two hundred years." Here Mr Rogers paused, to flourish the will already held in his hand. "His brother, Richard, was quite clear that he did not wish Henry John to be appointed guardian. It would seem immoral to go against the wishes of Ada's father at this juncture."

Mr Bradshaw, Henry John's lawyer, bristled at the word "immoral", for there was absolutely nothing immoral about his client, who was a model citizen in every respect. He objected to this hinted slur on Henry John's character. He looked as if he were about to speak, but one forbidding look from Mr Justice Davies curtailed his intention and he remained silent, though disgruntled.

Mr Rogers fistled about in his document-case, eventually producing three sheets of paper. "Your Honour, I have here three testimonials as to the character of my client, Mrs Priscilla Sellers. With the court's permission, I should like to read them out."

Mr Justice Davies nodded his acquiescence, and Mr Rogers dramatically read out the words of each of the three testimonials, as if his life depended on a perfect performance. Mr Braithwaite's appraisal of Priscilla, "a model landlady, whose compassion and common sense in times of trouble" had kept him "sane and on the straight and narrow", sounded positive and compelling, though the judge raised a quizzical eyebrow as he considered the implications of the clichéd inferences.

The Preston bank manager, Mr Basil Wilson, had written a dry, practical evaluation of Mrs Sellers: she was a "shrewd businesswoman, whose accounting was exemplary". Short and to the point, Mr Wilson had not seen fit to be flowery or over-complimentary. Like Mr Gradgrind in Charles Dickens's *Hard Times,* he only dealt with facts, hard facts.

Joshua Margerison's testimonial was read out last. A Lancashire man through and through, of steady Methodist stock, Joshua Margerison had been the founder of a successful soap manufacturing business. Mr Rogers was not going to waste any opportunity to lay emphasis on the importance of this referee's testimonial to the good character of his client.

"The Margerison soap manufactures of Preston have been distinguished by our revered monarch. The company's 'White Windsor' soap now bears the inscription 'By appointment to Her Majesty Queen Victoria'. I also understand that Joshua Margerison is to attend a special gathering at the Palace, for his firm has been selected to produce a commemorative toilet soap for Queen Victoria's diamond jubilee. Mr Margerison's testimonial is beyond question; it asserts Mrs Sellers's suitability, indeed her right, to be Ada's guardian henceforth."

Mr Rogers read out the words that sang Priscilla's praises, with a flamboyance which grew with the confidence of a poker player who knows he has fortune on his side. His coup de grace was delivered with the observation, "Your Honour, it appears that my client has three excellent testimonials in support of her application. The other applicants have none."

If Mrs Pankhurst had only known of his existence, how she could have used his skills in helping women in their political moves for equal rights! Mr Joseph Rogers had used the demand for three testimonials for his divorced female client to his advantage, as the Official Solicitor had not considered it necessary to seek such endorsement of the men's applications.

The corners of Mr Justice Davies mouth twitched a slight smile, perceptible only to those who knew him well. The Official Solicitor "had been brought down a peg or two", as he later chuckled in Chambers to his judiciary cronies.

Ada had listened to all the praise which had been publicly read out about her Aunt Priscilla and was enjoying the sensation of feeling familial admiration when The Honourable Mr Justice Theobald Davies announced that it was time for a decision to be made.

"Ada," he ordered, "stand please!"

Ada got to her feet, a lone figure in blue facing the judge. She was wide-eyed: all the court's attention was now on her; she was the centrepiece; she could feel everyone's eyes pierce her back.

Addressing her severely, Mr Justice Davies said, "Now, Ada, by the statutes of The Custody of Children Act of 1891, it is you who must decide. The court has brought before you four persons who wish to be your guardians. Of those four, the court rules that only two are considered satisfactory, namely Mr Henry John Porter, your uncle on your father's side, and Mrs Priscilla Sellers, your aunt on your mother's side. These appear to be two applicants of equal merit in this case. Now, child, do you understand what it is you must do? Do you understand that you must decide?"

"Yes," Ada answered monosyllabically, and then, remembering her manners, "your Honour."

That she, Ada, had only to say a name to decide her future was almost too good to be true. She wanted to pinch herself again to see if she really was awake. She did not dare, for fear it was only a dream.

"Good, good. So which of the aforementioned persons do you choose as your guardian?"

There was a pregnant pause.

"Go on, Ada!" urged Alice softly. "Say who you want to be your guardian."

Ada looked across the courtroom. There was Uncle Henry John smiling encouragement, his eyes sparkling in the electric light. It was almost as if he were willing her to choose him. She felt drawn to him; she liked him, she liked Vine House, she liked her cousin Hilda.

"Now's your chance to be in charge of your destiny, child," prompted Mr Hawkins in a hushed yet urgent whisper. "Go on!"

And there was Aunt Priscilla in her tall maroon hat. She had only the trace of a smile, a gentle upturn to her lips, but when Ada made eye contact with Aunt Priscilla, the honest steadfastness which she saw in those grey eyes was all she wanted. She wanted to be with Aunt Priscilla.

Loud and clear, so there would be no mistake, no misunderstanding, Ada made her choice, her heart bursting with unparalleled, euphoric emotion.

"My Aunt Priscilla, if you please, your Honour."

Ada waited, holding her breath, while the judge looked at her thoughtfully. Then he slowly removed his monocle and nodded his assent.

"Let it be known that this is a landmark case, a precedent in the provision of justice for women and children of this sovereign land. This court so rules that Mrs Priscilla Sellers be appointed the guardian of Miss Ada Porter, minor of the Parish of Ely."

Ada suddenly felt ten feet tall. Had she drunk from Alice Liddell's other Wonderland bottle? Could this really be happening? She wanted to sing and dance; she could have hugged the judge; she wanted to wave across to Mr Rogers and shout her gratitude out so loud that it would echo round and round the courtroom for ever!

Aunt Priscilla was smiling now, her hand extended in an elegant, almost regal wave of victory across the courtroom to Ada.

Ada stood there with a widening smile on her lips.

Striking his gavel upon the desk before him, the Honourable Mr Justice Theobald Davies announced with an air of finality,

"Case closed."

"All rise!" commanded the court usher.

As the judge left Chancery Court Number Seven, Ada turned to Alice and Mr Hawkins to share her happiness with them. Dear Alice! She was laughing and crying all at the same time, wiping her eyes on her monogrammed lace handkerchief. Only Mr Hawkins looked grave and sad, his comforting arm round his daughter's shoulders, for he foresaw the void which was to be his and his daughter's life from now on, without sweet Ada to bless their days.

Ada was suddenly chastened. Her new-found elation mixed with sombre thoughts: happiness intertwined with sadness. A new life with her Aunt Priscilla made her happier than words could ever express. But oh how she would miss Alice, her dear friend and confidante!

Here in the Royal Courts of Justice, Libra equally balanced gain and loss. Mr Minns had been right, thought Ada, as a new understanding was born in her.

Life was indeed bitter-sweet.

CHAPTER 7
ADA

Part 1

Prestonians were undecided. Should they be flattered or insulted that the celebrated author, Mr Charles Dickens, had chosen their town as the model for Coketown in *Hard Times*? Should they enjoy a feeling of honourable fame or ignominious notoriety?

"It was a town of red-brick, or of brick that would have been red if the smoke and ashes had allowed it," Mr Dickens wrote, *"but as matters stood it was a town of unnatural red and black like the painted face of a savage.*

"It was a town of machinery and tall chimneys, out of which interminable serpents of smoke trailed themselves for ever and ever, and never got uncoiled."

The very first impression which Ada had on her approach to Preston across the North Union Railway Bridge, was that of dirt and grime. Chimney upon chimney belched out soot-laden smoke along the skyline, drifting up into the upper air and then falling again, depositing its greasy black specks over the town. There were cotton mills too, answering to Mr Dickens's description of *"vast piles of building full of windows"* and she imagined she could almost hear the pulsating factory noise, *"a rattling and a trembling all day long, and where the piston and the steam-engine worked monotonously up and down like the head of an elephant in a state of melancholy madn*ess." Several foundries and coal yards, numerous engineering works and builders' yards, all contributed to the dirty atmosphere.

Ada remembered Mr Hawkins's scathing remarks back in Cambridge, when they had been taking turns to read from *Hard Times* on a cold winter evening in January.

"That's industrialisation for you, nothing but *'dark, satanic mills'!"* he had said. "All dirt and grime, hard labour and miserable faces."

"My Aunt Priscilla's face is not miserable!" Ada had risen to her aunt's defence.

"I know that," he agreed, "for your Aunt Priscilla is a lady, but in the poorer areas where the working-classes live, the faces are miserable. Your face would be miserable too, if you lived in one of those northern back-to-back houses with open cess-pools right beside you, with cinders and ash all around, choking you to death!"

Ada's face was set. After all, if luck went her way, she would go to live in Preston!

"Yes, Father," Alice had said, trying to alleviate the tension, "but that was Preston fifty years ago! Things must have changed."

But some things had not changed. Monotony and sameness in the lives of the ordinary people had not changed, for all the humanitarian reforms of the previous forty years. Cinders, the bi-product of all of the coal-powered industries, were piled high all around in shifting mounds; a mixture of dry clinker and ash was used as surface material for paths and lanes, and strewn across waste ground between housing blocks. In the dry weather the air would be filled with dust whipped up by light summer breezes, and locals would have to go out "degging" the cinders, a process of spraying water from specially constructed watering-cans with wide rose spouts, in order to douse the choking particles.

Proud Prestonians would have argued that Preston was the first provincial town to have gas street lighting; that it was the hub of commercial activity and success with some of the finest engineering works in the land; that there were three mainline railway stations, and docks opening the town up to foreign trade; that Richard Arkwright, who had developed the spinning-frame that enabled cotton yarn to be spun mechanically, was born and bred in Preston. They rejected Mr Dickens's disparaging remarks outright when he referred to their Preston to Lancaster Canal as "a black canal", although the main passenger barge was named the Water Witch. His Coketown was simply a fictional town in their estimation.

Mr Hawkins had been undeterred. "I remember when I was a boy. Such stories we heard about Preston, up north, terrible stories that beggared belief: exploitation of the poor, unfeeling cotton lords. Why, the spinners and weavers eventually had to go on strike after their wages had been reduced by ten per cent."

Then, much to the amazement of Ada and Alice, he had broken into song:

"In eighteen forty-seven, my boys
I am sorry for to say
They took from us the ten per cent,
Without so much delay.
And now we want it back again,
Our masters in a pout
Said they would not grant it us,
So we're everyone locked out."

During the Preston Lock-out, as it was called, the bosses brought in black-leg workers called "knobsticks" to keep their factories running. The strikers were not to be beaten, gathering support for their cause with *The Cotton Lords of Preston*, a fund-raising song written at the time, casting aspersions on the "mighty men" and "swells of Fishergate" as nothing more than "a set of stingy Blades". Each verse had been followed by a chorus, blaming the Cotton Lords for the working man's misery.

But Preston was not all doom and gloom to Ada. As she and Aunt Priscilla were driven on that first day from the station to her new home in Ashton, the April sunshine reflected off the light stone-work of the recently erected municipal buildings and off the polished shop-front windows of the grand facades of modern retail premises. As they went down Fishergate Hill towards the stately River Ribble incandescently shimmering in the bright light, nothing could have been further from Mr Dickens's description of *"a river that ran purple with ill-smelling dye"*.

In the weeks to come, Ada was to get to know the pleasant suburb of Ashton, where Oundle Villa was situated, where houses had front gardens and there was a luxurious park in the centre. They would often wander further out into the countryside of Cottam, listening to the corncrakes shrieking to one another across the fields of young corn and wheat.

In Preston itself there were some lovely areas, discovered as Aunt Priscilla took her for long walks through Avenham Park, past the bandstand where Michael Entwhistle and Thomas Hinton still regularly sat smoking their pipes and telling the time by the trains which traversed the North Union and the East Lancashire Railway bridges.

Ada and her aunt would walk round the smart new suburbs around Avenham Park, salubrious avenues like Ribblesdale Place and cotton-poplar tree-lined Bushell Place, deliberately built upwind of Preston. Here there were expensive properties, inhabited by the upper and middle classes. There was one house which Ada liked more than all the others in Ribblesdale Place.

"Look, Aunt Priscilla!" Ada had stopped dead in her tracks as they saw the end house on the corner of the square. "Isn't it just like the house where I was born?"

"I believe it is very like Waddington Terrace!" Priscilla noted the similarities of the Georgian design. When she looked at her niece, Ada's expression was one of wistfulness. Such a catalogue of loss in her young life, thought Priscilla. She led the way up into the town to view the new, Gothic revival style Town Hall built in 1867, where she had once had the privilege to attend one of Franz Liszt's many performances in that very building.

Ada was allowed to wander round the newly completed Harrris Museum and Library every Saturday morning as a special treat, though she would often feel sad on these occasions, for she was reminded of her library and museum visits with Alice in Cambridge. In the afternoon, after she and Aunt Priscilla had been for afternoon tea in The Bull and Royal Hotel, Ada would be allowed to sit in the parlour with her own lap-escritoire, to write to Alice to enthuse about all the treasures she had found, and what she had learnt of the history of the town.

"In 1888 Preston became a County Borough," she wrote to Alice in late May, *"but I'm not too sure what that means! And did you know that every twenty years the town holds a Guild Fair. It goes right back to the middle-ages and beyond. I can hardly wait till the next Guild in six years time. Next century! 1902!"*

As a Cambridgeshire lass from Ely, Ada knew much about Cromwell who had lived on St Mary Street, and she began to feel at home when she heard that he had won his most decisive battle at Preston in 1648. But when she asked Mr Braithwaite, the lodger in her aunt's house and a self-styled local historian, exactly where the battle had been fought, he looked askance at her.

"We have never marked the battlefield," he answered.

"Why not?" asked Ada.

"It's not something we Prestonians feel proud about."

"Why not?"

"Because we're Royalists! Charles the Second was proclaimed king at the market cross here in Preston in 1649."

Ada knew her history of the Civil War. "But he wasn't king then!"

"No, he wasn't, but he was proclaimed king at that time. When he was finally restored rightfully, mark my words, *rightfully* to the throne in 1660, there was dancing in Preston's streets all day and carousing all night into the small hours."

"Like the Guild celebrations?" asked Ada.

"The Guild?" Mr Braithwaite was taken aback. "Nothing is like the Guild. There's carousing all day as well as at night. None of your teetotalism applies then!"

"What's teetotalism?" Ada suddenly remembered Aunt Caroline's passion for Ceylindo tea. Where was Aunt Caroline now?

"You young girls today, you know nothing!" Mr Braithwaite tended to have a restrictive view of the world, which stopped at the banks of the River Ribble, similar to those in London for whom the world stopped at the Watford Gap. Those who were not as intimately acquainted with Preston, its inhabitants, history and ways were regarded as uneducated by Mr Braithwaite. "Taking the pledge," he explained.

"Pledge?" Ada was none the wiser.

"Not drinking! Total abstinence from alcohol, as put forward by Mr Joseph Livesey, only he had a stutter and said at a public meeting, 'T-total abstinence' and so the name stuck and it became teetotalism!"

To Ada, whose family had been master brewers for countless generations, this was as odd a notion as she had heard of. "You mean not drinking beer and wine and such like? That's unnatural!"

Mr Braithwaite was a reformed alcoholic who had followed Mr Livesey's fanatical example and had taken the pledge. Now, in his darkest moments, when he still yearned for a tipple, Mr Braithwaite might have agreed with Ada that such a way of life was unnatural, but Temperance Society meetings and the kind understanding which Mrs Sellers had shown him over the past ten years, kept him on the straight and narrow.

"Quite the reverse!" he severely pointed out. "Mark my words, young lady, quite the reverse!"

He sounded so cross that Ada was not sure whether she really liked Mr Braithwaite or not. She had felt much more comfortable with Mr Minns with his fund of quaint proverbs to assist one through the vagaries of life.

That evening, before the May sun had set she wrote to Mr Minns to keep him informed. She realised that if it had not been for him, she might never have met her dear Aunt Priscilla, and her life would have taken a very different course. In her letter she itemised in summary diary form what she had done since she had arrived in Ashton: namely *"walked round Preston with Aunt Priscilla, visited the sights, got to know Ashton, started at Ashton Elementary School. Got to know cousin Mabel, who will be eighteen on the 24th of the month. She is a governess."*

To have described her differing thoughts and feelings would have been beyond her powers of expression, and the letter would have been too long. She was only allowed to write one sheet, which together with the small envelope would have weighed half an ounce. Any heavier, and there would have been double the postage to pay, and Aunt Priscilla, as frugal with Ada's annuity as with her own money, would not have allowed that under any circumstances.

Ada went to Ashton Elementary School on the day after she arrived in Preston. There had been no time to get to know anyone, not even the neighbours and their children. As a new entrant almost at the end of the school year, and all alone again, consequently her first day at school had been traumatic. This was her third first day at a new school in as many years, so she was an expert at dealing with the stares and taunts which accompany such moments. She sighed inwardly as a few big girls stuck their tongue out at her at morning break time. She had always heard that people up north were puny, dark-haired descendants from diminutive Romans, who had been the remnants of a garrison left behind in Chester at the demise of the Roman Empire, but these girls were tall, flaxen-haired and large-breasted, probably descendants of some marauding Vikings. However, she stood her ground in her own indomitable, unmovable way and an uneasy stalemate ensued, until the school hand-bell was rung and they were forced to retreat and line up for the rest of the morning's lessons.

At lunchtime, as the boys and girls were once again in the playground quadrangle, one of the girls, a Mavis Nobblet, hurled an insult at Ada. "Why, you're more like a catlick than a prodidog! Only real prodidogs go to this school!" Then she spat at Ada's feet.

Ada looked at the frothy spittle on the ash and cinder ground, and then stared into Mavis's smirking blue eyes, trying to pretend that she knew exactly what a prodidog was. Whatever it meant, it must be some word peculiar to Lancashire. A crowd of children now swarmed round the pair of girls, like gamblers round an illicit cock fighting pit, waiting for a fight. Ada moved not a muscle.

"Leave her alone!" A boy's voice broke the silence, and a dark-haired youth, no more than eight years old, bravely forced his way to the front of the circle. "You're such a bully, Mavis. Leave her alone!"

Mavis and her friends towered above him, leering and sneering, looking as if they could have had his head on a platter.

"Ooh, hark at him!" Mavis jeered. "Who's a mummy's boy, then?"

The unutterable had been uttered. There was a horrified hush and the children fell back and hung their heads, disassociating themselves from Mavis Nobblet as quickly as they could. The boy's face turned scarlet. It was an unwritten law in school that you never mentioned anyone's dead relatives. This boy's mother had died quite suddenly in November. His name was Harry.

On the way home Ada asked Aunt Priscilla, "Am I a prodidog?"

"Wherever did you hear that expression?"

"Mavis Noblett. She said I was more like a catlick. What's a catlick?"

Aunt Priscilla was almost laughing. "A prodidog, my dear, is a protestant, and a catlick is a catholic!"

Later, when Ada was looking out through her bedroom window, she saw the boy who had stood up for her entering the front door of the house opposite, where she knew cousin Mabel worked as a governess.

"Who's the boy who lives opposite?" she called to her aunt.

"There are two. Which one?"

"Come and see, quickly."

"That's Harry Margerison," Aunt Priscilla said. "He's a very serious young man, but has got his head screwed on."

"Is he a mummy's boy? Mavis said he was."

"Far from it, I'm afraid. Those poor children have no mother."

"Oh!" Ada whispered sympathetically.

"She died just before Christmas. Margaret, she was called. She was a dear friend of mine." Then she took Ada by both hands and looked earnestly into her dark brown eyes. "You and I owe her much," she said. "She made the court case possible. Without her we would not be here together."

Sadness, happiness, gratitude and satisfaction all mingled together in Priscilla's heart. To show that she understood, Ada put her arms round her aunt and gave her a long, long hug.

Ada had learnt that nothing in life is for free: happiness comes at a price.

Part 2

"Don't worry!" announced Mabel airily, sitting on her side of the double bed which she and Ada shared. "We won't have to put up with one another for long."

"What do you mean?" asked Ada with a sinking feeling. Was she to be taken away again? Move somewhere else? Go away from the haven here with Aunt Priscilla? She was happy and secure here. It was where she wanted to be, and had told the judge that she wanted to live with Aunt Priscilla. Surely the judge's decision was final?

"I have grand plans," was Mabel's cryptic reply as she nodded her head knowingly through the window towards the house opposite.

"At the Margerisons?" Ada asked. "You mean, become a live-in governess?"

Mabel conspiratorily tapped her nose. "Wait and see!" And she terminated the conversation and began to file her long tapering finger-nails.

Mabel was vain. She would spend much time looking at herself in the three hinged dressing-table mirrors, adjusting the glass so that she could see herself from every angle. She parted her dark brown hair in the middle, from her widow's peak to the nape of her neck, gathering her tresses into a soft loop behind each ear. It was not a particularly modern or fashionable hairstyle, but it suited her and gave a softness to what might otherwise have been classified as hard features for a young woman. Mabel was also hard-working and ambitious, and had promised herself that she would get on in the world. Already educated, and highly thought of in the Harris Museum where she had worked as a clerk and guide, she would secure for herself a solid husband: a man who would not run off to America on a whim, like her father and brother had done.

Since the death of Margaret Margerison, there could be no doubt that both Mabel and Priscilla had played a considerable role in helping George Margerison through difficult times. Their two families had even spent Christmas together at Priscilla's house, to ease him and his family through that festive season, in the face of their recent loss.

Shortly after the New Year, Mabel had offered to be a weekday governess to the two youngest children, Edith and Bessie, suggesting that she worked from eight o'clock in the morning until five o'clock in the afternoon. George, still in mourning and distraught, with no-one other than Stella the housemaid to look after his small girls, was grateful for all the help that was offered. Mabel had immediately given up her employment in the Harris Museum, and had begun her work as governess straight away. Even though Priscilla had regarded this as a retrograde career move, away from the public eye where suitors might be found, she knew that once Mabel's mind was made up, there would be no dissuading her. Like mother, like daughter. Both as stubborn as mules when it came to tenacity.

One Saturday, the week before Ada's ninth birthday on July 20th, when Priscilla, Mabel, Mr Braithwaite and Ada were sitting down to lunch, they began to discuss birthday treats for her.

"What would you like for your birthday treat?" Aunt Priscilla asked.

Ada closed her eyes. A picture of a little girl in a frilly white dress picking flowers in Wicken Fen flitted through her mind. What she really wanted was unattainable: her Papa was long gone, a fond, dim memory; and Mr Stokes and Maud Harrison were figures becoming hazy with the passing of time; and the colours of the pressed flowers had faded. Wouldn't it be lovely to go back in time, to revisit the past every now and then and say hello. It would be even better to be able to bring the past into the present. Perhaps a picnic would help to bring everything back.

"You're having a real long think, any road," said Mr Braithwaite. "We're all agog, waiting!"

This thought process was getting out of hand. "Only in fairytales!" she said inwardly.

Everyone was waiting for her answer. Shaking herself out of such a silly day-dream of things impossible, she said, "I'd like to go on a picnic."

"My word, that's a good choice!" Mr Braithwaite was impressed. "No wonder it took so long!"

"That would be fun, wouldn't it?" Ada asked.

"We could go to Blackpool sands and take a hamper with us." Priscilla had not been on a picnic for many a year, and already was excited at the prospect. "Weather permitting, of course."

"This hot spell is bound to last!" asserted Mr Braithwaite, though meteorology was not one of his strong points.

"And we could ask George and family along too!" suggested Mabel, blushing.

Priscilla turned to her daughter. "George?" she exclaimed, a distinct note of surprise in her tone of voice. "So it's 'George' is it? Since when did you start calling Mr Margerison 'George'?"

"Not to his face, I don't," snapped Mabel, clearly enraged that her mother should think she had no sense of decorum. She was embarrassed too, for having let slip her innermost feelings of affection for the man who was her employer. He might be twenty-two years older than she, but what did it matter? He was a handsome man, in need of a wife, someone to look after his children, and he was rich.

"I should sincerely hope you don't. He's your employer, and an older generation."

"No he's not, he's only…" Mabel trailed off the sentence. She had said too much already. Close to tears, she excused herself from the lunch table and ran from the room.

"Now there's a turn-up for the books!" said Mr Braithwaite, whose fork had been poised halfway between his plate and his mouth for the duration of that intriguing verbal exchange.

Ada wondered what all the fuss was about. "Do you think Mabel is going to get married to Mr Margerison?" she asked with interest, the conversation she had had with Mabel on that first night now making sense. "Is that what she meant by her grand plans?"

Aunt Priscilla looked thoughtful. "What grand plans? I never heard about any grand plans." Priscilla was astute enough to now understand the motivation behind Mabel's sudden decision to leave her job at the Harris Museum. She was pragmatic enough to consider that it might have been the right one after all: a nice gamble that might just pay great dividends! She would keep a watchful eye on developments and do her best to support her daughter in her 'grand plans'.

It therefore came as no surprise when George appeared on the doorstep the following Tuesday afternoon. She had been half expecting a visit.

"Good afternoon, Mr Margerison," Priscilla greeted him formally, as she always did. "What a pleasant surprise! Please come in!"

"Yes, a surprise! I suppose it is!" He looked nervous.

She led him through to the parlour.

"Please won't you sit down!" Priscilla indicated the armchair beside the fire, as she herself sat at her rose-wood desk in the bay-window.

"Indeed, no!" he said too quickly, looking distinctly uncomfortable. Recollecting himself, he smiled and said more gently, "No, I prefer to stand. What I have to say has to be said standing!"

"I see! This sounds very ominous!" observed Priscilla, but, from the evident anxiety diplayed by her visitor, she was beginning to suspect the reason for his visit.

"Not ominous, dear me no!" Here he took a deep breath and launched into what was the purpose of this unexpected visit. "I have come to ask you something special, regarding matrimonial matters."

"Ah yes!" said Priscilla, nodding. "I thought as much!"

"Am I that transparent?" George looked relieved that she had at least understood why he was here, and also had not shown any sign of disapproval.

"Please go on!" she coaxed him.

More confident, he continued, "In other words, I have come to ask for your consent… to ask… to ask…"

Here he stopped and loosened his collar, for now the moment had come, his face had become red and his eyes looked like those of a desperate man. Priscilla felt for poor George's awkwardness, and to spare him further embarrassment and worry, she finished his sentence for him. "My consent, to ask for my daughter's hand in marriage?"

George Margerison looked stunned, as if he had been thunderstruck. He corrected her, "Not your daughter's hand, but *your* hand in marriage."

Now it was Priscilla's turn to look stunned: she was truly dumbstruck.

"My dear Priscilla, will you do me the honour of being my wife?"

Part 3

Ada wished she could remember what Mr Minns used to say about 'strange bedfellows'. She had forgotten what it was that made strange bedfellows. Was it adversity or common causes or kindred thoughts or perhaps war? In the continuous excitement of the ever-changing present, now that she was eleven years old, her early childhood was fading fast, the memories were fraying round the edges and the details were becoming blurred.

Unlikely though it may have seemed to outsiders, Ada and Mabel, cousins with nine years between them, as different as chalk from cheese, had become friends.

"Will you be my bridesmaid?" Mabel asked over a cup of afternoon tea and hot scones dripping with butter and strawberry jam, during their weekly Saturday rendezvous in Oundle Villa.

"Me?" Ada was surprised. "Why me? Why not one of your friends at the Harris Museum?"

"Of course, if you'd rather not..." Mabel looked ruffled; she had been expecting an out-and-out affirmative response.

"I'd love to be your bridesmaid. Does Aunt Priscilla know that you've asked me?"

"Not yet."

There had been an uneasy relationship between Mabel and her mother during the last two years. Since the day when her George and her mother announced their engagement, to be precise.

Mabel never referred to her love for George Margerison: it was her little secret, unspoken. Yet Priscilla had understood, and was aware of how difficult it would be for Mabel to live under the same roof as them after they were married. However, in her genuine attempt to solve the problem, she had inadvertently made things worse. Her suggestion that Mabel take over Oundle Villa and continue to live there, taking in lodgers, had been misconstrued as a practical means of getting rid of her, thus removing the competition, so to speak. Even though Mabel had agreed to the arrangement, the whole affair had made her very angry. She had felt betrayed.

But Mr Braithwaite knew what she was thinking. He often scolded Mabel. "Your mother had nothing to do with it! I doubt if she even knew where your heart lay."

On another occasion, while they were eating what Mr Braithwaite called his "special high tea", a meal of ham and eggs and fresh bread and butter, he had said, "She didn't know anything about your so-called 'grand plans', as you call them. I can tell you that." He had remembered that it was Ada who had innocently mentioned them.

It was only now that Mabel was betrothed to her young beau, the handsome Mr McKeune who had bowled her off her feet the minute he had stepped into the Harris Museum, where she had resumed her employment, that she was able to meet her mother on equal terms with none of the hitherto unspoken friction, which had infiltrated and spoilt the mother-daughter friendship for so long.

Ada was honoured to be Mabel's bridesmaid. She believed that they were two kindred spirits who had been hit by the same lightning, and had clung together in stormy, perilous seas.

Just as Ada had begun to feel secure in her new home in Oundle Villa, her whole world seemed to fall apart, when Aunt Priscilla had announced that she was to marry Mr Margerison.

"What do you say, girls? Is this not wonderful news?" asked Aunt Priscilla, a look of exhilaration on her finely-chiselled features.

Both Ada and Mabel had been united in that frozen moment of horrified time, too shocked to say anything.

"We are to marry on August 31st by special licence, at the Town Hall," she continued, like an excited schoolgirl. "Our two families are to become one!"

Both Ada and Mabel experienced the same sense of lost future security. Mabel had lost a potential husband; her 'grand plans' had come to nought. She cast her eyes down and pretended to examine her fingernails, unable to look at her mother. Congratulations, or even a smile, were beyond this dejected young woman.

Ada's haven was being pounded by crashing waves. Her cosy new life with Aunt Priscilla was foundering. She had a sinking feeling. She did not want to share her life with strangers on an unknown shore. More strangers! She wanted things to stay as they were. Her life-saving decision made on April 23rd, which had sounded so important and forever binding, was floating away. Saint George's Day! Well, George certainly had his day now, and hers was slipping away, she thought ruefully, the tears of bitter disappointment pricking the back of her eyes.

"Now, let's get down to the business of names!" said Priscilla briskly, trying to lighten the perplexing, sullen atmosphere of disapproval.

"Names?" was all that Mabel could muster, looking up, but not meeting her mother's eye.

"Since he's marrying me, and I'm your mother," Priscilla sounded rather foolish, even to herself, with this silly observation, but she was desperate to get Mabel's approval, "you should call George 'Father'."

It seemed simple.

Mabel might be cast adrift in her own turbulent sea of uncertainty, but of two things, however, she was absolutely sure: she would never live under the same roof as George with her mother as his wife, and she would never call him 'Father'. Her own father may have been a selfish wastrel who had deserted her mother, but he was her father nevertheless. The whole idea was preposterous. She too had a sinking feeling. The future looked bleak.

"And you, Ada, will have to call him 'Uncle', since he's marrying your aunt."

It seemed simple.

"What's Harry going to call you?" Ada queried.

"All the Margerison children will call me 'Mother'." Priscilla was quite decided. There would be no arguments about that.

So Ada would be an outsider again: Mabel and Harry and Gilbert and Edith and Bessie would all call Aunt Priscilla 'Mother', while she alone would call her 'Aunt'. However, in all this tossing on an ocean of insecurity, one thing was certain: she was glad that she had to call Mr Margerison 'Uncle George'. She would never have called him 'Father', for he was nothing like her dear, dead Papa.

Ada and Mabel instinctively knew on that day that they mirrored each other in disappointment and loneliness. Clinging together, to save themselves from going under, a new friendship had been born.

Now, two years on, they were in calm blue waters, afloat and buoyant. Mabel had recently been betrothed to an up-and-coming young man of means, and Ada was to be a bridesmaid and catch the bride's bouquet!

"What colour would you like your frock to be?" Mabel asked.

Ada immediately answered, "Light blue, like the sea on a calm, sunny morning."

It had taken only a few weeks for Ada to settle into her life with the Margerisons. Haydock Grange was now their new home. It was a rambling eighteenth century country residence with mullioned windows, set in two acres of lawns with a sweeping driveway bordered by hundred year old elm trees. Since their move to this large, luxurious country house in Cottam on the outskirts of Preston, life had in fact been good.

Ada had to admit that her worries had been mainly unfounded. Her angry thoughts – that nothing was for ever, nothing lasted; that happiness was a temporary state and would pass; that past events and people all had their day – had diminished. What had been a cynical philosophy of life, borne of cyclical disappointment and sadness, had become but a few niggling thoughts which she had cast to the back of her mind, where they now quietly slept.

In her new life of constancy and comfort, with a never-ending round of parties and celebrations, and surrounded by people who loved her and depended on her, life was indeed good.

The Queen's diamond jubilee firework display in Avenham Park just the previous year had brought twenty thousand people from the town and the surrounding districts to watch the explosive brilliance of the firecrackers and rockets shoot high over the bandstand, up into the night sky. Schools and businesses were given special holidays in order to celebrate with their monarch, the grand old lady who ruled the greatest empire in the world.

Spud Saunders, who normally sold scoops of delicious ice-cream served in glass shell dishes during the summer months, reverted to his winter trade of selling piping hot baked potatoes from the same hand-cart for the evening fireworks.

"He'll be makin' a bob or two," remarked Michael Entwhistle from the comfort of a folding canvas chair, on the higher ground overlooking the park. The bandstand was no place to sit on this night.

"Ay, that he will," agreed Simon Hinton, with a Black Watch tartan rug over his knobbly knees. "Always had a good nose for business!"

"How he can stand old saw-bones beside him, I'll never know!" Michael nodded towards Preston's oldest resident street musician, who played eerie, melancholic dirges on a twenty-eight inch carpenter's saw blade with a frayed violin bow. Some said he was a Russian immigrant from Saint Petersburg, who had stowed away on a cargo ship, and some said he was a descendant of Antonio Stradivari, the Italian violin maker. But no-one knew for sure, for he was dumb. Some local gossips of an insensitive and vitriolic nature, purporting to be sensitive music critics, also said he must have been deaf... tone deaf!

Passers-by, however, would toss a copper into the moth-

eaten fur hat of dubious origin, more out of pity than
appreciation of his music. So too did Ada. Now that she had
coppers to spare, she was generous to a fault. Uncle George
handed out excessive amounts of pocket money each Saturday,
"far too much for the children", in Aunt Priscilla's estimation. In
his defence, he protested that he had never been any good with
money: neither as a young man living in an end-terrace in Grafton
Street, when he had little; nor now that he had plenty, with
Margerison soap world famous, commissioned by the Queen
for her Diamond Jubilee and by the Cunard Line for the cabins
of their trans-world passenger liners.

"It doesn't grow on trees, you know," Aunt Priscilla had
reminded Ada. "And you remember that too, Bessie," she added
to the five-year-old, whose hand she now held.

But just then, the nearby trees in the park were lit by a
mushrooming, dazzling firework floret, and all the leaves
shimmered like thousands of pieces of gold ripe for the picking.

"Yes it does, yes it does. Look!" cried Bessie gleefully.

"Guineas on every tree!" Edith agreed, her eyes wide with
the firm belief that now all things were possible. Only last week
she had written a jolly little verse, for her *If Only* anthology. She
had read it out to Ada, who was her friend:

"If only money grew on trees,
We'd grow rich and fat and glad,
Our pockets would be full of gold,
And folks would not be sad."

"Thousands of golden guineas!" Edith spread her arms wide,
as if she would gather them all in.

Priscilla and George had laughed, enjoying this bit of
childhood make-believe, as they all sat together as a family on
the grassy slope around the bandstand lawns eating their baked
potatoes, watching the kaleidoscopic blaze of colours.

As the last twinkles and sparkles flickered and fell, Ada
suddenly felt cold in the ensuing darkness. Although she cupped

her hands round the potato to warm herself, she knew the shivers were from within her very being. For suddenly her insecurities had woken from their contented slumber. She was remembering Edith's other *If Only* poem:

> *"If only mother was still alive,*
> *How happy we should be,*
> *We'd laugh and sing and run about*
> *Each day till half past three."*

The goblins of Ada's past were stalking in the undergrowth. Was her fairy-tale world of happiness only make-believe after all, and would she waken to find she inhabited a dark and alien world, once again lonely and sad?

She found herself composing a simple stanza:
> *"If only time could stay quite still,*
> *And joys could last forever..."*

"What are you thinking?" Harry's face was close to hers, peering at her in the gloom.

"I was just thinking," she said evasively. Harry was always so serious and grown up, even though he was a year younger than she was, that she did not want to admit to indulging in infantile pursuits like composing rhymes.

"What about?

"Just make-believe and fairy-tales."

Gilbert chimed in. "You're far too long in the tooth for that, old girl," he said digging her affectionately in the ribs.

He could always make her laugh with his yarns and his antics. His passion for sailing ships and all things nautical would often dominate his speech. He would talk about quinqueremes, Spanish galleons and *The Victory* with an air of intimate knowledge, as if he had been one of their crew. When he saw Harry reading, he would call him a "land-lubber", and when he wanted the girls' attention, he often hailed them as "me hearties". Ada was fascinated as Gilbert discussed sailing manoeuvres like "tacking" and "jibing" and "goose-winging".

He would shock her sometimes too when he whispered naughty words like "bloody", and referred to his father as "the old cock"!

Gilbert was two years older than she was, worldly wise and very handsome. Ada loved this fun-loving fellow: but of course it was just brotherly love.

"If only…" she hummed to herself.

Part 4

Ada inwardly swore that she would cry for a week. This was undoubtedly a gross exaggeration, because she was not the sort of girl who wept. But she did go as far as to lock herself in her bedroom. It all seemed to accord with the behaviour of a maiden whose love has been thwarted by the cruel hand of fate.

Gilbert had been sent away to boarding school.

Not only that, but he had been sent overseas to boarding school. In actual fact, it was King William's College in the Isle of Man! But to Ada, he might as well have been sent to Australia, for she would no longer walk the two miles from Cottam to Ashton School and back with him, listening to the springtime mating calls of the corncrakes, wandering along the summer lanes where the butterflies danced, passing the whispering ears of autumn wheat in Farmer Glossop's fields, and crunching through the winter ice puddles.

He had started his new school in September. And life would be exceedingly dull until the Christmas Holidays and the centenary celebrations, when he would be home again.

Ada would never forgive Aunt Priscilla and Uncle George for sending him away to school. No, never! And the reasoning which she had overheard was highly suspect, if not downright wrong. She had been sitting, unseen, in the summer house on the lower lawn one Sunday afternoon at the beginning of July, when her aunt and Uncle George had passed close by on their customary walk.

"You're too easy-going by far. He's in with a very rough and ready set of boys and girls, George, whose language is appalling and behaviour unseemly. Is that what you want? A son who learns nothing but vulgarity and coarseness in school?" Priscilla was deliberately overlooking all the well-mannered boys and gentle girls who made up the majority of pupils in Gilbert's class.

"That's not what I want, of course, but surely our influence at home should count for something?"

"It should, and to a certain extent it does, but his trouble is that he's too gregarious and impressionable. If he were more like Harry, there would be no problem; Harry's hard-working and self-sufficient, and settles to his studies. He doesn't get led astray. But with Gilbert it's a different matter. No, my mind is made up. The sooner he goes away to school the better."

For the love-sick Ada, now bereft of her hero and pining daily, Harry was a very poor substitute, with his intense reading of any novel he could lay his hands on, from Charles Dickens and Thomas Hardy to Bram Stoker and Jane Austen. His in-depth discussions about military campaigns and historical facts which had changed the world were dry compared with Gilbert's joviality. She knew deep down that Gilbert was too whimsical and superficial, but he was fun to be with.

Harry was fanatical about walking fast too: no congenial dandering to and from school with him. "Come on, Edith, don't dawdle!" he would say, when she stopped to pick a few cowslips to put in a little vase she kept on her bedroom windowsill.

"Bessie, you're so slow. Pick up your feet, and look lively!" he would say when his little sister was trotting beside him, as fast as her little legs would carry her.

Ada's long legs had no trouble keeping up with him. She actually enjoyed outdoor activities like walking and cycling, and in the coming winter they would go skating, for Uncle George had promised to buy them all skating boots for Christmas. But she could not appreciate why Harry always had to stride everywhere, always in a hurry, always at break-neck speed.

"Let me carry your books for you," he had said to Ada one day the previous June, on their way home from school.

Gilbert had laughed and said, "You're an idiotic Sir Galahad."

"No he's not, Gilbey," said Edith, rallying to Harry's defence. Gilbert flinched. He still hated to be called 'Gilbey'.

"Watch out, Ada," he laughed, "for a medieval knight in shining armour is lurking in our midst!" Then he had tried to push Harry into the ditch at the side of the lane. Harry, far more nimble and athletic than his brother, who was tending towards plumpness, side-stepped and Gilbert hurtled forward, somersaulted and landed on his rump, amidst the wild garlic growing rampant on the sides of the ditch.

But now, when Harry asked Ada so seriously and in such a gentlemanly manner if he could carry her books, something told her that it would be unladylike to decline the offer. So she graciously accepted and walked tall by his side, her arms swinging freely. She felt almost like a lady! Ada never felt like a lady with Gilbert, but she still missed him and his fun-loving ways.

"You stand tall and see just what a lovely and graceful lady you're becoming. Just like your Mama," Mr Minns had once said to her.

She wondered who had carried her Mama's books when she was a girl.

Part 5

One Sunday afternoon in November, There was a knock on Ada's bedroom door.

"May I come in?" Aunt Priscilla called.

"Yes, of course, Aunt."

"I'm glad that you've stopped locking your door!" she said with a raised eyebrow and a twinkle in her eye.

Ada blushed. Her love-sickness had long since diminished, and she thought of Gilbert now only as a good-natured, if forgetful, brother. He had forgotten to write to her, even though he had promised he would write every week, and even though she had written to him without fail every Sunday.

Sunday was now Ada's correspondence day, and after attending church in the morning, and eating a sumptuous Sunday lunch of roast beef served on a silver salver with slices of crisp Yorkshire pudding and steaming fresh vegetables, Ada would spend two hours writing to her friends and relations, her favourite and most frequent correspondents being Alice Hawkins in Cambridge, Cousin Hilda at Vine House, Mr Minns back in Ely, her sister-in-law Nina in Chertsey and her niece Ethel in Clapton. She still used her miniature escritoire and her fountain pen with the golden nib, which her Papa had given her seven years ago on her sixth birthday.

"There's something I want to tell you," Aunt Priscilla said with an air which suggested that what she had to say was of great magnitude. She sat down on the brocade occasional chair near the fire.

"Is it bad news?"

Ada braced herself for the worst by sitting up very straight and placing her hands demurely in her lap. It was her way of dealing with unwelcome news and disappointment.

"Good heavens, no, far from it, but it's something which will have a considerable effect on all our lives" Aunt Priscilla said. "I wanted you to be the first to know, as you are the oldest in the family here at the moment, with Gilbert being away."

Ada liked the sound of that phrase "in the family". She visibly relaxed and waited for her aunt to explain.

"Your Uncle George and I have decided to embrace the new century by moving to a new house in Preston. Now what do you say? Is that not wonderful news?"

Ada loved living in their present county house in Cottam amid the fields with the corncrakes calling, but it would have been churlish to have shown any disapprobation about a move to a new house in town. She recalled with chagrin her dreadful behaviour when Aunt Priscilla had said she was to marry George Margerison. She had to make up for that now.

"Indeed it is wonderful," Ada said, hoping that her voice betrayed not an iota of disquiet.

"The house is Georgian, an excellent property, with spacious rooms, servants' quarters, electric light, a garden at the back and a coach house and stable yard. Now wait till you hear the next part. Would you like to know the exact location of the house?"

Aunt Priscilla's excitement was catching. Ada nodded enthusiastically.

"Well," Aunt Priscilla said, drawing out her surprise, "it's in Ribblesdale Place…"

"You mean…?"

"Yes, my dear, it's the very house which you so admired, the one which is almost identical to Waddington Terrace, the house where you were born."

Ada put her hand up to her mouth to quieten her trembling lips.

When she finally spoke, her voice was a whisper. "Am I dreaming?"

"Pinch yourself and see!"

"It will be like going home."

"It *will* be home."

"Oh thank you, Aunt!"

"Don't thank me! Thank your uncle! It was all his idea. He wanted to move closer to the soap works, for it will not be long before Gilbert and then Harry will be of an age to join the board of directors. When your special house was put up for sale, it seemed the best place for us to buy. We move in at the end of January, in the new year."

"In the next century! Just imagine, nineteen hundred and one!"

Part 6

It was happening all over again! Her throat hurt horribly and all her joints were stiff and sore. She was so hot, oh so hot, that she thought she must have fallen down the primrose way to burn in Hell, forever surrounded by a sea of faces staring and lunging at her.

The Prodidogs were chanting "Stand up for Jesus" in the Whitsuntide procession, and the Orangemen's banner of King William on his white charger was flapping in the demonic flames, where a painted replica of Joan of Arc smiled blithely.

"No-one can lick the catlicks!" the dumb saw-musician was shouting, but Ada couldn't hear what he said.

"Tirra lirra," said Mr Braithwaite, raising his pint tankard of Porter beer to the Temperance League officials. "Bottoms up!"

"When I was in the kitchen doin' a bit of stitchin' in came the bogey man and knocked me out," sang Mavis Nobblett with no tune, skipping with a crocus chain rope.

"Books are for burning!" sneered Sir Galahad, as he tossed *The Lady of Shalott* into the Vine House fireplace. "Tirra, lirra!"

"Rheumatic fever, eh?" nodded Uncle Philip. "Ceylindo tea's the only cure!"

"She died of a fever, and no-one could save her," sang Molly Malone, clutching a shamrock leaf.

"How's the patient, doctor?" Uncle George's face momentarily swung into focus. "She mustn't die," he said, biting his lip.

"T-too early t-to t-tell, I'm afraid," said Doctor Livesey, adjusting his monocle. "Ada, it is you who must decide... must decide..."

"Off with her head!" shrieked the Queen of Hearts, and the

Mad Hatter gave her ten shillings and sixpence for her trouble.

"Is she going to die?" Edith tried to muffle her sobs.

"Of course not." Aunt Priscilla's voice was distant.

"Wake up, Ada! Wake up Ada!" Alice was poking and prodding her. "Don't go down with the sinking ship!"

"Everything will turn out all right," Mr Minns quietly assured her. "God is watching over you!"

"Rheumaticky knees, rheumaticky knees!" wheezed Simon Hinton, waving a Black Watch tartan flag.

"This is the way you catch your death," Maud sang, "catch your death, catch your death!"

"Who'll buy my black taffeta?" cried Miss Sneed from the fairground stall, spitting pins.

The Town Hall bells were ringing in time to the pounding drum-beat of her pulse at her temples.

Mr Dickens was saying, "This barbarous jangling of bells is driving the sick and the nervous mad. Hard times! Hard times!"

There were so many people careering before her watery, bewildered eyes that Ada knew not what was real and what was imaginary, but slowly, as her temperature dropped, the faces faded and disappeared from view. When she opened her eyes, just one face remained, smiling at her.

"Are you feeling better?" It was Harry.

"What day is it? Ada asked, for time seemed to have stood still.

"Friday, February 8th."

It was the anniversary of the day that her mother had joined the angels in Heaven. The pale pink roses in Ada's cheeks faded. "The day my mother died."

"Mine died in November," offered Harry, by way of comparison. "Better to die in February than in November though."

"Why is that?" asked Ada.

"There are more flowers in February to put on the grave." Then he walked over to the dressing-table and brought over the little posy of flowers, which he had picked in the garden

214

specially to cheer her up. "Look! These are for you."

They were snowdrops. Horrid snowdrops! Reminders of the dead and dying.

"Why, they're the very worstest flowers in the world!" she cried, reverting to her childish grammar of years ago.

Harry recoiled. He was trying very hard to make her feel better and here she was being quite impolite! And quite out of character too!

He corrected her. "You mean the very worst flowers."

Now it was her turn to be taken aback, for were not those the very last words which her Papa had uttered? His kindly, regretful face swam before her eyes.

Then Harry suddenly changed his mind and said with a decided tone, "No they're not. They're pretty, just like you."

"They're nature's teardrops, and very, very sad!" she cried, tears welling up in her eyes, her Mama's pale face coming into view.

"Nonsense!" Harry disagreed, not wanting to see her cry. "Snowdrops are nature's little pearl drops."

Ada was shocked. Her life-long belief was being challenged.

"Allow me, milady," he said, ever so politely, just like a real Sir Galahad. Then he leant forward and proceeded to hang a snowdrop on each of her ears. "Look, dangly earrings. That's what they are. Earrings fit for a princess."

When she saw herself in her hand-mirror, which he handed her, she looked so silly with the delicate petal-heads bobbing up and down over her ear lobes that she could not help but giggle.

Mama and Papa were there with her, inside her head, smiling. And when Harry draped two snowdrops over his ears, Ada laughed till she thought her sides would burst.

No need to wait for nature's teardrops to dry. No need for the yellow and purple crocuses to bloom under the beech tree. No need to wait for the spring flowers, to be happy.

Sad tears and happy laughter ran hand in hand across the sweet meadow of life.

Ada reached out her hand towards his.